The Cutler Brothers Series

Book 1: Cade
Book 2: Madoc
Book 3: The Cutler Brides

By Paige Tyler

Published by Blushing Books ®,
a subsidiary of
ABCD Graphics and Design
977 Seminole Trail #233
Charlottesville, VA 22901

The trademark Blushing Books ® is registered in the US Patent and Trademark Office.

Paige Tyler
        The Cutler Brothers Series
ISBN 978-1-935152-08-8

Cover Design: Rae Monet

Thank you for purchasing this copy of The Cutler Brothers Series by Paige Tyler

Please check out our websites sites, including Spanking Romance, located at http://www.spankingromance.com. A completed novel or novella is published here each week.

We also operate Bethany's Woodshed, located at (http://www.herwoodshed.com) the Internet's oldest and largest spanking story site. In operation since 1998, Bethany's has published hundreds of full length spanking romances, all professionally written. Please check out our website for more wonderful stories by Author and other fine authors.

We also run an eBook site at Romantic Spankings (http://www.romanticspankings.com). Here you will find hundreds of eBooks for immediate download.

Our print book site is located at SpankBooks. (http://www.spankbooks.com)

Paige Tyler is a full-time writer of erotic romance. She and her research assistant (otherwise known as her husband) live on the beautiful Florida coast.

For more of her sexy erotic fiction visit
www.paigetylertheauthor.com

TABLE OF CONTENTS:

THE CUTLER BROTHERS SERIES
BOOK 1

CADE

CHAPTER ONE

"Cutler, my office! Now!"

At the order, Cade looked up from his computer, his brow furrowing. *Shit*, he thought. He'd barely been at the job two weeks and he was already being called into the boss's office. Figuring he couldn't have done anything this soon that would get him fired as a U.S. Marshal, Cade pushed back his chair and got to his feet. Extremely aware of the other Marshals looking quizzically at him, he crossed the room and walked into the Deputy Chief's office.

Still wondering what he'd done that would have his boss bellowing across the office for him, Cade was tense as the older man closed the door and walked over to his desk.

"I've got your first assignment for you," Pete Conner said, picking a folder up and tossing it down on the desk in front of Cade. A middle-aged man, he had graying hair and a stocky build that made him look like he'd be right at home on a football field. "A woman in the WitSec Program called in saying she thinks her identity has been compromised, and I want you to go check it out," he told Cade. "She's probably making a fuss about nothing, so I think it's a case you can handle on your own."

The momentary high that Cade had felt at the mention of an assignment for the Witness Security Program, or WitSec as it was called, disappeared in a flash. He tried to control his disappointment, though. He had known coming into this that he was going to have to prove himself. How well he had done on the Marshals' written exam or the physical fitness test didn't mean a thing to the Deputy Chief. Neither did the wealth of experience he had brought with him from the Dallas Police Department. He was starting from the bottom rung again and being the new guy, it wasn't like his superior was going to give him the best assignments right off the bat. But just because he knew that didn't mean he liked it. After all of the stories his father and older brother, both of whom had been Marshals for years, had told him, he'd hoped things would be a little bit more exciting. All he'd done since he'd been hired was sit at a desk all day.

Cade frowned as he opened the folder and glanced down at the file. Might as well do this by the book regardless of how unimportant it was, he thought. "Why do you think she's overreacting?" he asked, scanning the first page of the thick folder.

"Because she's been moved almost half a dozen times in less than five years," the other man replied. "None of her claims that someone had tracked her down could ever be verified, but she insisted, so we had to move her. As you can guess, that's kind of earned her the reputation for being paranoid. Since this is the fourth call to our office in the six months she's been in our district, I'd have to agree." He sighed. "The others all turned out to be wild goose chases, so this one probably is, too. Just take her statement and tell her that we'll look into it. That should keep her satisfied for a little while."

Cade nodded. "I'll get right on it."

Though new to the Marshals Service, Cade could understand his supervisor's frustration with the woman. Regardless of what Hollywood depicted, the Witness Security Program was very successful. No one in it had ever been harmed while under the protection of the Marshals, or even had their new identity discovered. The Program was a well-run operation, so it was highly unlikely that Riley Barnett, or Katherine Jones, as she was now called, was in any real danger. But he would check it out. At least it would get him out of the office for a little while, he thought.

Taking the file his supervisor had given him back to his desk, Cade read through it quickly. Finding the name of the district attorney that had prosecuted the mobsters Riley Barnett had testified against, Cade gave the man a quick call to see if there was any reason to think the woman was in danger. The DA had seemed surprised by the question and told him that the organization Riley Barnett had testified against was completely defunct and that there was no one interested in going after her. Thanking the man, Cade hung up. Even more convinced that Conner was probably right about Riley Barnett overreacting, Cade wrote her address down on a piece of paper, and then headed over to her apartment.

Riley Barnett lived just north of Seattle, and since traffic leaving the city wasn't heavy at that time of day, it didn't take long for Cade to get to her apartment. Pulling into an empty parking space, he got out of his SUV and walked over to the building, taking in the surroundings as he did so. He did it more out of habit than because he thought there might be a threat, but nonetheless, he automatically found himself making mental notes of the area as he walked up the front steps and into the building. Certainly, nothing seemed out of place, he thought.

Riley's apartment was on the second floor, and as he made his way upstairs, Cade wished he had taken the time to read her file more thoroughly. Not that he needed to, he supposed. Pete Conner had been doing this a lot longer than he had, he reasoned, so if the other man thought Riley Barnett was being paranoid, then she probably was.

Taking out his badge as he came to a stop in front of her apartment, Cade reached out to ring the doorbell. A moment later, he heard a woman's soft voice.

"Who is it?"

Her tone was cautious, even a little nervous. But then Cade had expected no less.

"Cade Cutler, U.S. Marshals Service," he said.

As he spoke, Cade held his badge up to the peephole so that she would be able to see the silver star on it. He waited patiently, figuring that if she was as paranoid as the Deputy Chief seemed to think, it would take her a while to open the door. When she finally opened it, however, it wasn't to let him in, but to peak out at him through the crack.

"Hand me your badge," she directed.

Cade's brow furrowed. He had to admit that he was a little taken aback at the question at first, but he should have realized she'd be a little suspicious.

Flipping his badge closed, Cade handed it over to her. He expected her to give his photo-ID a cursory glance, and then let him in, but instead, she closed the door in his face. He was just starting to wonder if she might be calling the District Office to check him out when he heard the chain being slid from the lock. A moment later, the door opened.

The apartment was small and simply furnished, with few personal touches. Which made sense, Cade thought as he let his gaze roam over the living room and eat-in kitchen adjacent to it. She had just been moved half a year ago, so it might take her a while to get comfortable. Of course, he suspected that even after she did settle in, it was likely that the place would never feel exactly homey. When witnesses were relocated, they left their old lives behind, so that meant no family photos or keepsakes from the past.

"I called you people yesterday. What took you so long to get here?"

Cade turned to find Riley Barnett holding out his badge, an annoyed look on her face. Despite the fact that she was glaring at him, Cade couldn't help but notice that she was extremely attractive. For some reason, he hadn't expected that. Tall and slender with curves in all the right places, she had long, blond hair and big, blue eyes, and what he decided were the most kissable lips he'd ever seen. *Whoa, get a hold of yourself, dude*, he chided harshly. *Focus on the job, not what the witness looks like!*

"Well?" she demanded impatiently when he didn't answer her question fast enough.

Cade reached out to take the badge from her outstretched hand, telling himself to stay cool. "I came as soon

12

as I could, Ms. Barnett," he said, slipping his badge inside his jacket pocket and taking out the small, spiral notebook he carried.

Riley folded her arms with a disdainful snort. "I suppose that's your way of saying I'm no longer a high priority," she sneered.

Cade felt his ire rise at the derision in her tone, and he had to clench his jaw to bite back the sharp retort that immediately came to mind. This was his first assignment, he reminded himself. He wasn't going to blow it because he lost his temper.

"Well, I'm here now, Ms. Barnett," he said calmly. "Why don't we sit down and you can tell me what the problem is."

For a moment, Riley didn't move. Everything that had happened over the past five years was finally beginning to take its toll, and the fact that the Marshals no longer seemed to be taking her concerns seriously wasn't helping. She had been at this long enough to have developed an intuition about this kind of thing, and someone was definitely out to get her.

But yelling at this cute Marshal wasn't going to help her cause, she told herself. So, she might as well do as Cade Cutler had suggested and sit down. Realizing the man was waiting for her to do just that, Riley gave him a nod and gestured toward the couch. At the movement, he edged around the coffee table and took a seat on the overstuffed couch.

Cade Cutler was different than the other Marshals she'd met, Riley thought as she sat down on the opposite end of the couch. For one thing, he was younger than the others, probably three or four years older than her own twenty-eight, she decided. And good looking, too. Actually, that was putting it mildly, she thought. Tall with broad shoulders and dark hair, he looked like he'd be better suited to modeling than law enforcement. In fact, the reason she'd taken so long to let him into her apartment after he'd handed over his badge was because she'd been staring at the photo on his ID. Even though the picture was barely bigger than a postage stamp, she'd been fascinated by his chiseled features and wide, sensuous mouth.

On the opposite end of the couch, Cade flipped open his spiral notebook and looked at her. When he'd first come inside, Riley had thought his eyes were dark, but up close, she could see that they were more gold than brown. Wow, she thought. She'd never seen eyes quite that color.

"So," he said. "What makes you think that your identity has been compromised, Ms. Barnett?"

He spoke with a slight accent – a drawl, her mother would call it – and Riley wondered where he was originally from as she reached up to tuck her hair behind her ear. "I've seen a black SUV parked outside my apartment building every night for the past week," she explained. "And then yesterday, I saw the same vehicle parked across the street from the bank where I work. That was when I knew I had to call you."

Cade waited for her to continue, but when she didn't he pointed out, "A lot of people have black SUV's, Ms. Barnett. Are you sure it was the same one?"

Though his tone in no way suggested that he didn't believe her, Riley still bristled. She was frustrated that no one in the Seattle office seemed to believe anything she said. Each time a Marshal had come out, they had displayed less and less concern.

"Of course, it's the same one," she said sharply.

Cade glanced up. "Did you get a look at who was inside?"

She shook her head. "The windows were tinted."

He scribbled something down on the notebook he was holding. "What about a license plate?"

Again, she shook her head. "I didn't see it," she told him.

"What about the make and model of the SUV?" he asked.

14

Her brow furrowed. She'd been too frightened to even think about looking at stuff like that. Besides, she wasn't very good with cars. She shook her head.

Cade closed his notebook and slipped it into the inside pocket of his suit jacket. "We'll look into it, Ms. Barnett, and get back to you," he said, getting to his feet.

Riley did the same, her frown deepening. "How are you going to look into it? Will you be posting Marshals outside my apartment building then?" She really hoped so; she hadn't slept well the past couple of nights.

He inclined his head. "If we determine that you're in danger, then you'll be given protection," he told her. "But I don't think you have anything to be concerned about. As I said, a lot of people own black SUV's."

Riley stared at him in disbelief. Did she have to end up at the bottom of some river somewhere before they believed her? She opened her mouth to argue, but Cade Cutler was already walking toward the door.

Annoyed, she followed after him. "How will you know if there really is a threat from the SUV if there's no one here to see it?" she persisted.

In the small entryway, he turned to give her a placating smile. "Like I said, we'll look into it."

She folded her arms to glare at him. "You're not going to do a damn thing, are you?" she said sharply. "Now that you people have already gotten my testimony, you couldn't care less about what happens to me."

His jaw tightened. "I'll be in touch," he said, ignoring what she'd just said as he turned to leave. He was just reaching for the doorknob when the greeting cards on the table along the wall caught his eye.

Riley watched in confusion as he picked one up and read it, and then did the same to another and another. But before she could ask what he was doing, he turned to fix her with a hard look.

"What the hell are these?" he demanded, holding up the cards.

Her brow furrowed. "Birthday cards," she said, her tone implying that it should have been obvious to him.

"I can see that!" he growled. "But this one's from your mother! And these," he added, gesturing with the others, "are from the rest of your family!

She shrugged. "Duh! Who do you think sends birthday cards?"

His eyes narrowing, Cade tossed the stack of birthday cards back onto the table and strode toward her. "How about, duh, you're in the Witness Protection Program? Which means that you're not supposed to tell anyone where you are. That includes your family! You're so worried about your identity being compromised and here you are broadcasting it to the world!"

Ignoring the implied insult, Riley lifted her chin to glare up at him. "My mother would never tell anyone where I am," she told him coldly. "And neither would any of my sisters."

His brows drew together. "Really? How reassuring," he scoffed. "What about the people who might be snooping through your family's mail to find out where you are? Have you thought about that?"

She frowned at the words, wondering if that could be true, but then told herself it was ridiculous. Nobody, not even Albert Donatti, the main mobster she had testified against, would bother with digging through the mail just to find her. Besides, even if he had, her family had addressed the envelopes to her new name.

Riley gave Cade another shrug. "That would be impossible because my mom and my sisters didn't put my real name on the envelope," she said. "I'm not stupid, you know!"

"That's debatable," he retorted. "So, how many relatives does your family have living on the West Coast?"

She gave him a confused look. "What are you talking about?"

He held up the card from her mother. "It doesn't matter what the name on the envelope says," he told her. "The card says *Happy Birthday to My Daughter* on the front. I think people will figure out that it's you."

Before she could say anything, he added, "I'm going to have to call my boss and let him know about this."

"Good," she muttered. "Because I want to talk to him, too. That way I can tell him that you don't know what the hell you're doing, and that he needs to send someone out here who does!"

At her words, Cade paused in the act of reaching into his pocket for his cell phone, his eyes narrowing. "Okay, that does it!" he growled.

Riley braced herself for another one of his snide comments, and was totally surprised when Cade grabbed her by the arm and marched her over to the couch instead.

"What are you...?" she began as he sat down, but the rest of what she'd been going to say came out in a rush of air as he gave her arm a quick tug that sent her tumbling headlong over his knee.

Riley was so stunned that she simply lay there draped over his lap as she tried to catch her breath. When she finally came to her senses a moment later, it was to push herself upright, but a strong hand on her back held her down. What the hell was he doing?

Outraged, she turned to glare over her shoulder at him, only to let out a startled gasp when she felt his hand come down hard on her jean-clad bottom. Oh my God, the brute was spanking her!

"Of all the...*owwwww!*" she cried as his hand connected with her other cheek. "Let me go right now! You can't do this!"

Cade only ignored her demand, instead smacking her ass again, even harder this time. "No, I'm not letting you go," he ground out. "And I can do this. You are without a doubt the most irritating female I've ever met and I'm damn well going to do something about it!"

As he spoke, Cade punctuated every other word with a hard smack that had Riley squirming and protesting after each blow.

"I'll...*owwwww!*...have your...*owwwww!*...badge...*owwwww!*... for this, you jerk!" she yelled.

Riley had hoped that threat would be enough to make Cade stop, but to her dismay, he continued to spank her. Over and over, his hand came down on her upturned bottom, first one cheek, and then the other until they were stinging! And the more she squirmed, the tighter he held her. He was so strong that there was no way she could break out of his grasp.

Smack! Smack! Smack! Smack! Smack!

On and on and on it went until her bottom was really starting to sting from the relentless punishment. Despite the fact that her struggles had absolutely no effect on him, she refused to give up. Reaching back with one hand, she beat against his leg with her fist. It didn't do any good, of course, but it certainly made her feel better.

"It seems obvious to me that someone should have done this a long time ago," Cade told her. "If they had, maybe you wouldn't be such a brat right now."

Even though he had been spanking her the whole time he was talking, he stopped lecturing her briefly so that he could focus on applying some really hard smacks right to the part of her bottom where her cheeks met the tops of her thighs. *Ouch!* She never knew that area was so sensitive. It stung like crazy even through her jeans!

"I can appreciate how difficult it is for you to be in the Witness Protection Program," he continued. "But that doesn't give you the right to be so obnoxious!"

Riley opened her mouth to spit out a retort, but the only thing that came out was a yelp as his hand connected solidly with both cheeks at the same time. God, she hadn't realized his hands were so big. That really stung!

And then, finally it was over and Riley was back on her feet. Torn between slapping Cade Cutler across that handsome face of his for what he'd just done, and rubbing the sting from her throbbing ass, she chose the latter. She was afraid that if she tried to smack him, she'd be right over his knee again anyway.

As she stood there rubbing her bottom, Riley thought that she should at least be telling Cade off, but for the first time in her life, she was speechless. The man had given her a spanking! What kind of brute had they sent to protect her?!

CHAPTER TWO

Well, he had probably just set the record for having the shortest career in the history of the U.S. Marshals, Cade thought bitterly. His family would be so proud. Then again, getting fired might be the least of his worries. After all, spanking a protectee was almost certainly on the shortlist of absolute dumbass things to do. Because of what he'd done, it was likely that he might never get another job in law enforcement of any kind ever again. It wouldn't matter to his supervisors that the dang woman had completely deserved the spanking he'd given her. Cade seriously doubted they would understand.

Even if Riley Barnett had deserved it, he was still surprised with himself for letting her get to him like that. He'd never done anything like that to a woman before. But she seemed to have an almost unnatural talent for pushing his buttons. Hell, she'd been doing it ever since he'd first walked into the apartment! And then she'd made that snide comment about him not knowing how to do his job. That had really hit a sore spot and before he knew it, he'd found himself dragging her over his knee and spanking that tight, little bottom of hers. He had to admit that it had definitely been satisfying.

And there was a part of him that felt the spanking had even been justified. To say that Cade had been shocked when he'd seen the birthday cards from Riley's family was putting it mildly. She had been in the program long enough to know what to do and what not to do. That she'd actually been in contact with her mother and sisters had to be the dumbest thing he'd ever heard. He wouldn't have thought anyone could be that stupid.

And now, he had to tell the Deputy Chief about it. *Shit.* Reaching into his jacket pocket, Cade took out his cell phone and flipped it open. Punching in the number, he kept one eye on Riley as he waited for Pete Conner to answer.

Cade was actually a little surprised that the blonde was still standing where he'd left her. He would have thought she'd run off to the bedroom and slam the door in a snit. Instead, she just stood there rubbing her freshly-spanked bottom, a pout on her full lips. He could see her wince now and then as she explored his handiwork. Good. He hoped it still stung.

"Conner," a gruff voice said in his ear.

Cade dragged his attention away from Riley. "It's Cutler," he said. "I'm at Riley Barnett's apartment."

"Is there a problem?" his boss asked.

Cade glanced at Riley. "You could say that," he told the other man. "There's not much substance to her claims that someone's been watching her, but her identity has been compromised." Quickly, Cade told him about the birthday cards he'd found, and the fact that she had admitted to telling her family where she was.

On the other end of the line, Conner swore. "You've got to be kidding me!"

"I wish I were," Cade said grimly.

The other man sighed. "We're going to have to move her again," he said. "And she can't stay at her apartment until we do, which means that you'll have to take her to a safe house."

As his boss rattled off the address for the safe house the Marshals Service had in Puyallup, Washington, Cade automatically wedged the cell phone against his shoulder so that he could write it down on the spiral notebook that he'd taken from his jacket pocket.

"Sir," Cade said when the other man had finished. "You might want to have another Marshal meet us there so that he can stay with Ms. Barnett. She and I got off on the wrong foot. I don't think I'm the best fit to work with her."

There was silence on the other end for a moment, then, "Are you telling me that you can't handle a simple babysitting job, Cutler?"

Cade felt himself flush. "No, Sir," he said tightly.

"Good!" Conner barked. "Then do your job, or go find another one!"

Cade's gaze went to the blonde as he snapped his cell phone shut. From the smirk on her face, it was obvious she'd overheard his boss yelling at him. Great, he thought irritably. Not only was Conner pissed at him, but he was going to be stuck with Riley Barnett for who knew how long. Just fucking great.

It was obvious from the yelling on the other end of the line that Cade Cutler's superior was chewing him out. Despite the fact that her bottom was still stinging like crazy, Riley took a great amount of pleasure in seeing the Marshal get berated over the phone.

On the other side of the room, Cade was slipping his cell phone back into his pocket. "I'm taking you to a safe house, so you'll need to pack a bag," he told her curtly. "And make it quick. We're leaving right away."

Riley blinked. If he thought she was going to some safe house with him after the spanking he'd given her, then he was crazy! "I'm not going anywhere with you!"

He regarded her for a moment in silence, his jaw tight. "I'm sure you overheard the conversation on the phone. No one else is being assigned to your case, so that means you're stuck with me."

She lifted her chin. "Why do I need to move again?" she demanded petulantly. "You just told your boss that you don't think the SUV is anything to worry about."

His jaw tightened even more. "And I'm probably right," he said. "But I might be wrong, too. And by telling your family where you are, you've made the chances that there is someone after you a hell of a lot more likely. Regardless, the Witness Security Program is founded on one fundamental rule – never compromise your identity. Yours has been, Ms. Barnett. And since I have no intention of failing on this assignment, you're going to that safe house with me, one way or another." He lifted a brow. "Now, which is it going to be? Are you going to voluntarily pack a bag and come with me, or do I need to spank you until you change your mind?"

Riley gasped, blushing hotly as she remembered how easily Cade Cutler had put her over his knee and spanked her bottom a few minutes earlier. "You're a real jerk, you know that?" she said.

Turning on her heel, Riley stomped down the hall and into her bedroom, slamming the door shut behind her. She leaned back against it, seething.

Great, Riley thought miserably. Now, she was going to have to move again. And she really liked it there, too. Not only did she have a terrific job, but she had finally started to make some friends. She'd even had a date lined up for that weekend; the first in over a year. *Dammit!*

Not for the first time did she wonder what her life would be like if she hadn't stuck her nose in where it didn't belong all those years ago.

She had been working late one night at the Manhattan financial firm where she was a junior stockbroker when she had overheard a conversation between her boss and some other men. Normally, she wouldn't have paid much attention, but it had seemed like odd time to be having a business meeting. So without them noticing, she had crept closer to the office to listen to what they were saying. When she had realized they were talking about money laundering, she had immediately gone to the police. The next thing she knew, she was wearing a wire and planting bugs for the Feds.

At the time, the whole thing had seemed so exciting, like she was a spy or something. Talking her way into upper-level meetings, skulking around in the middle of the night making copies of incriminating documents, and hacking into her boss's computer to find evidence had all seemed like so much fun. Especially being fresh out of college like she had been. But then the real world had intruded and she found herself testifying against not only her boss, but a high-powered mob figure as well. That was when it hadn't been fun anymore. Her life had become hell at that point.

That had been five years ago. Since then, she had been moved from one city to another, one apartment to another, one job to another, one identity to another. And now, it was going to start all over again.

To make matters worse, Cade Cutler had spanked her! She could still feel every spot on her bottom where his hand had come down. It was a good thing she had on jeans instead of a skirt. As it was, she was probably going to have marks, maybe even bruises. She had never been so manhandled in her life! And to think she had actually thought he was cute!

Suddenly realizing that she'd been standing there for at least five minutes, Riley gave herself a mental shake. Half afraid that the Marshal would come in to check to see what was keeping her and make good on his threat to spank her again, she hurried across the bedroom to the closet and took out her overnight bag. Going over to her dresser, she pulled open her underwear drawer and taking out a dozen pairs of bikini panties, put them in the bag. Closing that drawer, she opened the one next to it and picked out a couple of lacy push-up bras before pushing it closed again. Opening the drawer below that one, she took out a pair of shorts and a cami-top, then went to the closet and grabbed several T-shirts and an extra pair of jeans, all of which she packed into the bag. Satisfied that she had enough clothes, she went into the adjoining bathroom to grab her toiletries, and added them to the bag as well.

Glancing at her reflection in the mirror above the sink, Riley was surprised to see that not only was her face flushed, but that her long, blond hair looked as if she'd just turned her head upside down and given it a good shake. Then again, she reminded herself, she had just spent a good ten minutes draped over Cade Cutler's lap getting spanked. Brute, she thought as she took the brush from her overnight bag and ran it through her hair. Dropping her hairbrush back into the bag a moment later, she zipped it closed, and then left the room.

Cade was just checking his watch when Riley walked into the living room, and he looked up at her entrance. "It took you long enough," he grumbled. "I was just about to come in and get you."

Riley gave him a glare. "Good thing you didn't," she said as she set the bag down on the floor and walked over to pick up her shoulder bag from the chair. "It would have taken me even longer with you giving me packing advice."

Cade said nothing, but only stood there waiting impatiently while Riley dug through her purse. She was probably deliberately being slow, he thought. God, she was irritating, he thought. And now, he was going to be stuck in some safe house with her. The thought was enough to make his jaw clench.

Over by the chair, Riley took her sunglasses from her purse and put them on before rummaging through her shoulder bag again. Coming up with her keys a moment later, she announced that she was ready to go.

Finally, Cade thought to himself as he bent to pick up her overnight bag. Opening the door, he held it for her so that she could walk out ahead of him. Riley stood where she was for so long that he thought he was going to have to prompt her, but after giving her small apartment one more wistful look, she brushed past him and stepped into the hallway.

They made their way down the stairs in silence. Once outside, Cade led her over to his Jeep, his gaze automatically checking to see if the black SUV that Riley had said she'd seen was anywhere around. She was looking for it, too, he noticed. But it was nowhere in sight. Not that he had expected it to be.

Neither of them spoke on the drive down to Puyallup, which suited Cade just fine. The less interaction he and Riley Barnett had, the better.

As safe houses went, it wasn't bad, Riley thought as Cade pulled into the driveway of a small two-story house an hour and a half later. It was in a crowded part of town with a couple of strip malls and stores just down the street. Not a bad place to be stuck. Not that she'd probably spend much time there anyway; the other times, she had been moved within a few days.

Walking up to the door with Cade several moments later, a thought abruptly occurred to Riley. They hadn't stopped for a key, and she wondered how they were going to get inside. She was about to ask Cade that same question when she noticed the keyless-entry pad beside the door.

Riley watched as the Marshal punched in the four-digit code, automatically making a mental note of the combination. Numbers had always come easy to her, which was one of the reasons she had enjoyed being a stockbroker so much. Well, at least that was one thing she could say about the Marshals. They always found her a job related to money and investing.

Walking into the entryway, Riley stood for a moment to survey her new surroundings. The house was a simple design, with a living room, an eat-in kitchen, and a small room down the hallway that was probably a bathroom taking up the downstairs, while a narrow staircase directly off the entryway led to the second floor. Toward the back of the house, she could see another door that led to the backyard.

Beside Riley, Cade set down her bag as he swept the house with his gaze. "I'm going to go check out the upstairs," he told her.

As he headed for the steps, Riley wandered into the kitchen. She had been too nervous that morning to eat much of anything for breakfast and now that it was nearing late afternoon, she was starting to get hungry. Hopefully, the pantry was stocked.

But both the pantry and the cabinets were empty, much to her dismay. Her brow furrowing, she opened the fridge, but besides an old carton of baking soda, it was empty, too. Great, she thought.

Hearing Cade's footsteps behind her, she turned to frown at him. "There's nothing to eat," she said as he walked into the kitchen.

He shrugged. "We'll get pizza delivered."

Riley looked at him in surprise. "Three times a day?"

He shrugged again. "Why not? What's wrong with pizza?"

"Nothing, but no one could eat pizza that much," she protested. Admittedly, she liked pizza a lot, but even she didn't want to eat it for breakfast, lunch, and dinner. "Besides, I have to eat more often than that, anyway. If I don't, then my blood sugar gets too low, and I get grumpy."

Cade lifted a brow at that, but before he could say anything, she continued.

"Can't we just run to the store and go shopping?" she asked.

His mouth tightened. "What part of witness protection don't you understand?"

She sighed. "Then how about you go to the grocery store?"

"And leave you alone?" he asked incredulously. "I don't think so."

Riley folded her arms. "They call it a safe house because it's safe, right? And you said yourself that I'm not in danger, so why can't I stay here while you run to the store?" she demanded. "It's not going to take you any more than thirty minutes, tops. I'll be fine."

When Cade made no reply, she took that to mean he was giving the whole thing some thought, so she added, "You won't like me when I'm grumpy. Trust me."

28

He shook his head with a sigh. "Okay, I'll go to the store," he agreed. "But only if you promise to stay put."

She made a show of looking around. "Where would I go?" she said.

Cade gave her an annoyed look. "Just do it, okay?" he told her. "I'll be back in thirty minutes."

Riley followed him to the door, quickening her steps to keep up with his long strides. "Aren't you going to ask me what I want?" she said.

He turned to face her. "I was just going to get some peanut butter and a loaf of bread."

She opened her mouth to protest, but then changed her mind. Cade had agreed to go shopping for her; she supposed she should at least be gracious. And besides, she did like peanut butter. "Okay," she said. "But make sure the peanut butter is the reduced-fat kind. And that the bread is one-hundred percent whole wheat."

Cade's mouth tightened, but he said nothing.

"Oh, and get some skim milk, too," she added as he turned the doorknob. "And yogurt. Maybe a box of cereal, too. Anything that's whole-grain." She paused. "And some fruit and vegetables."

He lifted a brow. "Anything else?" he asked dryly.

She thought a moment. "Chocolate," she said, and then added, "Maybe you should write all that down."

"I got it." He opened the door. "Remember, stay put. And don't open the door to anyone."

After Cade had left, Riley considered unpacking, but then decided it would just be easier to live out of her suitcase. Wishing she'd remembered to bring a book or two with her, she went into the living room and grabbed the remote from the coffee table. Flopping down onto the couch, she turned on the television.

Surfing through the channels didn't take her long since the house was only set up with basic cable. Darn it, she thought. She should have asked Cade to stop at the video store on the corner and get some movies while he was out. Then again, maybe it was a good idea that she hadn't. He'd probably come back with a bunch of action movies that had lots of stuff blowing up and no real story. Still, watching a movie or two would have helped to pass the time.

Suddenly, an idea came to her. Why not go to the video store herself?

Because Cade told you to stay put, a little voice in her head reminded her.

He'd also told her that she wasn't in any danger, Riley pointed out. And besides, it was only a short walk to the video store. She'd seen on in the strip mall down the street. Come to think of it, there was a bookstore, too. She could grab a couple of videos and some books and still be back well before Cade. And if he didn't like it, well, then that was tough. He might be able to drag her off and uproot her whole life all over again, but that didn't mean she had to be bored the whole time they were at the safe house.

Her mind made up, Riley turned off the television, picked up her purse, and started for the door.

Cade was pretty sure it wasn't procedure to leave Riley alone at the safe house while he went grocery shopping, but it had seemed easier than listening to her complain all night. Besides, as much as he hated to admit it, she had been right. They couldn't eat pizza the whole time they were there. Besides, it hadn't taken more than thirty minutes to run to the store and back. And in reality, she was right about something else, too. Even if procedure dictated that they move her again, she wasn't really in any danger. So, this run to the grocery store wasn't that big of a deal.

Pulling into the driveway, Cade shut off the engine and grabbed the two grocery bags full of food from the back seat. As he neared the house, he shifted them to one arm so that he could use his free hand to punch in the entry code on the keypad beside the door.

Riley was standing in the living room when he walked in, and she turned at his entrance. His gaze immediately locked on the DVD's in her hand, and his eyes narrowed.

"Where the hell did you get those?" he demanded.

She set them down on the coffee table. "From the video store on the corner," she said.

Ignoring the scowl he gave her, Riley took one of the bags from him and walked into the kitchen to put it down on the counter.

Cade followed. "You went out to the video store after I told you to stay put?" He put the bag he was carrying down on the counter beside hers with a thud. "I didn't spank you hard enough before, did I?"

Riley whirled around, her face flushed with embarrassment at the mention of the spanking he'd given her. "I don't know what the big deal is!" she snapped. "You said that the SUV was nothing to worry about, so I'm not in any danger. Or were you wrong about that?"

Cade clenched his jaw. "I said that the SUV was probably nothing to worry about," he corrected. "But that doesn't mean I want you traipsing around all over town, completely disregarding everything I tell you."

She folded her arms to glare up at him. "I didn't go traipsing around all over town. I only went to the video store on the corner," she protested, and then, turning back to the bag of groceries, mumbled, "I won't do it again."

"Damn right you won't!"

Biting back a retort, Riley reached into the bag, only to let out a gasp of surprise as Cade's hand closed over her arm.

"What...?" she started to say, but the words trailed off as he marched her over to the kitchen table and the straight-backed chairs there. Her eyes went wide as she realized what he intended. "Oh, no you don't!" she told him.

Riley tried to hang back, but Cade had already sat down and was pulling her over his knee. She tried to resist, but it did no good. He was way too strong for her. That didn't stop her from flailing and kicking at him, but within moments, she was staring down at the linoleum floor, her bottom in the air and his hand on her back.

"Dammit!" she yelled, beating her fist against his muscular thigh. "Let me go!"

"Not until you and I come to an understanding!" Cade told her. "Because if you don't start doing what I tell you, then this cute, little ass of yours is going to be sore the entire time we're stuck here."

For some ridiculous reason, Riley felt herself blushing at his words, but before she could open her mouth to say something rude in return, he brought his hand down hard on her jean-clad bottom.

"*Owwwww!*" she yelped.

But the sound was lost as another resounding smack echoed throughout the kitchen. Having just gotten spanked a few hours earlier, her bottom was already beginning to sting, and Riley squirmed as he brought his hand down over and over.

"*Owwwww!*" she protested. "You can...*owwwww!*...stop now! I already...*owwwww!*...told you I wouldn't...*owwwww!*...go to...*owwwww!*...the stupid video store again!"

"Somehow, I don't really believe your promises. So, this is to make sure you think twice before you go anywhere without my permission again!" he told her in between spanks. "Going to that video store was foolhardy and dangerous. No one may be after you now, but if someone did manage to find you through those dumbass birthday cards, then they could track you by that damn video-rental card of yours. But you didn't think of that, did you? Of course not! Because you're too busy telling me that I don't know how to do my damn job!"

Between her protesting and the sound his hand made as it smacked down on her ass over and over, Riley barely heard half of what Cade said, but when he paused a moment later to ask her if she understood, she nodded her head emphatically.

32

"Yes, yes, yes!" she told him.

She thought that after the lecture that he was done, but then he continued to rain hard smacks down all over her bottom.

"Hey!" she protested. "I said I understood!"

"Good," he said, bringing his hand down again. "Now that we have that part taken care of, I want you to give me your solemn word that you won't go anywhere without my permission?"

She nodded her head vigorously. Right then, her bottom was stinging so much that she thought she probably would have agreed to just about anything.

"I didn't hear you," Cade insisted, giving her a particular hard smack right on her sit-spot.

Riley blinked at both how hard the spank was, as well as what he obviously expected her to say. He actually wanted her to say the words out loud? She'd thought that being put over his knee for a spanking was the ultimate in embarrassment, but this was even more humiliating!

When she continued to hesitate, he prompted her with another hard smack, this time to both her cheeks. "I don't think I'm getting through to you," he told her. "Maybe you can't feel the full effect of the spanking through the jeans. Maybe I should pull them down."

Her eyes went wide at that. "*Nooooooo!*" she cried, her face turning bright red. "Okay, okay! I promise that I won't go anywhere without your permission! Are you satisfied now, you jerk?!"

Riley regretted the words as soon as they were out of her mouth. Though she really did think Cade was a jerk, calling him one while in her present position probably wasn't the smartest thing to do, and she held her breath as she waited for him to start spanking her again. But to her surprise, he took her arm and put her back on her feet. She immediately reached around with both hands to cup her throbbing asscheeks, only to gasp. If anything, they seemed to sting even more now that he had stopped spanking her. And that threat to pull down her jeans had been unbelievable! He really was a brute, she thought.

CHAPTER THREE

After the spanking Cade had just given her, Riley had been sure there would be marks on her bottom, but when she stormed off to the bathroom afterward, she was surprised to see that there weren't any. Her bottom was really pink, though, she thought as she pushed down her jeans and gazed at her rosy asscheeks in the mirror above the sink. And, she found out a moment later when she reached back with one hand to rub, they were tender to the touch, too.

She couldn't believe that Cade had spanked her again. And for something as stupid as going to the video store, too! Like someone was really going to track her down using her video-rental card! That wasn't even logical! Well, one thing was for sure, when she got settled in her new place, wherever that was, she was going to call his boss and tell the man that Cade Cutler was completely out of control! She'd pull out her cell phone and call his boss right then, but the knowledge that she was going to be stuck with this guy a little while longer made her realize that wouldn't be a very good idea. But she'd get him in the long run, she promised herself

Pleased at the idea of getting back at the Marshal for manhandling her, Riley allowed herself a small smile as she wiggled her jeans up over her hips and buttoned them. She had never realized that denim was so rough until the material rubbed against her tender bottom. *Ouch!*

Though part of her would rather have spent the rest of the night in the bathroom rather than have to face Cade again, the other part of her refused to be intimidated by him. So, after checking her reflection in the mirror, she tucked her long, blond hair behind her ear and walked out of the room.

Cade was standing at the counter pouring milk into two large glasses when she walked into the kitchen a few minutes later, and he looked up at her entrance. He had taken off his suit jacket and rolled his sleeves up to reveal nicely muscled forearms. Oh yeah, she thought. He might be a jerk, but he was a good looking one. He should definitely be modeling instead of working in law enforcement.

"I made you something to eat," he said, glancing at the table.

Riley's gaze went to the peanut-butter-and-jelly sandwiches on the table. For a moment, she considered telling him to take the sandwich and shove it, but at the sight of food, her stomach began to growl loudly, and she wisely decided to give in to her hunger and eat instead. Murmuring a soft, "thank you," she pulled out a chair and sat down, wincing a little as her bottom touched the seat.

At least he had remembered to get whole-wheat bread, she thought as she slid the plate closer to her. And skim milk, too, she noticed as he opened the fridge to put the plastic container on the shelf.

Closing the door, Cade picked up the two glasses and walked over to the table. Setting one of them down in front of Riley, he pulled out the chair across from her and sat down.

They ate in silence, the hum of the refrigerator the only sound in the room.

"So," Cade said after several long minutes. "How did you get into the Witness Protection Program?"

Riley looked up in surprise, taken aback not so much by the question, but by the fact that the Marshal was actually bothering to talk to her. As she sipped her skim milk, she considered that maybe he was trying to make up for being such a jerk earlier. "I testified against a mobster," she answered.

Cade's mouth quirked. "I figured that much," he said. "I was referring to the particulars. I didn't really have time to read the whole file before I came over to your apartment."

She said nothing for a moment, not sure if she felt like having a conversation with the man who had given her not one, but two spankings that day. Then she decided, why not? It was either that or sit there in silence for the rest of the night. And it had been a long time since she'd been able to talk to anyone about it.

"I was a stockbroker at a Manhattan investment firm," she explained, setting down her glass and sitting back in her chair. "I was working late one night when I heard my boss talking to some men in his office. It wasn't odd for him to be in the office at that time of night, but it was kind of unusual for a client to have an appointment that late, so being a little curious, I wandered down the hall to hear what they were talking about." She let out a sigh. "I wish now that I hadn't."

Cade waited for her to continue, and when she didn't, he prompted her. "What did you hear?"

She chewed on her lower lip, remembering. "They were talking about laundering money," she said. "Apparently, my boss had been in bed with the mob for years."

"And they realized you were listening in on their conversation and came after you?" Cade surmised.

Riley shook her head. "Actually, they had no idea I had heard anything at all. They didn't even know I was there," she said. "Being the upstanding citizen that I am, I decided to go to the cops and tell them what I'd heard. It never occurred to me that I would have any further involvement. But the next day, the FBI showed up at my apartment wanting me to go undercover for them."

Cade was stunned by that. He'd been surprised enough when Riley had said she'd been a stockbroker, but hearing that she had gone undercover for the Feds was something he would never have thought someone like her would do. After how careless she'd been with keeping her identity a secret, he had to admit, he'd thought her a rather dim bulb. He supposed that he was going to have to reassess his opinion of her. At least in some ways.

Across the table from him, Riley ran her hand through her long hair, pushing it back from her face. "If I had known then that my whole life would get turned upside down and I would end up in the Witness Protection Program, I never would have done it," she said. "But at the time, it sounded exciting, so the FBI didn't have to work too hard to persuade me to wear a wire for them." Her lips curved into a small smile. "I was really naïve back then, and I got caught up in the whole spy thing, thinking I was saving the world." Her smile faded. "But after the FBI got all the evidence they needed, the real world came crashing down. When they showed up at my door with U.S. Marshals and told me about the Witness Protection Program, I finally realized what I had gotten myself into. I lost my job and my friends, and I haven't seen my family since then. Plus, I've been moved all over the place and forced to live under a different assumed identity every time. It's enough to make anyone wonder if it had been worth it."

Cade frowned. He had never really thought about what people in the Witness Protection Program gave up. He knew how close he was to his family, though. If someone told him that he could never talk to or see them again, he might not go along with it any better than Riley had. That thought almost made him regret yelling at her earlier about being in contact with her family. He probably would have done the same thing in her position.

For a moment, she looked so forlorn and alone sitting there that he had resist the urge to reach across the table and cover her hand with his. "What you did, going up against the mob, took a lot of courage," he told her quietly instead.

She regarded him in silence for a long moment, her blue eyes sad. "Maybe," she agreed. "But it was also stupid."

Cade felt like telling her that it hadn't been stupid. That it had been brave and unselfish. But he didn't think she really wanted to hear something like that, particularly not when she was feeling so down, so instead, he said nothing.

38

Pushing her chair back, Riley picked up her half-full glass of milk and went into the living room, leaving Cade alone at the table. He sat there, watching as she picked up one of the movies, popped it into the DVD player, and then sat down on the couch, kicked off her shoes, and curled her legs under her.

With a sigh, Cade pushed back his chair and got to his feet. Picking up their empty plates, he rinsed them off, and then set them in the rack to dry before grabbing his glass of milk from the table and going into the living room.

The movies Riley had picked out were standard chick flicks, all sappy story and no action, and Cade was bored senseless by them. But since there was little else to entertain him, he sat on the couch and watched them with her. Sitting through two of them was almost more than he could take, however, and he was relieved when Riley finally announced that she was going to bed after the second one.

Grabbing the remote from the coffee table, Cade flipped through the channels disinterestedly. He should probably go to bed, too, he thought. Despite the fact that the house had two bedrooms, he had decided he would sleep on the couch downstairs. He supposed it was silly really, since Riley wasn't in any danger, but it was standard procedure and he thought he should probably follow the book regardless of the threat.

Before he turned in for the night, Cade did a sweep of the house, checking all the doors and windows to make sure they were locked, as well as pushing aside the curtains to take a look outside. Except for the occasional car driving by, it was quiet.

Cade was just about to let the curtain on the living room window fall back into place when he noticed a dark SUV coming up the street. His eyes narrowed as it approached, but though the vehicle slowed a little as it passed the house, it didn't stop, and he felt himself relax as it drove off. A lot of people drove dark SUV's, he told himself, including his own brother.

The ground floor secure, Cade turned away from the window and headed upstairs to check on Riley before going to bed himself. The door to the bedroom on the right had been left slightly ajar, and he could see the soft glow of light through the opening.

Not wanting to wake Riley if she were asleep, Cade didn't knock on the door, but instead, quietly pushed it open just enough to poke his head in. If she were still up, no doubt she'd have a few choice words for him about barging in on her, he thought.

But to his surprise, Riley was sound asleep. It turned out that the light wasn't coming from the bedroom at all, but from the one in the adjoining bathroom, which she had left on. That made sense, he thought. As scared and paranoid as she was, she probably always slept with a light on.

In the soft glow, Cade could see her slender form outlined beneath the covers. She was curled up in a ball with the blanket tucked up under her chin and to his surprise, the image touched his heart. She looked so small and vulnerable, he thought. And at the same time, very sexy.

Abruptly, Cade was reminded of the spanking he'd given her earlier that evening. Though he had been really angry at how stupid she had been, he suddenly felt badly about putting her over his knee again. Then again, she had deserved it, he told himself. If someone really were after her, they would have had the perfect opportunity to grab her the moment she'd stepped foot outside the safe house. Even so, she'd had a pretty hard time of it lately, he reminded himself, so maybe he should cut her a break.

And yet, even as he decided that spanking her again might have been a little overboard, there was a part of him that was secretly pleased Riley had given him a reason to do it. Standing there now, with her looking so sexy, he could admit that he had enjoyed spanking her. When he had put her over his knee the first time back at her apartment, Cade been too intent on what he was doing to pay much attention her ass.

40

And though he'd been no less angry with Riley when he'd spanked her when he'd come back from the store than he had been in her apartment, he had found himself taking the time to admire her curves while she'd been wiggling around on his lap. No doubt about it, her ass was amazing! Well-rounded enough to fill out her jeans nicely, but still firm enough to show that she definitely worked out. He could just imagine what she'd look like under those jeans.

Too bad she hadn't given him a reason to pull them down, he thought. Then again, it was probably just as well, because he would have had a really hard time concentrating on actually spanking her. He was getting hard just thinking about it.

Cade swore under his breath and backed out of the bedroom. Get a grip on yourself, man! You're a U.S. Marshal, not some dude looking for a hot lay! It was his job to protect Riley Barnett, not bed her.

Annoyed with himself for even having those thoughts, Cade went back downstairs and checked the doors one more time. Emptying his pockets, he dumped everything including his cell phone onto the coffee table. Then he slid his gun holster from his belt and set it down on the table as well.

Sitting down, he lie back on the couch and pillowing his head on his arms, closed his eyes and tried to fall asleep. But thoughts of the beautiful Riley Barnett sleeping just upstairs kept him awake long into the night.

Cade was still asleep when his cell phone rang the next morning. Immediately reaching for it, he flipped it open and held it to his ear.

"Cutler," he said.

"It's Conner." The man's voice was gruff in his ear. "Everything going well?"

Cade couldn't help but notice that the Deputy Chief didn't actually wait for him to reply before continuing.

"Riley Barnett's a low priority, so it'll take us a little while to find a more permanent place to put her," the other man said. "The bean counters really don't like the idea of spending the money to move her again when there's no definitive threat. I know that you couldn't give a crap about that, but nevertheless, it means you'll be stuck with her for a while longer."

"How much longer?" Cade asked, trying to keep his voice steady.

Conner sighed. "I don't know," he said. "Maybe a week or more. You have a problem with that?"

Cade's jaw tightened, but he knew better than to voice his displeasure to the Deputy Chief. The man would only take that to mean he couldn't do the job. "No problem, Sir," he told his boss.

Conner grunted, obviously expecting Cade to complain, and surprised when he hadn't. "Good," he said curtly. "I'll be in touch."

Cade flipped his phone closed with a sigh. A week or more at the safe house with Riley, he thought. God, that was going to feel like forever. He wondered how many chick flicks that would equate to.

A thought suddenly occurred to him then. He didn't have any clothes with him. Hell, he didn't even have a toothbrush. He was going to have to go back to his apartment, he realized. Which posed a problem of a different kind; he couldn't leave Riley at the safe house while he went all the way back to Seattle. Who knew what kind of trouble she would get into if he did? Of course, if he had another Marshal backing him up on this like he was supposed to, it wouldn't be a problem, he thought. But he didn't. He was completely on his own, which meant he'd have no choice but to take her with him. It wasn't exactly procedure, but what else could he do?

CHAPTER FOUR

Cade was in the kitchen when Riley came downstairs. Last night had been the first time she'd slept well in a long time and as much as she didn't want to attribute it to the Marshal's presence, she knew he was the reason. He might have a nasty habit of spanking her, but she couldn't deny he made her feel safe.

He glanced at her as he poured coffee into mugs. "I talked to my supervisor this morning," he told her. "It's going to take a while to get you set up with a new identity, so until then, we'll be staying here."

Riley nodded, but said nothing as he handed her one of the mugs. Well, at least she'd get a few more days in the Pacific Northwest before they moved her off to wherever it was they decided to put her, she thought.

"The thing is," Cade continued. "I don't have anything with me other than what I'm wearing, so we're going to have to take a run up to my apartment so I can get some things."

She frowned at that. It was a bit unusual that the Marshals weren't sending out anyone to relieve Cade. Maybe there was a budget crunch or something at this time of year. Or maybe it just showed how low of a priority she really was to them, she thought bitterly. But she supposed she couldn't blame Cade; it wasn't his fault. She was sure it wasn't any picnic for him, either, and she couldn't help but wonder who he had peeved off to get stuck on this assignment all by himself.

So, after a breakfast of whole-wheat toast and coffee, they drove up to Cade's apartment in Seattle. At least it was nice to get out, she thought. At first, Riley simply enjoyed the scenery, but as they neared the city, she found herself thinking out loud.

"Do you know where they're going to be relocating me?" she asked, turning her attention from the window to Cade. His hair was a little tousled from sleep, but even with bedhead, he still looked incredibly handsome for this early in the morning.

He gave her a sidelong glance. "Not yet," he said. "But in all honesty, I doubt they would tell me even if they knew."

She sighed and looked out the window again. "I hate having to move," she said. "I really liked living in Seattle."

Cade said nothing for a moment. "Where did you live before this?"

Riley turned away from the window to look at him again. "Indiana first, and then Wisconsin for about a year," she said. "After that, I lived in Iowa for a little while, and then Utah. They were okay, but I really like the Pacific Northwest the best. I'll miss it."

Beside her, Cade nodded. "I know what you mean," he said as he took the exit that led into downtown Seattle. "When they assigned me to the Seattle office, I wasn't too thrilled with idea of moving here. I thought it was going to be gray and rainy all the time, but when I got here, I decided that the place was actually pretty great."

Her lip curved into a small smile. She hadn't been too keen about moving to a place where it was cold and rainy all the time, either, but then she'd been pleasantly surprised to learn that it didn't rain all year round, but was sunny and warm for the spring and summer months.

"You're not originally from around here then?" she said to the Marshal.

He shook his head. "I grew up in Dallas," he told her.

Her smile broadened. "I thought I detected a slight accent."

Cade chuckled. "That's not an accent," he told, giving her an offended look. "It's called a drawl."

44

Riley had to laugh. "My mistake," she said. "A drawl, then."

He glanced at her. "Speaking of accents, you don't sound like a typical New Yorker."

"That's because I grew up in Connecticut," she explained. "I moved to Manhattan after I graduated from college."

Turning onto a side street, Cade pulled up outside an apartment building. Though it looked like it had been built decades ago, inside it was well kept, and Riley thought it very charming as he led the way up the stairs to the second floor. Cade's apartment had a breathtaking view of Puget Sound and the Cascade Mountains beyond, and Riley found her gaze drawn to the window the moment she stepped inside.

"I'll just be a couple of minutes," Cade told her as he closed the door.

Riley nodded absently as he strode across the living room and disappeared down the hallway and into what she assumed was his bedroom. As bachelor pads went, it was nice, she thought as she looked around. There were the requisite television, CD player, and various other electronic equipment, of course, but there were no piles of dirty clothes on the floor or dishes in the sink like she had would have expected to see.

Maybe that was because Cade didn't live alone, she thought. Maybe he shared the apartment with a girlfriend. That would make sense, considering how clean and put together the place was. For some strange reason, though, the notion of Cade having a girlfriend bothered Riley. Which made no sense. It wasn't like she was jealous or anything. Actually, she didn't even like him. That being the case, she pushed the errant thought aside. Besides, it made sense that the Marshal would have a girlfriend; he was too good looking not to have one. But as Riley let her gaze wander around the living room, she couldn't help but admit she was relieved to find there weren't any obvious feminine touches anywhere. Maybe he didn't have a girlfriend.

Catching sight of the framed photos on one of the shelves on the built-in bookcase along the wall, Riley gave in to her curiosity and walked over to look at them. One was of a smiling, older couple standing in front of what looked like a horse corral. The man was wearing a cowboy hat and had his arm around the woman's shoulders while she leaned into him slightly. From the man's angular jaw and the woman's warm golden-brown eyes, it was easy to figure out that they were Cade's parents.

Riley turned her attention from that photo to the one beside it. This one was of Cade and another man that could only be his brother. Besides being tall and broad-shouldered like the Marshal, the man also had the same dark hair, chiseled features, and golden-brown eyes that Cade did. A girl would have a hard time resisting either of them, she thought.

A noise behind Riley interrupted her musings, and she turned to see Cade coming out of the bedroom, overnight bag in hand. Embarrassed to be caught looking at his personal things, Riley flushed and quickly set the picture fame back on the shelf.

"I-I'm sorry," she stammered. "I didn't mean to..."

But Cade only shrugged. "That's okay," he said.

Riley tucked her hair behind her ear. "Is this your brother?" she asked, glancing at the picture.

Cade set his suitcase down on the floor and walked over to stand beside her. "Yeah," he said. "That was taken a couple of years ago out at my parents' ranch."

She nodded. "Does he live in Texas then?"

"Madoc?" Cade shook his head. "No. He's a U.S. Marshal out in Denver."

Riley looked at him in surprise. "Your brother's a Marshal, too?"

His mouth quirked. "Yeah," he said. "I'd guess you'd say I'm following in his footsteps, though I'd never admit that to him."

46

She smiled, her gaze going back to the photo again. "You two sound like you're close."

"I suppose you could say that," Cade replied. "We fought like crazy when we were younger, and we're still competitive as hell, but there's nothing we wouldn't do for each other."

Riley's thoughts automatically went to her own family, and she chewed on her lower lip. "My sisters and I are really close like that, too," she said softly. "Before I was in Witness Protection, I'd get together with at least one of them every weekend. Sometimes, they'd come to Manhattan and we'd go shopping or see a show, and then, sometimes, I'd go up to Connecticut to spend the weekend with one of them." She shook her head. "God, it seems like a lifetime ago."

Beside her, Cade furrowed his brow. Once again, he realized how hard being in the program had been for Riley. He suddenly had an almost irresistible urge to take her in his arms. Then, surprised he had felt that strongly for her plight after what she had put him through, and unsure what to make of it, Cade cleared his throat. "We should get going," he said.

Over the next several days, Cade and Riley fell into a routine of sorts. With little to keep them occupied, they spent the time either watching television or reading the books they had brought with them. By the afternoon of the second day, however, they had exhausted both forms of entertainment, so they had ended up talking instead.

Riley was a lot more open than he thought she would be, especially considering they hadn't gotten off to a great start with each other. Not only did she tell him about herself and her family, as well as the small town in Connecticut where she had grown up, but she also confessed to him about how nervous she'd been moving to Manhattan after she'd graduated from college, and how she had feared she wouldn't be able to make it at the financial firm where she'd gotten hired.

As Cade listened to her talk, he found himself reassessing his opinion of her again and again. Despite what he had first thought when he'd met her, Riley Barnett was actually a lot more likeable than he had ever expected her to be.

In turn, Cade found himself opening up to Riley about his own life. Not just about his childhood back in Texas, either, but about what it was like growing up in a family where becoming a Marshal was almost a forgone conclusion. He'd never been able to talk to anyone about the doubts he'd had when he'd applied to the Marshals Service, but to his surprise, he found himself telling Riley about all the fears and reservations he'd had when it came to living up to his family's expectations. He wanted to think that the only reason he was talking this freely to Riley was because there was nothing else to do at the safe house except talk, but the truth was, he just found her extremely easy to talk to.

And she wasn't hard on the eyes, either, he had to admit. The other night, he'd gotten a glimpse of her in those little shorts and tank top she slept in. The sight had brought him to a full stop just outside her bedroom door. She'd been leaning over the bed, straightening the sheets when he'd walked by on his way to the shower. The position had pulled her skimpy shorts even tighter and given him a glimpse of her absolutely awe-inspiring asscheeks. He'd almost groaned out loud and probably would have if he hadn't thought she would hear. So, instead, he'd taken a cold shower, and then gone back downstairs where he spent half the night staring at the ceiling.

For her part, Riley was becoming just as enamored with Cade. She was amazed by how well they were getting along. She hadn't spent this much time talking to a guy in five years. Even though she and Cade came from different backgrounds, they shared a lot of the same viewpoints and had a lot more in common than she would have thought possible. Not only was family very important to both of them, but they also had the same taste in things like movies and books. They were also both into physical fitness, particularly jogging.

Of course, talk of getting out and running reminded Riley even more of how she hated being cooped up in the safe house. But then something dawned on her. Cooped up in a safe house or not, it was the most fun she'd ever had with a man, and she had to admit that Cade really wasn't such a bad guy. When he wasn't spanking her, of course.

The thought of the spankings he given her made Riley blush and she quickly focused her attention on the cards in her hand. Cade had found the deck in one of the drawers in the kitchen that morning and had asked if she'd wanted to play a game or two. Riley didn't play cards that often, unless one counted solitaire, of course, but she'd been up for something new, so she'd eagerly joined him at the kitchen table.

They started out with gin rummy, but after a few games, Cade suggested poker.

"I don't know how to play," Riley said.

He looked up from shuffling the cards, surprise in his golden-brown eyes. "You've never played poker?"

"I never learned," she admitted with a shrug.

He shook his head. "Well, you can't spend this much time with a man from Texas and not learn how to play poker," he told her with a grin. "It would be considered a crime against my cowboy heritage."

So, Cade spent the next several hours teaching her. Though Riley had to admit she was having a difficult time paying attention to most of what he was trying to teach her, especially when he came around to her side of the table to look at her cards. With the hard wall of his chest pressing against her back as he leaned over her chair, she couldn't seem to focus on anything but how amazing he felt. How she managed to learn the first thing about playing poker under those circumstances, she couldn't even begin to guess, but after a dozen or so hands, she had finally begun to get the hang of it.

"You know," she said as she picked up one of the M&M's they were using as chips for the game and popped it into her mouth. "These are great, but we have nothing in the way of real food to eat for dinner tonight."

On the other side of the table, Cade stopped shuffling the cards to look up at her. "Really?"

She almost laughed. "Really," she said. "We have been here for almost a week, you know."

He shrugged. "We'll just order pizza again."

She shook her head. "I didn't think I'd ever say this, but I'm sick of pizza," she told him. "We had it three nights this week already. I've got to have something different. Besides, we're out of milk, too."

He sighed. "If I go to the store, will you promise to stay put this time?"

Riley felt her face color at the memory of what had happened the last time Cade had gone shopping, or more precisely, what had happened after he'd come back. "No more runs to the video store," she said, and then added, "Promise."

Cade's eyes narrowed warningly. "You'd better not," he told her.

Riley watched as he got to his feet, her gaze traveling down the length of his body and back up again. Since going by his apartment to pick up some clothes, Cade had traded in his business suit for jeans and a button-up shirt, and though she had to admit that while he looked extremely handsome in the suit, he looked even more gorgeous now. She especially liked the way those tight jeans showed off his great butt.

Blushing at the direction of her thoughts, Riley pushed back her chair and stood up, then followed Cade to the door. Once it closed behind him, she leaned against it and breathed out a sigh. God, what a hottie! She could really fall for a guy like him. Darn it, why did she have to move again just when she'd found someone she liked?

50

Though Cade didn't think Riley would be foolish enough to leave the safe house again, he wasted no time getting what they needed at the grocery store. Even so, it was almost dark by the time he turned down the street where the safe house was located. As he neared the house, he saw a dark SUV just pulling away from the curb.

Cade's gut clenched. Was it the same SUV that Riley claimed she'd seen outside her apartment building? The same one that he'd seen driving by the other night? He had no way to be sure.

Cade tightened his grip on the wheel, torn for a moment as to what he should do. Should he follow the SUV, or check on Riley first? he wondered. His fear for the beautiful blonde outweighing his desire to check out the SUV, he pulled into the driveway and hurried up the front steps.

Seeing no signs of forced entry, Cade felt himself relax a little. But that didn't stop fear from continuing to grip him. The thought that even now Riley could be lying on the floor bleeding to death from some hit man's gunshot made Cade's hand tremble as he hurriedly punched in the code to unlock the door.

Hand resting on the weapon on his hip, Cade took a deep breath and threw open the door.

For a moment, Cade just stood there in disbelief. Whatever he had expected to find, it wasn't the scene that met his gaze. Riley was leaning against the back of the smaller of the two couches, talking on her cell phone. She looked startled to see him, as if she hadn't expected him to be back quite so soon, but at the glower he gave her, she hastily brought her conversation to a close.

"I have to go, Mom. I'll call you when I get settled in my new place," she said quickly, and then, without waiting for a reply, snapped her cell phone closed and dropped it back into her purse with a hasty nonchalance that suggested she would rather he not have seen her talking on the phone.

And with good reason, Cade thought as he slammed the door shut.

"What the hell are you doing?" he demanded.

"I...uhm...I was just talking to my mom," Riley stammered.

Cade ground his jaw. The relief he had felt at finding Riley safe and unharmed when he'd walked in had been replaced by anger at seeing her on the cell phone. "That much I figured out," he growled. "What I meant was, what the hell were you doing talking to your mother after everything I told you?"

Riley shrugged. "Well, she called me," she explained. "And I couldn't just hang up on her. It would be rude. Besides, I had to tell her that I was moving again, and that we couldn't use the mail anymore because it was too dangerous."

"And calling her on the phone isn't?" he said incredulously, unable to believe how Riley could be so smart, and yet be so stupid at the same time. He shook his head. "You know, I could give you a fifteen minute lecture on how easy it is for someone to tap into a cell phone conversation, but I don't think it'd sink in. It seems that the only time I can get through to you is when I'm spanking you, so I'll take that approach instead."

At his words, Riley's eyes went wide, but before she could so much as take a step back, Cade closed the distance between them and grabbed her arm. Jerking her forward, he bent her over the back of the couch in one swift motion, and then held her there while he peppered her jean-clad bottom with quick, hard spanks.

She began protesting immediately, squirming and kicking to free herself. But Cade ignored it, instead wrapping his arm around her slender waist so that he could hold onto her more tightly as he continued to bring his hand down over and over on her wiggling bottom. Somewhere in the back of his mind he remembered telling himself that he should cut her a break, but seeing her talking on her cell phone had made him

52

forget all about that. Once again, she needed to be reminded what the rules were and why it was important that she follow them.

But the sight of that incredible ass of hers wiggling all over the place was almost enough to make him completely forget about spanking Riley altogether. A growing tightness in his jeans had him wanting to just yank down her jeans and thrust himself inside her instead. But he knew he couldn't do that. Not only would he never force himself on Riley like that, but the reality was that she needed this spanking. If she didn't learn to start doing what she was told and being more careful, she was going to get herself killed. That thought steeled his resolve.

"*Owwwww!*" she protested as his hand came down again. "That really...*owwwww!*...hurts!"

"Good!" Cade growled. "Then maybe you'll remember this the next time you want to go off and do something else foolish!"

She let out another high-pitched yelp. "You can't...*owwwww!*...expect me to just...*owwwww!*...cut all ties with my...*owwwww!*...family!" she told him. "I won't...*owwwww!*...do it!"

Cade's jaw tightened. "You'd damn well better do it, Riley, because if you don't, you're going to wind up dead," he said harshly. "Is that what you want?"

He could tell from the way Riley stiffened that he had finally gotten her attention, but that still didn't stop him from delivering a hard smack to the sweet-spot right where her asscheeks met the tops of her thighs.

"Is it?" he demanded.

In the silence, there was a sound outside, like the crunching of gravel underfoot, and Cade jerked his head up to listen.

Unaware that he was no longer paying attention to her, Riley turned her head to glare at him over her shoulder. "Of course it's not, you..."

But the words were muffled as Cade clamped his hand over her mouth. Infuriated that he wouldn't let her finish calling him the nasty name he had coming to him, she began to struggle to free herself, but his hold on her only tightened.

"Quiet!" he hissed in her ear. "There's someone outside!"

Riley immediately went still at his words, forgetting all about her stinging bottom as terror gripped her. Oh God, she thought. They had found her!

Taking his hand from her mouth, Cade pulled her upright and slid his Glock from the holster at his side. "I'm going to go check it out," he said softly. "Stay here."

She caught his arm. "By myself?" she asked fearfully.

He gave her a hard look. "Just do as I tell you, and you'll be fine."

Riley opened her mouth to protest, but before she could get the words out, the door burst open and a man stepped in, a gun already thundering in his hand.

CHAPTER FIVE

Cade moved faster than Riley could ever have thought possible. Grabbing her around the waist, he threw her to the floor behind the couch and covered her body with his. Above them, the couch exploded in a flurry of stuffing as bullets tore through it with alarming speed. Huddled there behind it, she knew the piece of furniture was providing very little protection, and that the only thing between her and certain death at that moment was Cade.

Riley barely had time to think about his unselfish act before Cade was up and returning fire with his own weapon. She didn't know if he hit the assailant or not, but regardless, the would-be assassin stopped shooting. A moment later, she heard the sound of retreating footsteps.

From where she lay on the floor, Riley looked up at Cade. He still had his weapon pointed toward the door. "Is he gone?" she asked softly.

Cade looked down at her. "Stay here," he ordered. "And stay down."

Realizing that Cade meant to go after the gunman, Riley opened her mouth to protest, but the Marshal had already gotten to his feet and was racing toward the front door.

Her heart pounding, Riley knelt behind the couch, trembling. What if the gunman came back? she thought. Or what if there was a second man, and the first one had just been meant to lure Cade away? Without Cade, she knew she wouldn't stand a chance against a hit man.

Cade's order to stay where she was echoed in Riley's mind, and she chewed on her lower lip, debating whether to disobey it or not. To heck with this, she thought. Ignoring the

Marshal's command, she scrambled to her feet and ran out into the night after him.

It was raining when Cade ran outside, and in the dim light of the streetlamp, he could make out the figure of a man beside a dark SUV halfway down the block on the other side of the street. So much for Riley being paranoid, he thought bitterly.

Tightening his grip on the weapon in his hand, Cade raced down the street toward the man, only to slow his steps as he drew nearer. He watched in amazement as the man, who was clearly oblivious to Cade's presence, fumbled with his car keys. He had locked the doors? Cade thought in disbelief. What kind of idiot hit man was this guy?

Lifting his gun, Cade leveled it at the man. "Federal Marshal!" he yelled. "Freeze!"

Startled, the man jerked his head around to stare at Cade in surprise. The rain was really starting to come down now, and in the near darkness, Cade could make out a broad face with a long nose, and a pair of close-set eyes.

"Turn around and put your hands where I can see them!" Cade ordered.

The man didn't move. Probably weighing his options, Cade thought. His finger firmly on the trigger, Cade took a step closer to the man.

"Put your hands where I can see them!" he repeated. "Now!"

Letting out a heavy sigh, the man lifted his hands in the air and started to turn to face him. Then, without warning, he turned and bolted.

"Shit!" Cade muttered.

Deciding that it would be too dangerous to take a shot at the man with all the houses in the vicinity, Cade gave chase instead. Though the man took Cade down sidewalks and in between houses, it was obvious he wasn't in good shape because within minutes, he was already starting to slow down.

56

Cade was just about to pick up speed when he heard the sound of running footsteps behind him. Did the hit man have a partner? he wondered. Stopping in his tracks, he spun around, weapon at the ready, only to stare in disbelief when he saw Riley coming up behind him. Like him, she was soaked to the skin, her long hair wet, her T-shirt molding to the curves of her breasts. Damn, she looked good, he thought. Then he ground his jaw as he realized that she had deliberately disobeyed his order and followed him.

Throwing a quick look over his shoulder, Cade saw the fleeing assailant disappear around a corner in the distance. Swearing under his breath, he lowered his weapon to glower at Riley. "What are you hell are you doing?" he demanded angrily. "I told you to stay at the safe house!"

"I was afraid that the hit man might come back," she explained, and then looked around. "Did you get him?"

Cade clenched his jaw. "No!" he growled. "But I was just about to catch him. That was until you showed up. Now, I can't go after him."

She hugged herself with her arms and blinked up at him through the rain. "Why not?"

"Because I won't have you following behind me, and I won't leave you here in the middle of street, that's why!" he snapped, shoving his gun back into the holster on his belt. "I can't believe you came after me!"

"And I can't believe you let the guy get away!" she shot back. "I thought Marshals were supposed to be trained for this sort of thing. Why couldn't you catch up to him? It didn't seem like he was running that fast to me."

Cade clenched his jaw at her insult. This was the thanks he got for risking his life to save hers? Could she possibly be any more irritating? God, he couldn't wait to hand her over to another Marshal.

"If I didn't have to get you out of here, I'd put you over my knee and spank your ass right now for that, you ungrateful little brat!" he ground out.

Riley didn't even bother to look the least bit contrite as she glared up at him. "In case you haven't noticed, those spankings of yours don't have the effect you seem to think," she told him.

"That's just because I haven't spanked you hard enough yet!" he snapped.

Riley opened her mouth to retort, only to shut it again when he firmly took her arm and steered her back the way they had come. Staying at the safe house now was out of the question, he told himself, but they had to go back there long enough to grab his Jeep. Cade's first instinct was to take Riley to the District Office in Seattle, but then he realized that there probably wouldn't be anyone there at this time of night. So, he needed to come up with another plan until he could talk to his boss. He could only imagine what Conner was going to have to say when he heard about what had happened.

To Cade's relief, the local police hadn't shown up at the safe house yet, which saved him a lot of hassle and explanation. But they would be there soon enough and he wanted to be gone before they did.

As he led Riley up the street, he noticed that the black SUV that had been parked by the curb was gone. Damn. He had hoped to get the plate number.

"Where are we going?" Riley asked after they had gotten their stuff from the house and were safely in the Jeep.

Cade gave her a sidelong glance. Neither of them had changed out of their wet clothes, and she was shivering. "A hotel," he told her, reaching over to turn on the heat.

"Why aren't we going to another safe house?" she demanded.

His gaze flicked to the rearview mirror to see if they were being followed. "That has to be arranged. It's not like we have a dozen empty houses in every town, you know," he said dryly. "And for all I know, they might just want to get you completely out of the area. But I'll leave that up to someone else. Until then, we'll just stay in a hotel."

58

Riley supposed that made sense. Hugging her arms around herself, she turned her head to stare out the window. The concept of her life being in danger had always been just that, a concept. But after getting shot at tonight, she realized just how real the danger was. If Cade hadn't been there to protect her, she had no doubt that she would be dead right now. And she hadn't even thanked him for what he'd done. Instead, she had berated him for not running after the guy fast enough to catch him. Even as she'd said the words, she'd known they were untrue. If she weren't an avid runner herself, she never would have been able to keep up with Cade back there. The real reason Cade hadn't caught the guy was because she had followed him.

Feeling more than a little ashamed at the memory of what she'd said to Cade, she turned her head slightly to look at him beneath her lashes. She really wanted to apologize, to tell him it had been fear and stress that had made her say those things, but for some reason, she couldn't seem to get the words out. And by the time she did get up the courage to say something, Cade was already pulling into the parking lot of a well-known hotel chain.

Promising herself that she would apologize to him when they got settled into a room, Riley tucked her still slightly wet hair behind an ear in an effort to make herself more presentable as she walked into the hotel lobby with Cade. The Marshal registered for a room quickly, asking for one that was neither near the elevator nor the stairwells. If the desk clerk seemed surprised by the request, he made no comment as he handed Cade two key-cards.

Having grabbed their bags from his truck before they had gone into the hotel, Cade and Riley went directly up to the room. Holding the door open for her, Cade switched on the light in the entryway, and then instructed her to wait there while he closed the drapes.

Hugging herself with her arms, Riley let her gaze wander over the room. With its institutional-style furniture, it looked like every other hotel room she'd ever been in, she thought. Her brow furrowed a little when she saw that there was only one bed, though. She wondered if she should point that out to Cade, but then decided against it. He probably wouldn't be in the mood.

Pulling the heavy drapes closed, Cade turned back to her. "Why don't you get out of those wet clothes and go take a shower?" he suggested.

She chewed on her lower lip. A shower sounded really good about now, she thought. She supposed that apology could wait until later. "Okay," she said, and then, added softly, "You'll stay here, right?"

He nodded. "I'll be right out here."

Relieved to hear that, Riley picked up her bag and walked into the bathroom. Closing the door, she leaned back against it for a long moment. Out in the other room, she could hear Cade talking to his boss on the phone, his deep voice strong and sure as he explained what had happened at the safe house.

Considering that she had just gone through a real live assassination attempt, Riley was surprised she wasn't feeling more terrified at the moment. But she was actually remarkably calm, she realized as she stripped off her sodden clothes. Maybe she was just in denial, she told herself. Or maybe it was because she knew she would be safe with Cade. She wondered what it was about him that made her feel that way. None of the other U.S. Marshals guarding her had ever made her feel quite so protected.

Remembering the feel of Cade's strong arms as he had wrapped them around her to shield her from the hit man's bullets back at the safe house, Riley let out a sigh and stepped into the tub.

In the bedroom, Cade flipped his cell phone closed with a sigh. Well, that had gone better than he had thought it would. He'd fully expected Conner to ream him a new one for letting the shooter get away, but to Cade's surprise, his boss had commended him on the way he'd handled the situation. Conner had even been impressed with Cade for having the forethought to take Riley to a hotel.

But Cade wasn't as impressed, not with the hotel plan, and certainly not with letting the shooter get away. It had been pure luck, not his skill as a Marshal that had kept Riley alive today, he thought bitterly. He never should have left her alone at the safe house to begin with. If he had gotten there just a few minutes later or if one of those bullets had found their mark...

He swallowed hard. The thought of Riley getting shot, or worse, was too painful to bear thinking about.

As he stood there listening to the sounds of the Riley moving around in the bathroom, he suddenly realized that this assignment wasn't simply about just keeping a witness in the program safe anymore. He might as well admit it. Somewhere along the way, he had developed feelings for Riley Barnett. Feelings that were growing stronger by the minute. More than being unprofessional, though, which it definitely was, it was pointless, because nothing could ever come of it. Riley was going to be relocated soon, probably hundreds, even thousands of miles away. When that happened, he would never see her again.

Cade shook his head. He didn't even understand how it had happened. He could see being physically attracted to Riley; she was beautiful and sexy, not to mention having a great body. But the things he was feeling went way beyond physical attraction, and definitely way beyond anything he'd ever felt for a woman before. But how could he fall for a woman who irritated him so damn much? And Riley could infuriate him like no other woman he'd ever known. So, how could this have happened? He didn't know the answer to that; he just knew it had.

The bathroom door opened then, interrupting his thoughts, and Cade looked up to see Riley coming into the bedroom. She had showered and changed into those skimpy shorts and curve-hugging tank top that had caused him more than one sleepless night since he'd first caught sight of her wearing them.

Cade cleared his throat and forced himself to tear his gaze away from her long, shapely legs. "I talked to my boss while you were in the shower," he told her. "He's going to arrange for another safe house, but until he has one set up, we're going to have to stay here."

Riley nodded. "Okay." She wet her lips in what he was sure was an unconscious gesture, and he almost groaned. "I...I wanted to thank you for what you did back at the safe house. You saved my life."

His jaw tightened. "I was just doing my job."

She looked away "I know," she said. "But I haven't exactly made that easy for you, and I'm sorry."

Damn right you haven't, Cade wanted to growl, but instead, he simply shrugged off her apology. "It's okay," he said gruffly. And then realizing how hard it had been for her to apologize at all, he added, "I know this whole thing hasn't been easy for you. Your life has been pretty hard the past five years. It's understandable if you get frustrated with it every now and then."

She gave him a small smile. "Thanks for understanding."

"No problem," he told her. He ran his hand through his hair. "Do you think you'll be okay out here while I take a quick shower?"

She nodded. "I'll be fine."

He bent to pick up his bag. "Don't go near the window," he warned. "And don't open the door to anyone."

"I won't," she assured him.

Maybe Riley was finally getting it, Cade thought as he walked into the bathroom. Of course, all it had taken was someone shooting at her. But at least now, she would do as he told her.

62

Not wanting to leave Riley alone any longer than necessary, Cade made the shower a quick one. Pulling on the extra pair of jeans he'd packed and a clean shirt, he slid his gun holster onto his belt, and then shoved his cell phone, keys and wallet all back into his pockets. Picking up his overnight bag, he opened the door and stepped into the bedroom, only to stop in his tracks when he realized it was empty.

Fear gripped him. He couldn't have left Riley alone for more than five minutes, he thought. And in that time, he'd heard no screams and no scuffle, and yet Cade knew that the bastard must have taken her. But why would the man kidnap Riley? he wondered. Why not just shoot her and be done with it? Then again, did the man's reasons really matter? Cade had to find her!

Dropping his bag onto the floor with a thud, Cade crossed the room in two long strides and yanked open the door to see Riley standing in the hallway, the key-card in her hand outstretched as if she'd just been about to stick it in the slot.

Relief coursing through him, Cade grabbed Riley by the arm and pulled her into the room, letting the door slam close behind her. "Where the hell were you?" he demanded.

She looked up at him with those big blue eyes of hers. "I went to get some ice," she said softly.

His brows drew together as he noticed the plastic bucket in her hand. "Ice? You went to get ice?" he said incredulously. "After everything that happened tonight, you're still taking chances and foolishly risking your life!"

Her gaze dropped to the ice bucket for a moment. "I guess I wasn't thinking," she said.

Cade swore under his breath. How could he have thought she'd ever do as she was told? The woman had some pathological condition that prevented her from listening to anyone.

"That's your problem, Riley! You never think!" he growled. "You were almost killed back at that safe house tonight. If that bastard had followed us here, he could have grabbed you the moment you stepped foot outside the room, and there's not a damn thing I could have done. Hell, I probably wouldn't even have heard anything over the water running in the shower."

Riley chewed on her lower lip as she looked up at him. "I'm sorry," she said. "I'll be more careful next time."

Cade's jaw tightened. "I'm going to make damn sure that there isn't a next time!"

Taking the bucket of ice from Riley's hand, Cade slammed it down on the desk and marched her over to the bed. In one swift motion, he sat down on the edge of it and dragged her over his knee, then lifted his hand to bring it down on her upturned bottom in a flurry of quick, hard spanks. This time, he told himself, he wasn't going to stop until he was sure she wasn't going to ever do anything that foolish again.

Riley bit her lip to stifle her cries; they were in a hotel after all and she didn't want anyone to hear. The smacks stung fiercely through the thin material of her shorts, though, and part of her wanted to protest each and every stinging spank he gave her. But the other part of her knew she deserved this spanking. She couldn't believe she had been so stupid leaving the room like that. Cade was right. She didn't think. She just did whatever she felt like doing without any thought to the consequences. This wasn't about just some silly set of rules anymore. Someone had really tried to kill her tonight and she had just foolishly risked her life for a bucket of ice. Truth be told, she had been risking her life ever since she'd come into the Witness Protection Program. And her carelessness had finally caught up with her. A spanking was the least that she deserved, she thought bitterly. So, she submitted willingly to Cade's firm hand, hoping that this time, it would have an effect.

But as Cade's hand continued to come down over and over on her poor, defenseless ass, she couldn't help but start to squirm and kick. She might deserve it, but yikes, did it sting! It didn't help that her shorts seemed to be riding up even higher with each spank to give him easy access to her bare cheeks.

"*Owwwww!*" Riley finally squealed, unable to keep silent any longer when his hand came down on the tender area of her sit-spots for what must be the umpteenth time. "Cade, please..."

But it seemed Cade was determined to make sure she learned her lesson this time because he only spanked her that much harder, and Riley pressed her face into the soft bedding to muffle her squeals of protest. Her ass felt like it was on fire!

Just then, Cade stopped spanking her, and she breathed a sigh of relief, thinking that he was done. But to her shock, Riley felt him grab the waistband of her shorts. With one quick yank, he pulled them all the way down to the middle of her thighs! Oh my God, she thought. She wasn't wearing any panties!

Her face flaming scarlet, she craned her neck to look at him over her shoulder. "Wh-what are you doing?" she squealed.

Cade lifted a brow. "You said it yourself," he told her. "These spankings don't seem to be having the desired effect. So, I'm going to make sure this one does."

She opened her mouth to protest, but his hand was already coming down on her bare bottom. She inhaled sharply at how much more the spanks stung now than they had before. She wouldn't have believed that the shorts could have provided so much protection, but apparently, they had.

What made it even worse, though, was the knowledge that she was completely exposed to Cade now. Riley tried to clench her asscheeks tightly together, hoping to hide her pussy from his view, but that only made the spanks sting that much more, and she quickly gave up on the idea. To heck with it, she decided. He probably wasn't even paying attention to her more feminine attributes, anyway. Clearly, she thought as his hand found her tender sit-spots, he was only interested in spanking her.

Even so, he couldn't help but see her pussy, she thought. The idea alone was enough to start a rebellious tingle between her legs. It wasn't her fault, really. She hadn't been with a guy in a long time and regardless of the fact that Cade was in the process of spanking her right now, he was still utterly gorgeous.

Oh God, how could she even be thinking things like that? He was *spanking* her!

So what? she told herself. She shouldn't be complaining. This was the first time she'd been even half-naked with a guy in a long while. If a spanking was what it took, then maybe she should volunteer for one more often.

She suddenly realized the spanking wasn't stinging nearly as much as it had when Cade had first started. That wasn't a surprise, she thought. She was barely paying attention to anything other than her pussy, which was getting wetter by the second!

Riley wondered if Cade could tell she was becoming excited. God, she hoped so. Because if not, she was going to have to do something extreme. That thought brought her up short. Was she saying that she wanted to have sex with Cade? When had that happened?

Before she could puzzle that out, the spanking was over and Riley was back on her feet. She didn't bother to pull up her shorts, which were now in a puddle at her feet, but just stood there, panting for breath and cupping her flaming asscheeks with her hands. Lifting her gaze, she looked up at Cade from beneath lowered lashes. Her breath caught at the look of anguish on his handsome face. He wasn't mad at her, she realized; he was worried about her.

He pulled her close. "You scared the hell out of me when I walked out of the bathroom and found you gone," he said hoarsely. "Don't ever do that me again, Riley."

Riley gazed up at him. This wasn't just a U.S. Marshal talking, she thought. This was a man who was concerned about someone he cared for. She knew that in her heart and that made her want him even more. She leaned closer to him. "I'm sorry," she whispered. "It won't ever happen again."

But Cade didn't seem to have heard her. Instead, he was gazing intently at her mouth. Knowing the effect it would have on him, she slowly wet her lips with her tongue. He must have been as close to the edge as she was because that little bit was all it took.

With a groan, Cade slid his hand into her long hair and lowered his head to cover her mouth with his. Riley didn't resist, but instead pulled him even closer, and as he molded her against him, she could feel the heat from his body. It had been so long since she'd been with a man, and she reveled in the sensation.

The kiss went on and on until Riley didn't think she could breathe. Only then, did Cade lift his mouth from hers to trail hot kisses down her neck. His nibbling made her shiver and clutching him to her even more tightly, she tossed her head back with a sigh. God, that felt so good!

Still heady from his kisses, she was barely even aware that Cade had stopped nibbling on her neck to urgently slide his hands underneath the hem of her tank top. Desperately wanting to feel his hands on her naked body, Riley lifted her arms over her head so that he could take off her top.

Cade's eyes turned to molten gold as he studied her and Riley felt herself blush as he took in her rounded breasts and slender waist before his eyes dropped to the gentle curve of her hips and long, shapely legs.

Standing there completely naked while he was still fully clothed made Riley feel utterly wanton and terribly shy at the same time, and she would have reached for the buttons on his shirt, but he caught her hands in his and pulled her close to kiss her again. This time, his hands gently cupped her breasts for one long delicious moment before sliding down her back to cup her red-hot asscheeks. Riley gasped against his mouth as he squeezed her freshly-spanked bottom. She hadn't realized how tender it still was! And yet the firm pressure of his fingers had her pussy clenching with excitement, and she moaned as she realized how wet she was getting. Deciding that the foreplay had gone on long enough, she slid her hands up the front of his shirt and began to savagely pull at the buttons.

With a soft chuckle, Cade released her to lend his assistance and within moments, his clothes had joined hers on the floor. Now it was her turn to study him and Riley let her hungry gaze rove over his naked body. God, he was so gorgeous! From his broad shoulders and muscular chest to his tight abs and long, powerful legs, he was perfect, she thought. And to top it all off, his extremely hard cock was just waiting for her attention! She would have knelt down in front of him and taken him in her mouth right then, but he didn't give her the chance. Instead, he took her hands and nudged her backward until she was up against the edge of the bed.

More than ready to have him inside her, Riley lay back on the bed, but Cade surprised her by leaning down to slowly kiss his way up the inside of her legs. Perhaps a little more foreplay would be okay, she thought as he alternated from one leg to the other.

But Cade seemed determined to take his time and within moments, Riley felt herself grow impatient again. Sliding her fingers into his hair, she tried to urge him up to her pussy, but he refused to play the game her way. Instead, he stopped at mid-thigh to tease and nibble at the soft skin there. While what he was doing felt incredibly wonderful, it was also incredibly frustrating, and she heard herself groan in exasperation. Only then did he begin to kiss his way up her legs again.

But even once Cade reached the junction of her thighs, he continued to tease her. He slowly trailed his tongue along either side of her pussy lips, dipping inside occasionally, but never allowing himself to come too close to her throbbing clit.

Riley groaned again in even deeper frustration. At the sound, Cade lifted his head to look at her with amusement.

"Something wrong?" he asked softly.

"Stop teasing me, Cade," she begged. "Please."

His mouth quirking, he lowered his head to immediately focus his attention directly on her plump clit.

Sliding his hands up her legs, he cupped her still-stinging ass in a tight grip that made her gasp. The combination of sensations was so intense that it was almost too much, but at the same time, it felt so amazing that she didn't want him to ever stop. Lacing her fingers into his hair to hold him in place, she slowly began to rotate her hips in time with his licking.

It didn't take long for her orgasm to build and within moments, she was crying out as wave after wave of pleasure rushed over her. Somehow, Cade seemed to know exactly how she liked it and his light, feathery licks let her ride out the orgasm for an unbelievably long time. Only then did he stop and climb into bed with her.

Riley had planned to return the oral favor, but Cade didn't give her the chance, instead slipping between her legs to slide his hard cock up and down the opening of her pussy. Realizing that he meant to tease her again, she wrapped her legs around his hips.

"No more teasing," she growled, hooking her hand behind his head and dragging him down for another searing kiss. "I need you inside me. Now!"

Cade didn't argue, but kissed her passionately as he plunged himself into her pussy in one smooth thrust.

Time lost all meaning for Riley then as he moved in and out of her. As excited as he obviously was, she was amazed at his stamina. Her orgasm seemed to have no beginning or end, but was just one, long, glorious burst of pleasure.

Riley didn't think it was possible for it to get any better until she heard Cade groan with his own release. Knowing that she had the ability to make him come so hard made her own orgasm that much more powerful, and she clamped her legs more tightly around him as he pushed his hard cock deep inside her and held himself there. The pleasure that rippled through her as she came again was so intense that it almost brought her to tears. That had never happened to her before, and she could only wonder what it was about this man that had brought on such powerful emotions.

CHAPTER SIX

The next morning, Riley awoke to find herself curled up against Cade's side, her head pillowed on his muscular chest, her arm thrown over him possessively. With a sigh, she cuddled closer to him. It had been so long since she'd been with a man, especially one so strong and protective, and she had missed it more than she'd realized.

As she lay there, her lips curved into a smile. Last night had been amazing, she thought. No man had ever made love to her so passionately and completely as Cade had. That first frenzied lovemaking session had been followed by several more, each slower and more tender than the one before it. Oh yes, she thought again, it had definitely been amazing.

And, she suddenly realized with a sickening lurch, it had also been a really big mistake. While she could admit that the sex was the best she'd ever had, sleeping with Cade had definitely been a stupid thing to do. But she hadn't been able to stop herself. She had wanted Cade, plain and simple, and so she hadn't bothered to think about what it would mean.

She wasn't the type to sleep with a man on a whim. Usually, it took her weeks of dating a guy before she even considered it, and that was only after she really fell for him. When she did fall for a guy, though, she fell hard. And after making love with Cade last night, she had fallen for the sexy Marshal with a really big thud! She would have to keep her distance from him at the next safe house, she told herself, or else risk losing her heart to the man altogether.

As if on cue, Cade's cell phone rang. He seemed to be sleeping so deeply that for a moment, Riley wondered if he would even hear it, but when he immediately reached out to grab it, she realized he must already have been awake.

Though she had been expecting the Marshals Service to call, Riley couldn't help but let out a sigh as she listened to Cade talk to the caller about transferring her to another safe house. From what she could hear, it sounded like they wanted to move her right away. She had hoped she and Cade would be able to stay at the hotel a little while longer.

Assuring the caller that they would be there, wherever "there" was, Cade flipped his phone closed and set it down on the bedside table. Knowing she couldn't pretend to be asleep any longer, Riley held the sheet to her breasts with one hand and used the other to push herself into a sitting position.

Tucking her hair behind an ear, Riley tried to ignore the way her pulse leaped at the sight of Cade's tousled hair and dark stubble. She hadn't known it was possible for anyone to look that gorgeous the first thing in the morning. "Do they have another safe house ready?" she asked.

Cade nodded. "My boss wants us to meet him at the Seattle office."

Riley said nothing. She wondered if Cade was as uncomfortable as she was after the night of unbridled passion they'd spent together. She wished she could think of something to say to make the situation less awkward, but nothing would come to mind. So instead, she just sat there, clutching the sheet to her breasts. The same sheet that was riding low on his hips to reveal his well-muscled chest and tight, sexy abs, she noticed. Oh God! If she didn't get out of bed soon, she was going end up jumping him!

Riley was still trying to figure out how to make a graceful exit from the bed when Cade cleared his throat. "I told him we'd be there as soon as we could."

Her face colored. "I'd better go get dressed then."

Realizing she'd have to leave the sheet where it was or else leave Cade completely naked, Riley avoided his gaze as she blushingly slid out of bed. Naked, she scooped her clothes up from the floor, and then grabbing her bag as quickly as she could, she padded into the bathroom.

Cade watched Riley go, his body responding to the sight of her nakedness with an eagerness that made him groan. He'd like nothing better than to drag her back into bed with him and spend the day making love to her. She was just that amazing.

Last night had been incredible. Riley was not only more beautiful than he had imagined, but more passionate than he could have dreamed. He could make love to her a thousand times and still never get enough, he thought. And waking up with her in his arms that morning had felt good. Too good, he told himself.

As enjoyable as the sex had been, there was a part of Cade that regretted taking her to bed last night. He'd known all along that Riley was the kind of woman he could fall for, the kind of woman he could see himself spending the rest of his life with. He'd also known that nothing could ever come of their relationship, not when she could be leaving at any time. But he had allowed himself to get close to her anyway.

Sleeping with her had been stupid not just because the relationship couldn't go anywhere, but because having sex with a witness was just downright unprofessional. He was supposed to be protecting her, not sleeping with her. If this ever got out, his career in the Marshals would be over.

Swearing under his breath, he got out of bed and collected his clothes from the floor.

When Riley walked out of the bathroom half an hour later, it was to find Cade already dressed and waiting for her. He had ditched the jeans and button-up shirt she'd gotten used to seeing him wear in favor of his suit and tie, she noticed, but he still looked just as gorgeous.

"Ready to go?" he asked, and Riley nodded.

They drove up to Seattle in silence, Cade obviously as preoccupied with his thoughts as she was with hers. Was he regretting last night as much as she was? she wondered.

Once inside the building where the U.S. Marshals had their offices, Cade led her directly to the one belonging to his superior. At their entrance, the man got to his feet and came around his desk to join the two other men that were standing in front of it.

"I'm Deputy Chief Conner," he said, extending his hand to Riley. "And these are Deputies Thompson and Morris."

Riley reached out to shake his hand, and then did the same with the other two Marshals when they offered their hands as well.

Deputy Chief Conner glanced at Cade. "No problems on the way, I take it?" he asked.

Cade shook his head. "No, Sir."

The older man nodded. "Good." He turned his attention back to Riley. "You'll be staying at a safe house just south of Olympia with Deputies Thompson and Morris for a couple of days until we get you relocated, Ms. Barnett. With any luck, we'll have you on your way within the week."

Riley's brow furrowed at the mention of the other two Marshals. Did that mean Cade wouldn't be going with her to the safe house? She glanced at Cade to see him looking just as puzzled by Deputy Chief Conner's words.

"I thought I would be staying at the safe house with Ms. Barnett," he said to the older man.

Deputy Chief Conner shook his head. "I want you working on finding out who the shooter was," he said. "Deputies Thompson and Morris will take care of her until we can get her relocated."

Riley felt her heart sank at that. She might have thought sleeping with him was foolish, but nevertheless, she had hoped to be able to spend a couple of more days with Cade before she had to move. But maybe it was better this way, she told herself. If she were with Cade, she had no doubt she would end up sleeping with him again and that would only result in more heartache. It was easier to make a clean break of things, she thought. But as her gaze strayed to the handsome Marshal, she realized it wasn't going to be easy at all.

"Ms. Barnett," Deputy Thompson said from behind her. "If you're ready, we can go."

She glanced over her shoulder at the men, before turning back to Cade again. At the hotel that morning, she hadn't been able to think of anything to say Cade and now there was so much she wanted to say to him. Like how much she appreciated him saving her life. And how comforting it was to be in his arms, even if it had been only for a little while. But she couldn't tell him any of those things, not with his superior and the other two Marshals looking on.

Cade gave her a nod. "Take care of yourself," he told her.

Riley felt a slight pang of disappointment that he hadn't said something more personal, but she realized that he couldn't very well say anything in front of his coworkers either. She offered him a small smile. "You, too," she said softly.

Realizing that the other two Marshals were waiting for her, Riley swallowed hard and turned away. Surprised to feel tears welling in her eyes, she quickly made her way to the door before anyone could see. But unable to resist one more look at Cade, she paused and glanced back at him over her shoulder to find him studying her with those remarkable gold eyes of his. For a moment the urge to run back into the office and throw herself into his arms was almost too much to resist and she had to force herself to turn away.

Cade watched her go, his gaze following Riley until she disappeared around a cubicle and out of sight. He had hoped that she would look back at him once more before she left, but she hadn't. Well, what had he expected? He was just another in a long string of Marshals who had been responsible for keeping her alive.

"Do you think you got a good enough look at the shooter to sit down with a sketch artist?" Conner asked.

The words jerked him from his thoughts and Cade gave himself a mental shake as he turned to look at the other man. "I should be able to, yeah," he said.

"Good," Conner said. "While you do that, I'm going to talk to the DA who prosecuted Donatti and see if he can shed some light on this whole thing. There must be a reason if Donatti put out a contract on Riley Barnett at this point."

Taking that as his cue to leave, Cade headed for the door. Regardless of the fact that he'd told Conner he would be able to work with a sketch artist, he wasn't sure how much good it would do. Not because he hadn't seen the hit man well enough, but because he was too distracted with thoughts of Riley.

Cade had really been taken aback when Conner had announced that Thompson and Morris were going to be taking Riley to the safe house. He had just naturally assumed he would stay with her until she was relocated. But maybe it was better that he didn't. The more time he spent with her, the harder it was going to be on him when she left. Besides, Conner was right. It was more important to track down the hit man that had tried to kill her.

With that in mind, Cade spent the rest of the day focusing his attention on doing just that. He was just frowning at the drawing the sketch artist had made when Conner walked over to his desk. The older man studied the drawing for a moment.

"So, that's our shooter, huh?" the other man said when he'd taken a look at it.

"Yeah," Cade said. "This guy's face is really familiar for some reason."

He hadn't realized it when he'd first seen the man the other night, but after thinking about it, Cade was sure he had seen the hit man somewhere before.

Conner regarded the sketch thoughtfully. "Take a look through the NCIC database," he told Cade. "If we're lucky, maybe the guy has a record. Start with known mob enforcers."

Looking through the online National Crime Information Center database would be a whole hell of a lot easier than thumbing through old mug books. Of course, everything depended on the guy having a record and being in the database. If he didn't, things would be much more difficult, Cade thought.

"What did the DA have to say?" he asked Conner.

Conner shook his head. "He wasn't in the office," he said. "I'm waiting for him to call me back."

Cade knew that with the time difference between the east and west coast it could be awhile before the man returned Conner's call. Hopefully, Cade would have a solid lead on the hit man by then.

As it turned out, though, Cade had no luck finding the guy through the NCIC database. He came up with a lot of known hit men, mob enforcers, and just general bad guys with organized crime connections, but none of them resembled the shooter from the other night. Thinking that he was using too narrow of a scope, he broadened it, but again, his search yielded nothing but hours of wasted time.

"Anything?" Conner asked when he came up to Cade's desk later that evening.

Cade sat back in his chair with a sigh. "Not a thing."

The other man frowned. "I just got off the phone with the Manhattan DA. Turns out that Albert Donatti has been more interested in making deals than in taking out witnesses," he said. "He's in the WitSec Program himself now."

Cade's brow furrowed. "He flipped on someone else?" he asked. "If that's the case, then it doesn't make sense that he'd go out and hire a hit man."

"No, it doesn't," Conner said, and then sighed. "Maybe we're just looking at this the wrong way. Look, go home and get some rest. We'll look at it a different angle first thing in the morning."

Cade went, but only reluctantly. He would much rather have stayed and looked through the criminal databases some more, but as exhausted as he was, he'd probably only miss something if he did.

Despite being wiped out, however, Cade couldn't sleep at all that night. Finally tired of tossing and turning, he got out of bed a little after midnight and wandered into the living room to watch television. But despite having plenty of channels to choose from, none of them could hold his interest, and before long, his thoughts turned back to Riley.

After spending a week in the safe house with her, his apartment seemed incredibly quiet and empty. He had never thought of himself as the overly talkative type, but it turned out that he had really enjoyed the time he and Riley had spent together talking. And he couldn't help but remember what it had felt like to spend the night with her in his arms. It might have been foolish, but it had felt good.

He found himself wondering what Riley was doing at that moment. Had she gotten settled in at the safe house? Was she asleep or was she making the other Marshals sit through whatever chick-flicks she'd talked them into renting for her? That thought made Cade smile. But then almost immediately, it turned into a frown as he was reminded again of how much he missed her. Did she miss him as much?

Cade let out a derisive snort at that. He would like to have thought that the sex they'd had the night before had meant something to Riley, but her actions that morning had made it clear that it had been nothing more than a one-night stand to her. He wished it could mean so little to him.

Turning off the television a couple of hours later, Cade threw himself back into bed and tried hard to push thoughts of Riley from his mind. He did fall asleep, but only because he was exhausted. And even then, he slept fitfully and often awoke swearing he could feel Riley there with him, sleeping curled up at his side.

Cade woke up around five the next morning feeling even more exhausted than he had the night before. He wanted to sleep more, but decided that it would be a waste of time to try. So instead, he took a shower and got dressed, then left for work. At the office, he'd at least have something to distract him from thinking about Riley.

He logged back into the NCIC database the moment he got into the office, but even though he tried to focus, it did no good. He couldn't stop thinking about Riley. Or worrying about her. Thompson and Morris were more than competent, so Cade knew that logically there was no reason to be concerned for Riley's safety. But he also knew that he would feel a hell of a lot better if he checked on her. So, around mid-morning, he gave up on the database search and decided to get a status report on Riley. Cade didn't have either man's cell phone number, however, but rather than ask Conner, he went down to get it from the Support Division.

Maxine, the woman who managed most of the administrative functions for the Seattle office, wasn't at her desk, however. Not knowing when she'd be back, Cade was about to leave a note for her when he noticed the photograph on her desk. Cade stared at the picture, unable to believe what he was seeing. In it, a smiling Maxine was standing in front of a panoramic view of the Grand Canyon, and beside her, was the dark-haired man who had tried to kill Riley at the safe house the other night.

"Son of a bitch," Cade muttered.

Grabbing the photograph off the desk, Cade leaned over the cubicle to show it to Maxine's coworker. "Do you know who this guy with Maxine is?"

The woman smiled. "Sure," she said. "That's Maxine's husband, Tony."

Photograph in hand, Cade swore under his breath as he quickly weaved his way through the maze of cubicles. All this time he had been thinking that it was some mob hit man that was after Riley. No wonder he hadn't been able to get a match through the NCIC database.

Back upstairs, Cade made a quick stop at his desk to grab the composite drawing before heading to Conner's office. Not bothering to knock, he walked right in. Ignoring the other man's scowl, he held up the photo in one hand, and the sketch in the other.

"I finally have a name to go with the face," he said. "Tony Caruthers, who just happens to be married to Maxine from the Support Division."

Conner's brow furrowed as he glanced from the photo to the sketch, and then back again. "Are you sure?"

"Positive," Cade assured him.

The other man swore. "Is Maxine Caruthers in today?"

Cade nodded. "But she's not at her desk."

"Let's find her then," Conner said. "I want to talk to her."

It took nearly half an hour to find Maxine in the huge office building, but when they did, it was to take her directly to an interrogation room. It didn't take much prompting to get the woman to talk and within minutes, she broke down and admitted everything. It seemed that her husband wasn't a hit man for the mob by trade, but just some guy who thought he could get rich quick by killing federal witnesses. The fact that Maxine had the addresses and personal records on all of the witnesses had made the decision easy.

"Did Albert Donatti order the hit?" Cade asked curtly.

Maxine shook her head. "No," she sobbed. "Tony thought he should do the job first, and then go to Donatti and ask for the money." She sniffed. "I told Tony it was a stupid idea, but he was sure we could make a bundle, and that no one would ever know. I didn't want to do it!"

80

But she went along with it anyway, Cade thought bitterly. "Why Riley Barnett, then?"

The woman shrugged. "Tony thought she would be an easy target, a good way to get his feet wet, I guess," she said. "He thought it would be safer to start with a woman instead of a man."

"Where is your husband now, Maxine?" Conner asked.

She didn't answer, but only fiddled nervously with the tissue in her hand, and Cade ground his jaw.

"You're already an accessory to attempted murder, Maxine," he told the woman. "Tell us where your husband is and the district attorney will probably take that into account."

Maxine said nothing for a moment, but Cade could tell she was considering his words. "I don't know for sure, but I gave him the address for the safe house down in Olympia this morning," she said finally. "He's probably on his way there."

Cade felt his gut clench. Riley, he thought. He could hear Conner talking to someone on his cell phone, ordering the local PD to the safe house, but Cade didn't wait around to see what else the man said. Instead, he got the address for the safe house from Maxine and was out the door before Conner could stop him.

CHAPTER SEVEN

Riley never ate ice cream right out of the container, but that afternoon she found herself sitting at the kitchen table with a pint of chocolate chip mint, half listening to the two Marshals talk about the baseball game they were watching on television in the living room and feeling altogether miserable.

It had only been a day since she'd seen Cade, but Riley missed him so much that her heart ached. How was it possible to develop such strong feelings for a man she barely knew? she wondered. She'd only slept with him one time. And they hadn't even exactly hit it off in the beginning. But as she sat there eating the ice cream, she wondered if she and Cade would have ended up dating if they had met under different circumstances. Then again, she thought, it was highly unlikely that they ever would have met at all if she hadn't been in the Witness Protection Program.

As painful as it was to think about, Riley let herself imagine what could have been. If she weren't moving to parts unknown, would things have gotten serious between her and Cade? Would they even have gotten married? She liked the idea that they might have.

Tears abruptly stung her eyes. What was the use of daydreaming about something that wasn't going to ever happen? All it did was make her feel more wretched.

Angrily wiping away the tear that trickled down her cheek, Riley jabbed her spoon into the ice cream again, only to freeze when she heard a loud thud coming from the front of the house. It sounded like it had come from the living room, she thought. But before she could even begin to puzzle out what it could have been, she heard a series of loud bangs. Oh God, she thought. Gunshots!

With the colored lights on the dash flashing and the siren blaring, Cade made the two-hour drive to the safe house in half that time. The local police were already there, as was an ambulance, and Cade felt his blood run cold at the sight of the latter. Had that bastard Caruthers succeeded in killing Riley this time?

Cade barely put the Jeep in park before he was out and running toward the house, flashing the silver star on his badge to the cops standing along the perimeter as he did so. Taking the steps two at a time, he hurried into the house to find the paramedics kneeling down beside the Marshals that had been guarding Riley. Both men had been shot, Thompson in the shoulder and Morris in the stomach. Afraid to think what that meant for Riley, Cade strode over to crouch down beside the woman tending to Thompson.

"Where's Riley?" Cade asked.

Thompson jerked his head toward the rear of the house, only to wince at the movement. "She must have gone out the back," he said. "The shooter went after her."

Swearing under his breath, Cade got to his feet and raced through the living room and down the hallway to the back of the house, pulling his weapon as he went. The kitchen door was wide open and Cade immediately headed for it.

In the backyard, there were several uniformed cops standing around talking, and Cade hurried up to them.

"Has anyone gone after them?" Cade asked, referring to Riley and the man hunting her.

One of the cops shook his head. "No," he said. "We have some dogs that should be here any minute, though. We're waiting for them."

Cade stared at the other men in disbelief. The ground was soaking wet and the tracks through the mud were obvious to anyone. He could have stood there and chewed them out for their lack of police work, but decided that it would be a waste of time. Instead, he headed into the woods behind the house.

84

A path led directly from the backyard to a dense, wooded area and even if the ground hadn't been muddy enough from the rain they'd had earlier in the day for him to see footprints, Cade instinctively knew that was where Riley had gone. It was the only place to go really. And though Cade was grateful for the muddy tracks, he also knew they would give Caruthers an advantage as well. But Riley was a fast runner, Cade reminded himself as he set out after her. And if she had a good head start, there was no way Caruthers would catch up to her. Unless she ran out of places to run.

Cade had been running for at least twenty minutes through the wet, slippery forest, at the same time working hard to keep his eyes on the tracks in the mud, when a dark shape suddenly burst through the trees and over a small hill directly ahead of him. Skidding to a halt, Cade instinctively took aim with his Glock, only to let out a sigh of relief when he realized it was Riley. Her long hair was a wild tangle around her shoulders, and there was mud all over her clothes. But Cade didn't think he'd ever seen her look more beautiful.

For a moment, Riley just stared at Cade, unable to believe that he was really there. Then, with a cry of relief, she closed the distance between them and threw herself into his arms. He wrapped his arm around her tightly, enveloping her in his warmth, and she sobbed against his chest. She was safe now, she told herself.

"Oh God, I w-was so scared, Cade," she told him, her breath coming fast and hard, the words half-muffled against his chest. "I d-didn't know wh-what to do, so I ran. But he f-followed me..."

Cade smoothed her hair with his hand. "Shhh, you did good, sweetheart," he said softly. Then, still holding onto her, he took a step back to gaze down at her. "Where is he, Riley?"

She looked up at Cade through her tears. "Somewhere behind me, I think," she said. "I doubled back, but I think he must have realized it because as I was running, I could still hear him behind me every once in a while."

Cade's gaze quickly darted to the wooded area around them before going back to her. "Go back to the house," he told her. "The police are there, so you'll be safe."

Riley frowned up at him. "What are you going to do?"

His jaw tightened. "I'm going after the guy that tried to kill you."

She tightened her grip on his arm. "You can't!" she protested. "He's got a gun!"

"So do I," Cade told her. "Now, go back to the house."

"Cade..." she began, but he cut her off.

"Dammit, Riley, for once in your life just do as you're told!" he growled. "Now, go!"

His tone brooked no argument and this time, Riley obeyed. Still reluctant to leave Cade alone, however, she took off at a slow trot over the sloppy, uneven ground. She was exhausted and would rather just have waited and walked back with Cade, but she understood his desire both to keep her safe and to catch the guy who had been terrorizing her once and for all.

But that didn't mean she wasn't worried for Cade, and she couldn't help but stop when heard the sound of footsteps crashing through the forest behind her. The hit man had caught up to her already, she thought. Even though Cade had told her to go back to the house, Riley found herself turning around and heading back toward the clearing where she had left Cade. Heart hammering wildly in her chest, she got there just in time to see the hit man standing in front of Cade, gasping for breath.

"Drop the gun and put your hands in the air!" Cade ordered, leveling his own weapon at the man.

Riley held her breath as she waited to see what the man would do. For a moment, he just stood there, his weapon still pointed at Cade, and Riley felt fear grip her. Oh God, what if he shot Cade? But to her relief, the hit man tossed the gun onto the ground and slowly lifted his hand above his head.

Relieved that it was finally over, Riley jogged back over to where Cade was standing. Though it wasn't her intention to distract him, she did, and in the split-second it took for him to glance her way, the other man charged.

Riley opened her mouth to warn Cade, but it was too late. The other man had already knocked him to the ground and they were grappling.

Her eyes wide, Riley watched helplessly while the two men struggled with each other. She had to help Cade, she thought. But how? Not quite sure, she ran toward the men, only to jerk to a halt when she saw Cade's gun go flying into the bushes. Her first instinct was to go look for it, but she knew it would take forever to find it, so instead, she reached down and scooped up a heavy branch that was lying on the ground.

Gripping it tightly, she slowly approached the two men. They were rolling around on the ground, each of them struggling furiously to gain the upper hand. She had to be careful, she told herself; she didn't want to end up hitting Cade by mistake.

Suddenly, the hit man rolled on top of Cade and drew his arm back to punch the Marshal. Knowing she wouldn't have a better opportunity, Riley swung a vicious blow at the hit man's head, only to hit Cade across the shoulders instead when he rolled his opponent over.

"Dammit, Riley, what the hell are you doing?!" he yelled at her while he still grappled with the man.

"I'm trying to help!" she shouted back.

"Well, stop it!" he ordered.

Disregarding what Cade said, Riley tightened her grip on the branch, ready to whack the guy again if she got the chance, but it wasn't necessary. Within a few moments, Cade had the hit man subdued and cuffed.

Cade glared at her as he hauled the man to his feet. "I thought I told you to go back to the house," he growled.

She gave him a sheepish look as she dropped the branch on the ground. "I know, but I thought you might need help or something."

"Really?" he said sarcastically. "And how did that work out for you?"

The question really didn't require and answer, but Riley gave him an embarrassed shrug anyway. "I'm sorry I hit you," she said.

Cade gave her an exasperated look but made no comment. "Come on," he said.

Still pushing the hit man in front of him, he led the way back to the house.

When they got back, the place was a complete madhouse. There were dozens of police cars, as well as what looked like every Marshal from the Seattle and the Tacoma offices. Of course, there was already a lot of press there as well, but to Riley's relief, they were relegated to a spot behind the yellow tape at the bottom of the driveway.

Riley didn't really need any medical attention, but at Cade's insistence, she allowed the paramedics to check her out. To her chagrin, the EMT fussed over ever scratch and scrape. The man was just finishing up with her when Deputy Chief Conner walked over.

"The other Marshals that were with me," she said. "How are they?"

He nodded. "They're both in surgery, but they're expected to make a complete recovery."

She nodded, relieved to hear that. "That's good," she said. "So, what happens to me now?"

Conner shrugged. "Actually, that's up to you."

Her brow furrowed. "Up to me?" she said. "I don't understand."

"It turns out that Albert Donatti didn't hire Caruthers to kill you. after all," Conner explained. "As a matter of fact, Donatti is really no longer a threat to you at all. He turned evidence on some of his own and is now in the WitSec Program himself. We'll have to go through some bureaucratic procedures, but I would think that you would be removed from the list of protected witnesses."

It took a moment for Riley to wrap her mind around what Deputy Chief Conner had just told her. "So you're saying that I don't have to move then? That I can go back to using my real name again?"

The older man gave her a small smile. "I think that's all going to be up to you now," he told her. "We would certainly move you one more time, though, if you wanted us to."

Riley glanced at Cade to find him watching her with those remarkable gold eyes of his. "Actually," she said softly. "I kind of like it here in Seattle."

Conner nodded. "Then it's settled," he said. "I'll have someone take you home."

Riley hoped Cade would volunteer, but to her dismay, Deputy Chief Conner was already calling over another Marshal.

"Like I said, there's some paperwork we'll need to go over, Ms. Barnett, but we can do that another time. Deputy Brogan will take you home," the older man said to Riley, and then, giving her a nod, pulled Cade off to the side to speak to him before walking over to intercept the group of reporters coming their way.

Riley hesitated, giving Cade a glance out of the corner of her eye, but he was deep in conversation with the uniformed police officer who had come up to him. Disappointed that he wasn't even going to say goodbye to her, she followed Deputy Brogan toward his car.

She was just about to get in when she heard Cade calling her name. Her pulse skipping a beat, Riley tried to hide her eagerness as she turned to see him jogging toward her.

"I wanted to catch you before you left," he said.

Riley held her breath as she waited for him to continue. He glanced at the other Marshal standing by the driver's side door, and then back at her. "I can't really talk to you here, though," he said. "Would it be okay if I stopped by your apartment later?"

She was tempted to ask him what he meant when he'd said that he couldn't talk about it there, but Deputy Chief Conner was already calling Cade over to talk to the press. "Of course," she said. "That would be fine."

He looked relieved. "I'll see you tonight, then."

As she watched him walk away, Riley tried to tell herself not to read too much into Cade's wanting to see her, but she couldn't suppress the surge of excitement that began to course through her.

Riley changed clothes half a dozen times that night before finally settling on a simple skirt and camisole top. She had no idea why Cade had asked to come over and told herself again not to read to much into it. For all she knew, he might be bringing over the paperwork that Deputy Chief Conner had mentioned. God, she hoped not!

The doorbell rang then, interrupting her thoughts, and Riley felt her pulse quicken. Smoothing her hands over her short skirt, she gave herself one more look in the mirror before hurrying to answer the door. Once in the entryway, however, she paused to take a deep, calming breath. She couldn't ever remember being so nervous! Wetting her lips, she ran her hands over her skirt again, and then threw open the door.

Cade was dressed and jeans and a button-up shirt, and looking even more gorgeous than Riley remembered. She must have stood there gazing at him for a full minute before she finally managed to find her voice.

"Come in," she said, taking a step back so that he could do so.

He took in her outfit, his gaze lingering on her legs for a moment, and Riley felt herself blush. "You look nice," he told her.

"Thank you," she said softly.

He cleared his throat. "I didn't know if you'd eaten already, so I stopped by to pick up some Chinese food," he said.

Riley glanced down at the bag in his hand in surprise, realizing that she hadn't noticed it before. This was definitely not an official call, then. "No, actually I haven't," she said. Giving him a smile, she took the bag. "I'll get some plates."

"That'd be great," Cade said as he followed her into the kitchen. "But I was hoping we could talk about what happened the other night first."

Riley's heart plummeted, the smell of the food wafting up from the bag making her feel sick all of a sudden. This was the part where Cade told her that he hoped she hadn't read anything into what had happened between them at the hotel, and that while they couldn't have a relationship, he hoped they could still be friends, she thought. Swallowing hard, she set the bag down on the counter and turned to look at him.

Cade cleared his throat again. "I know that we didn't really get off on the right foot, and that there was a lot of stuff that happened between us at the safe house, but I think we have a connection," he said, and then immediately held up his hand. "Before you say anything, let me finish."

Riley almost smiled. She hadn't been going to say anything, but it seemed obvious that Cade had rehearsed whatever he was going to say quite a bit and she didn't want her to interrupt him. In all honesty, she didn't know where he was going with this, but the part about them having a connection definitely made her pulse quicken.

"Actually, there's more than a connection. As cliché as this is going to sound, I think we were meant to be together," Cade continued. "I know that when this started, you were just a witness I was supposed to protect, but even though you drove me crazy most of the time, I found myself drawn to you. And that feeling got stronger the more we were together. I don't know if you feel the same way, but I do know that for my part, I want you in my life."

She blinked up at him, suddenly unable to breathe. "What are you saying, Cade?" she asked softly.

Cade reached out to gently brush a strand of hair back from her face. "I'm saying that when you were in danger, I could barely think straight, and that made me realize what you mean to me." He paused and took a deep breath. "What I'm trying to say is that I'm in love with you, Riley Barnett."

Riley caught her breath, speechless. Of all the things she had expected Cade to say when he had come over tonight, telling her that he had fallen in love with her had definitely not been one of them.

In front of her, Cade suddenly looked unsure of himself. "I think this is the part where you're supposed to say something," he told her quietly.

She took a step closer to him, her lips curving into a smile. "Well, then how about this?" she said. "I love you too, Cade Cutler."

A grin spreading across his handsome face, Cade slid his hand into her hair and bent his head to kiss her on the mouth. Riley melted against him, parting her lips to urge him on with her tongue, and by the time he lifted his head a few minutes later, she was breathless.

"Now that we've gotten that out of the way," he said softly. "We need to talk about what happened in those woods behind the safe house today."

Her brow furrowed in confusion as she looked up at him. He wanted to talk about that *now*? "What about it?" she asked.

He lifted a brow. "I told you to go back to the safe house, and instead, you decided not to."

She chewed on her lower lip. "I told you," she said. "I was worried about you and thought you might need help."

92

Cade's jaw tightened. "Riley, you once again foolishly put yourself in danger," he said. "And more importantly, you refused to do what I told you to do."

Riley looked up at him from beneath lowered lashes. "I'm sorry," she said softly. "I promise I won't do it again."

He let out a sigh. "I know you believe that," he said. "But I need to make sure, and since the only way I can ever seem to get you to really listen to me is to give you a spanking, that's what I'm going to have to do."

She blinked at him in surprise. "A spanking?" she echoed. "You're not serious!"

Cade couldn't really mean to spank her, not after telling her he loved her, she thought. But he had already taken her hand and was leading her into the living room.

"But you said you loved me!" she protested.

"I do love you," he told her over his shoulder. "That's why I'm doing this."

That could only make sense to a guy, she thought. "But what about dinner?" she reminded him. "It'll be cold."

He turned to face her. "We'll reheat it," he said, and then his mouth quirked. "Right now, I'm more concerned about warming that sexy, little bottom of yours and making sure that you don't do anything as foolish as you did today again. At least until you forget how much a spanking stings."

Though her lips formed into a pout, Riley allowed Cade to draw her over his knee without too much more protest. Considering how that most recent spanking he'd given her at the hotel had culminated in some incredibly hot sex, she supposed she could put up with a sore bottom. But she really would have to talk to him about this habit of his to spank her every time she didn't do what he told her. He was going to have to learn that just because he was from Texas, he couldn't spank her like this was the old west.

But that would have to wait, she supposed, because he was obviously intent on spanking her right now. Wiggling into a more comfortable position, Riley pillowed her head on her arms and waited for Cade to begin.

Even though she knew it was coming, the first spank still caught her by surprise. Ouch, she thought. Couldn't he start a little bit softer? But before she could ask him about it, he landed a second smack to her other cheek.

"*Owwwww!*" she cried. "Cade, that stings!"

"Good," he told her, bringing his hand down again in another stinging smack. "That way you won't be tempted to do anything foolish for a long time."

After another dozen spanks, her bottom really felt like it was on fire, and unable to control herself, Riley reached her hand back to protect her tender asscheeks. But Cade only grabbed her wrist and held it pinned against the small of her back.

"You're not getting off that easy," he told her with a chuckle. "I tend to remember you hitting me with that branch pretty hard."

"But I didn't mean to hit you!" she protested even as his hand came down on her bottom again. "If you...*owwwww!*...had stayed still...*owwwww!*...for a minute, I would have...*owwwww!*...gotten him!"

"You know," he said, pausing to rest his hand on her stinging bottom. "I don't think you're getting the point of this spanking. Maybe I should try a different approach."

Before she could even ask what he meant by that, Riley felt Cade push up her skirt, exposing her skimpy black thong. She had worn it because she'd hoped they might end up making love that night, but the realization that he was seeing her wearing something so sexy was enough to get her pussy purring. Which was strange, she thought, considering that the spanking stung so much. She'd definitely have to give that some thought later, she decided.

"Very nice," he commented, running his hand over her bare bottom. "It's almost as if you knew you were going to get a spanking tonight."

94

Riley gasped and started to tell him that she knew nothing of the sort, but the words disappeared on her lips when his hand connected with her right cheek.

"*Owwwww!*" she yelped, going rigid over his lap. "Not so hard! You may not realize it, but that skirt provided a lot of protection."

Cade chuckled. "Then it's a good thing I pushed it up," he told her as he began to apply his hand firmly to first one cheek, and then the other in an easy rhythm.

That had her kicking and squirming all over the place. The spanking wouldn't have been nearly that bad if it weren't for the cell phone, or whatever it was he had in his pocket, jabbing her in the hip every time she wiggled.

"Okay, okay!" she squealed. "I get the point! I promise to be good and do exactly what you say from now on!"

"I really doubt that," Cade drawled, a hint of amusement in his voice. "In fact, I imagine you'll be getting yourself into trouble frequently. Which is fine with me, as long as you realize that you'll be getting a spanking every time you do."

He punctuated his words with one more hard spank to her bare bottom before he took her hand and helped her to her feet.

Riley gave him a pout as she stood there rubbing her sore bottom. Her poor ass was on fire! But just like with the spanking he'd given her at the hotel, her pussy was soaking wet. Of course, there was no way she was going to let Cade know that the spanking had gotten her all excited. He'd want to give her one every day! That thought made her face turn almost as red as her bottom.

"That was a really hard spanking," she pouted. "Next time, could you remember to at least pull the cell phone out of your pocket before you put me over your knee. That thing is really uncomfortable when I'm wiggling around."

Cade's mouth twitched. "Sorry about that," he said, getting to his feet. "It's not my cell phone, though. But I'm glad you mentioned it. I was actually going to give it to you later, but I think that now is probably the perfect time."

Riley watched as he pulled something out of his pocket, only to feel her heart begin to beat wildly as he dropped to one knee in front of her. The spanking she'd just gotten all but forgotten, she stared transfixed at the ring box Cade held in his hand.

"I know this might be kind of sudden," Cade said. "And I don't want you to feel that you have to give me an answer right now, but when I said that I wanted you in my life before, I meant forever."

With that, Cade opened the box in his hand to reveal the most beautiful engagement ring Riley had ever seen. Oh God, she thought, he was really asking her to marry him!

"Like I said, there's no rush to give me your answer," he told her. "But I hope that you'll think about it and that someday you'll agree to marry me."

Riley smiled down at him, tears of happiness in her eyes. "I don't need to think about it. I can give you my answer right now," she said. "Of course, I'll marry you!"

For a moment, Cade seemed surprised that she had given him an answer so quickly, but then he grinned. Taking the ring from its velvet-lined box, he slipped it onto the third finger of her left hand, then got to his feet and pulled her into his arms for a passionate kiss.

Lifting his head a moment later, Cade gave her a serious look. "You know what this means, don't you?" he said. "You'll have to change your name again."

Riley laughed. "That's okay. I'm used to it," she said pulling his head down to kiss him again.

The Cutler Brothers Series
Book 2

Madoc

CHAPTER ONE

Madoc Cutler still couldn't believe his little brother, Cade, had actually gotten married. When Cade had called to tell him that he was engaged, Madoc had been surprised by the news, but that had been nothing compared to how stunned he had been when he'd learned that not only was the woman his brother had fallen for in the Witness Security Program, but that he'd known her for all of a whole week before he proposed! What the hell had Cade been thinking? All that stuff Cade had spouted about knowing true love the moment he saw it and not being able to live without Riley just seemed downright insane to Madoc.

Madoc, being five years older and obviously much wiser than Cade, had tried to talk some sense into his brother, but it had done no good. Cade was completely head over heels for Riley Barnett. Though Madoc could certainly understand being attracted to the beautiful blonde, he couldn't understand why his brother had felt the need to marry her. In his opinion, Cade should have just done the smart thing and moved in with her. That way, he wouldn't have been tied down. But when Madoc hadn't been able to dissuade his brother from making one of the biggest mistakes of his life, he had finally agreed to not only attend the wedding, but to also be Cade's best man.

Of course, it didn't help that their parents absolutely loved Riley and were completely thrilled that Cade had finally found a nice girl and settled down. Now that he thought about it, Madoc supposed he should be happy Cade had gotten married. At least now his brother would be the one having to listen to their mother and father constantly harp about not having any grandchildren. That was a headache Madoc would happily let his brother put up with.

For his part, Madoc could never see himself having kids. Actually, he couldn't even see himself getting married.

He just wasn't the marrying kind. Sure, he liked women – a lot – but every one he'd ever gone out with seemed to want to rein him in. They all thought his job as a U.S. Marshal was a phase that he would get out of, and when it became apparent he wasn't planning to leave his job any time soon, his girlfriends usually started throwing around ultimatums. That hadn't worked out too well for them, though, because he had always chosen the job over them. He probably always would. What woman could produce the same thrill and excitement that he got from being a Marshal?

Madoc reached up with his free hand to rub the back of his neck. Deciding to drive from where he lived in Denver to Seattle for his brother's wedding had seemed like a good idea at the time, but he was barely halfway through Montana on the return trip and he was already exhausted. Staying up late partying the night before probably hadn't helped, he supposed, and now, it looked like the weather was turning against him. He frowned as he scanned the sky. It was getting really gray and looked liked it was going to snow at any minute. He had heard on the radio earlier that it was supposed to snow sometime that day, and he hoped it wasn't heavy. He still had a lot of driving to do before he got home.

He had hoped to make it to Billings before he had to stop for gas again, but glancing down at the gauge, he saw that it was almost on empty. As he took the exit for the next town, Madoc chided himself for not leaving Seattle earlier that morning. He had taken almost a week off already, and there would be a pile of work on his desk when he got back. Not only that, but his boss would be royally pissed if he called in to ask for more time off because he was stuck in the snow.

As he stood filling his gas tank a few minutes later, Madoc surveyed the small town of Flint Rock. It was one of those towns that had sprung up simply because there needed to be a gas station at that point along the highway. There were a few fast-food places and a diner, as well as the requisite tourist traps. Other than that, it didn't have much else to offer.

100

Thinking he should probably get something to eat as well, Madoc decided he wasn't really in the mood for fast food and settled on the diner instead. The place looked like it could have been any of a dozen different chain diners, and probably had been over the years. The building was at least thirty or forty years old and could use a little fixing up, but he didn't really care what the place looked like, as long as he could get something good to eat, fast.

Pushing open the door, Madoc scanned the inside of the diner. Other than a handful of people sitting at the counter, the place was empty, he noticed as he made his way to the restroom. When he came back out a few minutes later, he debated for a moment whether to sit at the counter, but then slipped into a booth near the window. That way, he could keep an eye on his truck.

Reaching for the menu resting against the napkin dispenser, he was about to look at it when he caught sight of the pretty, dark-haired waitress behind the counter. Daaaaang, Madoc thought. Well, she definitely stood out in a small town like this. Even wearing glasses and a drab waitress uniform, she was a knockout. Then again, he thought appreciatively as he took in her rounded breasts and slender waist, the uniform did hug her curvy figure in all the right places. And he had to admit that the oval-shaped glasses with their black frames were surprisingly flattering on her. It made her look like some tame librarian-type that had a wildcat inside of her just waiting to get out.

"What can I get for you, sugar?"

Startled, Madoc tore his gaze away from the girl behind the counter to see a short, plump, gray-haired waitress standing beside his table. He had been so distracted by the younger waitress that he hadn't even realized the woman was there. Or that she had set down a glass of ice water in front of him.

His brow furrowing, Madoc looked down at the menu in his hand and ordered the first thing he saw. "Uhm, I'll have the meatloaf."

"Do you want fries or mashed potatoes with that?" the woman asked, her pen poised above the order pad she had in her hand.

Madoc glanced over at the younger waitress behind the counter again to find her studying him with big, brown eyes. Tucking a strand of long hair behind her ear, she gave him an embarrassed smile and looked away.

Realizing that the older woman was still waiting for an answer, Madoc forced his attention back to her. What had she asked him? Oh yeah, what he wanted with the meatloaf. "Mashed potatoes will be fine," he told her.

She scribbled his order on the pad, and then tucked it into her apron before giving him a smile. "Coffee okay?"

He nodded. "Coffee would be great. Thanks"

"Coming right up," the woman said.

As the plump, little woman made her way back to the counter, Madoc found himself secretly hoping the younger waitress would bring his coffee over, and he was disappointed when the gray-haired woman picked up the coffee pot and started over to his table again. Even so, he couldn't help but play a little fantasy through his mind about the younger waitress. In it, she would slowly walk over to his table, her curvy hips swaying provocatively as she did so. Then, once she got there, she would lean way over to place the mug on the table, which of course would cause her breasts to strain against the confining buttons of her uniform. And then...

Unfortunately, the older waitress reached his table before Madoc's fantasy could go any further. Though he tried hard to concentrate on what the nice, old woman was saying, and even told her about his job and why he had been out to Seattle, his gaze kept being drawn to the girl behind the counter again. She was laughing with one of the customers, and the sound was warm and rich as it drifted across the diner and over to where he sat.

Telling himself that it wasn't polite to stare, Madoc picked up a packet of sugar and emptied it into his coffee, and

102

then turned to look out the window. But the gray sky and the tiny town of Flint Rock wasn't enough to hold his interest for very long, and every so often, he would let his gaze wander over to the pretty, dark-haired girl behind the counter again.

Madoc was just staring at the darkening sky outside, wondering how much longer the snow would hold off when he heard the sound of a plate being set down on the table. Realizing that his food had arrived, he turned to thank the waitress, and was pleasantly surprised to see the dark-haired girl standing there. Up close, she was even prettier, he thought, taking in her full lips, pert nose, and the light dusting of freckles across her cheeks.

"More coffee?" she asked with a smile.

Her voice was soft and sweet, just like the rest of her, Madoc thought. "Please," he said.

As she leaned over to pour the coffee, Madoc's gaze automatically went to her perfectly rounded breasts. His fantasy had been right on; they did strain nicely against the uniform. As he tried hard not to be too obvious about staring at her breasts, he caught sight of the plastic nametag on the front of her uniform, and frowned when he saw that her name was Jane. It wasn't that there was anything wrong with the name, of course. It was just that he had expected the pretty waitress to have a more exotic name.

"I don't think I've seen you around before," she said, giving him another smile.

He tore his gaze away from her perfect breasts. "Just passing through," he told her.

Madoc thought he detected a hint of disappointment in her dark eyes at his words, but it was gone before he could be sure.

"Where are you headed?" she asked.

"Denver," he said.

She looked at him in surprise. "Denver?"

He nodded. "Have you ever been there?" he asked curiously.

She reached up with one hand to adjust her glasses in what he was sure was an unconscious gesture. "Me?" she said. "No. I've never even been out of Flint Rock."

Madoc regarded her for a moment. That was difficult to believe. "Really?" he said. "You kind of look familiar. I thought maybe we might have run into each other back there."

That probably sounded like some sort of pick-up line, and a really lame one at that, Madoc thought, but it was true. Though he hadn't noticed it when he'd first seen her, the more he looked at the waitress, the more sure he was he'd seen her somewhere before. Then again, maybe it was just wishful thinking.

She let out a nervous, little laugh as she reached up to fiddle with her glasses again. "I don't think so," she told him. "I'm sure I would have remembered if we had."

He gave her a smile. "You're probably right," he agreed.

She returned his smile with one of her own. "Well, have a safe drive to Denver," she said, picking up the coffee pot from the table. "And be sure to watch out for the snow. I hear it might be a pretty bad storm. You wouldn't want to get stranded out here in the middle of nowhere."

"I don't know," he said, his grin broadening. "Maybe I would."

She gave him a sexy smile that immediately made his jeans feel tighter in the crotch, and then turned to head back to the counter, an extra little sway in her step.

Damn, Madoc thought as he watched her walk away. Getting trapped in the snow with a woman like her might just be worth the hell he'd catch from his boss for taking more vacation time. Drab it might be, but the curve-hugging waitress uniform she was wearing definitely showed off her feminine figure. He'd always been an ass-man, and the not-so-plain Jane had one hell of a sexy bottom. Not to mention extremely shapely legs, he noticed. Yep, getting snowbound in

104

the middle of nowhere with the cute waitress would be downright fun.

Picking up his fork, Madoc was about to turn his attention to the food he had ordered, but he couldn't resist glancing over at the counter again. Jane had set down the coffee pot and was talking to the older waitress. From the way the women glanced his way, he had a sneaking suspicion they were talking about him, and he found himself hoping Jane would come over to talk to him again, but a moment later, she disappeared into the kitchen.

As Madoc ate, the feeling that he'd seen the dark-haired waitress somewhere before came back to him. He was good with faces and usually didn't forget one, something that served him well in his line of work. But if he had met her, he told himself, surely he would have remembered such an attractive woman. Hell, he almost certainly would have asked her out.

A thought so absurd it was almost laughable popped into his head then, but it gave Madoc pause just the same. It was possible he might have seen her in passing somewhere, but it was also possible he might have seen her somewhere else – on the Most Wanted List. Where the hell had that thought come from? he wondered. He shook is head. *Dude, you're spending way too much time on the job.*

Madoc shook his head again. There was no way that cute waitress could be wanted in connection with anything more criminal than breaking a few hearts, he told himself. For all he knew, he'd seen her in a magazine somewhere; she was certainly gorgeous enough to be a model.

Putting the ridiculous notion that she was a criminal out of his head, Madoc finished his meal, then paid the check and left the diner. As he did so, he looked back one more time, just to get another look at the dark-haired waitress, but she still hadn't come out of the kitchen.

Outside, it was beginning to snow, hard. *Damn*, Madoc thought. He'd better get moving or he really would be stuck in this town. He quickened his step, only to halt beside his SUV, his hand on the door handle. What if he were wrong about the girl? What if she really were a fugitive? It wasn't really that big of a stretch. He was becoming more and more convinced that he had seen her face, and the wanted list was where he spent most of his time looking at people. It could actually be possible she was fugitive. And if she were, then it was his job to bring her in.

Knowing he wouldn't be able to leave without checking it out, Madoc was about to head down the street to the police station he'd passed on the way to the diner when he spotted the small public library across the street. Deciding it would be easier to log onto the U.S. Marshals' fugitive database there instead of explaining his suspicions to the local sheriff, he walked across the street and into the library.

Giving the elderly librarian at the desk a nod, he sat down at one of the computers and connected to the Internet. With his password, logging onto the Marshals' fugitive database was simple, and within a few minutes, he was typing the parameters into the search engine. His search came up with almost a hundred female fugitives fitting Jane's description, and as Madoc scrolled through each one, he found himself praying that the cute waitress wouldn't be among them.

But Madoc's worst fears were confirmed when he pulled up the next page of fugitives a few minutes later. Gazing back at him from the top row of photos was the cute, dark-haired waitress from the diner. Even without the glasses she'd been wearing as a disguise, he recognized her easily. Swearing under his breath, Madoc clicked on the wanted poster and began to read.

Name: Shayna Matthews
Alias: None Known
Description:
Sex...Female
Race...White
Date of Birth...June 4, 1976
Place of Birth...Colorado

106

Height...5'9"
Weight...125
Eyes...Brown
Hair...Brown
Skintone...Medium
Scars/Tattoos...None Known
Wanted for...Unlawful Flight – Embezzlement and Suspicion of Murder
Warrant Issued...District of Colorado
Date of Warrant...August 8, 2006
Matthews is wanted for Unlawful Flight to avoid prosecution and by the Denver County Sheriff for Failure to Appear. Matthews jumped bond after her arrest by the Denver, Colorado police for Embezzlement and Suspicion of Murder.

"Shit," Madoc muttered.

Despite what he had just read, he couldn't believe the sweet waitress he'd met at the diner was wanted on suspicion of murder. Or maybe he just didn't want to believe it. But there it was, in black and white, and as much as he wanted to just forget that Shayna Matthews, aka not-so-plain-Jane the waitress, was a fugitive, he couldn't. He was a U.S. Marshal, which meant that it was his duty to bring her in.

His hand tightening on the mouse, Madoc clicked on the print button, and then logged out of the database. Folding the wanted poster of Shayna Matthews, he shoved it into his coat pocket, then strode out of the library and across the street to the diner.

Shayna's hands trembled as she hurriedly shoved what little clothing she had into the small overnight bag she'd brought with her when she'd left Denver. Of all the men in the diner she could have flirted with, she had to pick a U.S. Marshal!

Tall and broad-shouldered, not to mention ruggedly handsome, she had noticed the Marshal the moment he'd walked into the diner, and had been disappointed when he had chosen a booth instead of taking a seat at the counter. So when Madge, the other waitress she worked with, had suggested she serve lunch to him, she had not only jumped at the chance, but had openly flirted with him. She'd figured that he was probably only passing through town, but had toyed with the idea of trying to convince him to hang around for a while. Little did she know he was there to arrest her, she thought bitterly. And if Madge hadn't learned that he was a U.S. Marshal from her conversation with him earlier, then Shayna would still be at the diner obliviously going on about her business.

God, she had been so stupid! Stupid to stay in Flint Rock for so long instead of going to Canada like she had planned. Stupid to think that a pair of ugly, non-prescription, black-framed glasses would be enough of a disguise to alter her appearance. Stupid not to dye her hair like her sister had suggested.

Still silently berating herself for her stupidity, Shayna grabbed her coat from the bed and put it on. If she hurried, maybe she could catch one of the truckers down at the gas station near the freeway and bum a ride with him. Anyone heading north would be fine with her.

She picked up her suitcase from the bed, and was just about to cross the small room she rented at the boarding house when there came a loud banging on the door.

"Federal Marshal!" a man's voice called. "Open up!"

Shayna froze, her hand tightening reflexively on the handle of her overnight bag as she stared at the door. Oh God, he'd found her, she thought. She couldn't go back to jail! She just couldn't! Just the thought of the small, gray cell was enough to make her stomach clench. She had to get out of there!

The Marshal banged on the door, louder this time. Heart pounding, Shayna looked around wildly for some other escape route. Her gaze immediately locked on the window on the other side of the small room. Not having to think twice, she dashed over to it. Instead of opening easily like it should have, however, the window didn't budge. Dammit, the darn thing was stuck!

Tears of frustration welling in her eyes, Shayna dropped her bag on the floor and tried to force the window open, but it did no good. The stupid thing probably hadn't been opened in ten years! Spotting a heavy bookend sitting on the low shelf beside the window, she grabbed it and was just about to use it to break the glass when the door burst open.

Still holding onto the bookend, Shayna whirled around with a startled gasp to see the handsome Marshal from the diner standing in the doorway, his weapon drawn and pointed at her.

"Shayna Matthews, you're under arrest," he told her. "Drop that and put your hands up."

Shayna knew she should obey, especially since the Marshal had a gun pointed at her, but she couldn't make herself do it. "You've got the wrong person. My name is Jane," she said, her voice trembling. "Jane Cooper."

His golden brown eyes went to the bag sitting on the floor beside her. "Nice try," he said sarcastically. "Now, drop what you're holding and put your hands up."

She swallowed hard, but still didn't do as he told her. "You've got the wrong person," she insisted.

The Marshal clenched his jaw. "I'm not going to tell you again," he warned her. "Drop what you're holding and get your hands in the air."

Shayna didn't move. She couldn't let him arrest her. Running had only made her look guiltier, and if she went back to jail, they weren't likely to let her out on bail this time. Her stomach churned.

Her gaze darted to the door and she wondered if she could somehow get past the Marshal. Apparently, he must have read her mind because he started toward her even as she tensed to make a run for it. Shayna's hand tightened on the bookend and before she even realized what she was doing, she drew back her arm and threw it at him.

Shayna just had enough time to see the Marshal's eyes go wide before he ducked. Knowing she would only get one chance at escape, she immediately ran for the door. But she didn't get more than a few feet before a strong hand closed over her arm and spun her around. With a cry that was half frustration, half rage, Shayna balled her hand into a fist and took a swing at the Marshal.

"What the...?!" he began, catching her arm before her fist could connect. "Dammit, take it easy!"

But Shayna wasn't about to take it easy. If she didn't get away from him, she was going to be spending a very long time in prison, maybe even the rest of her life. With that horrific thought motivating her, Shayna savagely tried to jerk free of the Marshal's hold.

"Stop it!" he ordered her, his grip tightening on her arms. "Dammit, I don't want to hurt you!"

"Then let me go!" she shot back, still struggling against him.

But it was obvious the Marshal wasn't going to let her go, so Shayna fought him wildly. Once she even managed to get her arm free long enough to try to scratch his face, but he quickly captured her wrist in his hand again.

Frustrated, Shayna tried to shove him away from her. To her surprise, she actually managed to catch the Marshal off balance long enough to knock him back onto the bed. She didn't catch him that unaware, however, because instead of releasing her like she hoped he would do, he tightened his grip on her wrists and pulled her down with him.

Ending up sprawled across his lap, Shayna was so stunned for a moment that she didn't even realize the Marshal had let go of her arms sometime during their fall onto the bed. As soon as she did, though, she immediately tried to push herself upright, but a strong hand on her back pushed her down again. She started struggling as hard as she could, anything to

110

keep him from grabbing her arms again. She knew the moment he did, she would end up in handcuffs.

But Shayna was surprised when the Marshal didn't even try to jerk her arms behind her back so that he could handcuff her. She thought for a moment that she might actually have a chance to get away, only to gasp in surprise when she felt his free hand come down hard on her jean-clad bottom. She stilled, her eyes going wide. Had he actually just *spanked* her? What the hell did he think he was doing?

Before she could say anything, though, he brought his hand down again on her other cheek, harder this time, and she yelped.

Her face flaming from both embarrassment and anger, Shayna tried to push herself off his lap again, to no avail. "Let me up, you jerk!" she demanded.

But the Marshal only gave her ass another hard smack. "Not until you agree to behave yourself," he growled.

Shayna cried out as his hand connected with her bottom yet again. "*Owwwww!* You have no right to spank me!" she told him.

"If you had just come quietly like I told you to, then I wouldn't be forced to do this," he retorted, punctuating each word with a sharp slap to her derriere. "But you leave me no choice. Trust me, spanking you into submission is a lot better than the alternative."

Shayna didn't know what the alternative might be, but she had certainly never been spanked in her life, and she couldn't believe how much it stung! But every time his hand came down on her ass, it felt like her cheeks were going to catch on fire.

"Now, if I let you up, are you going to behave yourself?" he asked, pausing momentarily.

Shayna gritted her teeth. Damn the man! "Yes!" she hissed. "Just let me up already!"

Taking Shayna's arm, he set her back on her feet. Though she really wanted to slap his handsome face, she settled for rubbing her sore bottom instead, only to stop when she realized the Marshal was reaching for his handcuffs.

CHAPTER TWO

Shayna knew if she were going to make a run for it then she was going to have to distract the Marshal somehow. He was standing right in front of her, though, and she knew she'd never get past him if she didn't come up with something good. But she had to try. She wasn't letting him take her in without a fight.

Her gaze darted to the open door and the empty hallway beyond, an idea suddenly springing into her head.

"Help me!" she screamed. "He's..."

Her shout had the desired effect. At her words, the Marshal half turned toward the door, clearly looking to see whom she was talking to. Wasting no time, Shayna immediately grabbed the clock from the bedside table and tried to hit him with it. Of course, it probably would have worked better if the clock hadn't still been plugged into the wall at the time, she thought grimly. Unfortunately, the clock didn't quite reach and instead of knocking the Marshal over the head like she meant to, all she did was knock everything off the night table, not to mention turn his attention back to her.

Clearly angry at her attempt to attack him again, the Marshal immediately snatched the clock from her hand and flung it to the floor. "You don't give up, do you?" he growled.

Shayna opened her mouth to retort, but before she could get the words out, the Marshal grabbed her arm and bent her over the bed. The next thing she knew, his hand was coming down on her ass again! What the heck was with this guy? she thought.

"I guess you didn't learn anything from that spanking I just gave you," he said.

He moved back and forth, administering a hard smack on first one cheek, and then the other, and she bit back a cry as she glared at him over her shoulder. She refused to give him the satisfaction of letting him know how much the spanks really stung.

"I learned that you're a brute!" she snapped.

His jaw tightened at that. "Still feisty, I see," he said. "Well, then I guess I'm going to have to make sure I don't let you up this time until I spank all the fight out of you!"

Obviously intent on keeping his word, the Marshal proceeded to do just that. Much to Shayna's dismay, he smacked her bottom over and over, and while she thought he had spanked her hard the first time, it had been nothing compared to how hard he was spanking her now. It felt like her bottom was on fire! Thank God, she was wearing jeans, she thought. She couldn't imagine what the spanking would feel like on her bare bottom!

But if he thought that a simple spanking would take the fight out of her, he was wrong! It might have stung like crazy, but Shayna still fought him wildly. She squirmed and wiggled as hard as she could, and yet it did no good. The Marshal had wrapped his arm around her waist and held her down more easily than she would have thought possible. She didn't think she'd ever seen a man so strong!

"Okay! Okay!" she cried. "I get it! I'll stop fighting you and go along peacefully!"

At her words, the Marshal stopped spanking her, much to her relief. "Really?" he said sarcastically. "How do I know you're not trying to trick me again?"

Her eyes widened at that. Actually, the spanking hurt too much for her to even think of tricking him. She had to admit, it was a good idea, though. But before she could cajole him anymore, his hand was coming down on her tender asscheeks again.

Shayna squealed as the Marshal continued to spank her. Right then her ass stung so much she thought she probably would have promised him anything, but all he wanted was her assurance that she would behave herself and go with him quietly. And if it would make him stop spanking her, then she would give it to him. But the moment his back was turned, she was out of there!

"Stop, please!" she begged. "I promise I won't try to run! Please just stop spanking me! *Pleeeease!*"

The miserable whine in her voice must have swayed him because he stopped, and Shayna let out a sigh of relief. She would have immediately reached back to rub her throbbing ass, but before she could move, the Marshal grabbed her arms and held them captive behind her back. So that he could handcuff her, she supposed. Every instinct told her to struggle, but she forced herself to remain still while he snapped the cold steel tightly around her wrists. Trying to escape while she was in such a precarious position would only earn her another spanking.

Taking her arm, the Marshal pulled Shayna to her feet and led her to the door. Once again, she had to fight the urge to try and run as he escorted her down the stairs and outside. She had to be smart about this and bide her time, and wait until the opportunity to escape presented itself. She wasn't going to get far with handcuffs on, which meant that she would just have to wait until he took them off during a bathroom break or something.

But to her surprise, and utter dismay, the Marshal didn't lead her to his vehicle like she had expected, but toward the sheriff's station down the street. Her steps faltered as panic set in. She had naturally assumed the Marshal would take her back to Denver. There was no way she would be able to escape locked up in jail.

Swallowing hard, Shayna allowed him to lead her down the street through the snow. As they passed the diner, she kept her head down. She couldn't bear to see people pointing at her and whispering behind their hands. It was going to be humiliating enough to be dragged before the sheriff; the man came into the diner every day for lunch.

The sheriff was talking to one of his deputies in the outer office, and both men looked up when they entered. Upon realizing that the Marshal had her in handcuffs, the sheriff's gray eyes narrowed. Before he could say anything, however, the Marshal showed the other man his badge and explained that Shayna was wanted back in Denver for embezzlement and suspicion of murder.

"He's confused me with someone else," Shayna told the sheriff after the Marshal had finished.

The Marshal tightened his grip on her arm and held her back when she tried to take a step forward. "Save it," he growled.

Turning to the sheriff, the Marshal produced a folded piece of paper from his pocket. At first, Shayna thought it was a copy of the warrant for her arrest, but as he handed it over to the other man, she saw that it was a wanted poster with her picture on it. She felt her heart sink as the sheriff read it over.

Madoc was watching the sheriff, too. At first, the other man had looked like he wasn't going to take Madoc's word that Shayna Matthews was a fugitive. It was one of the reasons he didn't like dealing with these small-town sheriffs. Sometimes they got really prickly about someone poaching on their jurisdiction. But it should be obvious from looking at the wanted poster that Madoc had made no mistake.

"Looks like you're right," the sheriff said as he folded the paper and handed it back to Madoc. "What do you want me to do about it?"

Madoc was stunned by the man's words. "I want you to hold her, of course," he said. "I'll talk to the district attorney when I get back to Denver, and he can arrange to have her transferred. It should only be a week or two."

"'Fraid not, Marshal," the sheriff said. "You're not gonna be able to leave her here."

Madoc frowned. "Why not?"

116

"Son, have you looked outside?" the older man said, gesturing toward the window. "There's a big snow storm coming. Me and my deputies will be pulling cars out of ditches and saving livestock for the next couple of days. Ain't gonna be no one around to watch your prisoner. I was just getting ready to close down the jail when you came in."

Madoc's frown deepened. How the hell could the sheriff just shut down the jail? "You're kidding me, right?"

The other man shrugged. "'Fraid not. I can't have her here if there's no one to watch her."

Madoc shook his head in disbelief. That had to be one of the most stupid things he'd ever heard. "That's why they put locks on the cell doors," he pointed out dryly. "So you don't have to watch the prisoners all the time."

The sheriff drew himself up to look Madoc squarely in the eye. "I'm not locking no one up without someone here to watch them, especially someone like this poor, little lady here," he said. "With the snow they're predicting, it could be days before me or my deputies can get back here to check on her."

Madoc wanted to point out to the man that Shayna Matthews wasn't a "poor, little lady," but a wanted fugitive, and then figured it would only be a waste of time. "If you won't lock her up, then what the hell am I supposed to do with her?" he said instead.

The sheriff shrugged. "Well, you can get a room at the motel, I suppose," he said. "Or you could just take her back to the boarding house. It's not like she's going anywhere in this snow."

Madoc stared at the other man, dumbfounded. What the hell kind of Podunk town was Flint Creek anyway? He shook his head. "Well, if you won't hold her, then I'll take her to the U.S. Marshals office in Billings."

The sheriff's eyes went wide. "Billings is almost two hundred miles from here," he said. "There's no way you'll make it that far in this snow. You'd be better off staying here."

Right, Madoc thought in disgust. "I'll take my chances with the snow," he told the other man. Tightening his grip on Shayna Matthews' arm, he turned toward the door. "Come on," he growled.

Outside, the snow had started to come down heavier, and Madoc swore under his breath as he led his prisoner to his SUV. Damn, he wished he'd never stopped at that diner!

"The sheriff's right," Shayna grumbled beside him. "It's crazy to try and drive all the way to Billings in this weather. We'll never make it."

Madoc gave her a hard look as they came to a halt beside his SUV. "I don't remember asking for your opinion," he said coldly as he brushed snow from the door handle.

"Well, I'm giving it to you anyway!" she shot back. "You might be willing to risk your life, but I don't want you risking mine!"

Madoc glared at her. "Like I said, you don't get a vote." He yanked open the passenger door. "Get in."

Shayna hesitated for so long that Madoc thought he would have to forcibly put her in the vehicle, but with a baleful look, she finally climbed into the SUV. With her hands cuffed behind her back, the whole thing was a little awkward, but she managed. Once she was inside, Madoc slammed the door, and then walked around to the other side and got in.

"You're making a huge mistake," Shayna said as he started the engine and put the truck in gear. "I'm innocent of those crimes."

He snorted. "That's what they all say."

"If I had done it, don't you think I would have run?" she asked.

Madoc gave her a sidelong glance. "You did run," he reminded her as he slowly merged onto the snowy highway.

Shayna sighed in exasperation. "I meant before I got arrested," she said. "If I had really stolen all that money, do you think I would have run off to Flint Rock, Montana?"

118

He shrugged. "Maybe you figured that no one would look for you there."

She shook her head. "That doesn't even make sense! If I had embezzled half-a-million dollars, I sure as heck wouldn't be working as a waitress in a diner."

Madoc didn't answer. Though he had to admit that waitressing at a diner in some Podunk town after stealing half-a-million dollars didn't make a whole hell of a lot of sense, he couldn't deny it had actually been rather smart on her part. If he hadn't decided to stop at that diner to get something to eat, Shayna Matthews would still be back there waiting tables, and no one would have been the wiser.

"Dammit, why won't you at least listen to my side of the story?" she snapped. "I was framed, I'm telling you!"

His hand tightened on wheel as the tires hit a slippery patch of road. "Enough already!" he told her harshly. "Save your conspiracy theories for the courtroom, Ms. Matthews, because I don't care. As far as I'm concerned, you're a fugitive and it's my job to bring you in. Now, shut up and let me drive."

Madoc waited for Shayna to argue her case further, but to his surprise, she fell silent. A moment later, he heard the soft sounds of crying. He swore silently. What did she think, that he would be moved by her tears and agree to let her go? *Yeah, right.* He didn't buy her innocent act or her fake tears. She could cry all the way to Billings, for all he cared.

Well, if that were true, then why the hell was he already trying to figure out what he could say to get her to stop crying? He tried to convince himself that it was just because he didn't like the sounds of her sniffling, but in reality, it was because he just didn't like a seeing her so upset.

So, what was he going to do? Take the cuffs off and let her go? Cursing himself for being so stupid, Madoc turned his attention back to the snow-covered stretch of highway before him and tried to ignore her crying. It stopped soon enough, much to his relief.

"Billings is a long drive," she said in a tearful voice. "Couldn't you at least take off these handcuffs until we get there? My hands are getting numb."

He slanted her a hard look. "No."

"I promise I won't try to escape," she added.

Madoc let out a harsh laugh. "I've heard that before."

"That was when we were back in Flint Rock and there were lots of places to go," she pointed out. "It's not like I can jump out of the truck. Besides, where would I go out here in this snow? Even if I managed to get away from you, I'd probably end up freezing to death." A pause, then, softly, "Please."

Madoc clenched his jaw. He had no doubt she was playing him. But, damn him, he had a weakness for beautiful women. And Shayna Matthews was definitely beautiful. What harm was there in uncuffing her? It wasn't like she could really go anywhere.

Fuck! If his prisoner hadn't been so dang sexy, would he even be considering taking the cuffs off? he asked himself. Probably not, he decided. But thirty seconds later, Madoc found himself slowing to a stop in the middle of the deserted highway and putting the truck in park. Shutting off the engine, he pulled the key out of the ignition.

"Turn around," he ordered Shayna.

She blinked, clearly surprised that he had agreed, but then scooted around on the seat so that her back was to him. Inserting the key into the lock, he undid it, and then took off the cuffs. Rubbing her wrists, Shayna shifted around in her seat again to look at him.

"Thank you," she said softly.

Madoc scowled at her, hoping he wasn't going to regret this. If she thought that doe-eyed Bambi look of hers was going to have some sort of an effect on him, then she was wrong. It didn't matter how damn sexy she looked in those black-rimmed glasses of hers.

120

"Just don't get it into your head to try escaping again," he said gruffly. "Because those spankings I gave you back at the boarding house will seem like love-pats compared to the one you'd get for making me chase you through this storm."

At the mention of the spankings he'd given her, Shayna's face colored and she quickly turned away. Thinking that the threat of another spanking should be enough to keep her from doing anything foolish, Madoc started the engine and slowly eased his SUV back up to speed on the snow-covered highway.

Though he tried to focus on driving, he couldn't get the image out of his mind of having Shayna over his knee. Even though he had been busy trying to subdue her at the time, he couldn't help but notice how great her ass had looked in those tight jeans she was wearing. Just the thought was enough to make him hard.

Madoc abruptly caught himself. What the hell was he doing? Shayna Matthews might be hot, but she was still a fugitive, dammit! He had no business fantasizing about her. And he sure as hell had no business putting her over his knee for a spanking again!

He wasn't even sure what had made him spank her in the first place. It certainly wasn't the way he usually dealt with fugitives, that was for damn sure. But when she'd ended up over his knee during their tussle, giving her tight little ass a smack had seemed like the most natural thing in the world. And he had to admit that it had gotten her attention.

Madoc supposed he could just blame the whole thing on one of his former girlfriends. He had heard of other couples spanking, of course, but he hadn't ever considered doing it until a girlfriend had told him that she liked it when a guy smacked her on the ass. He had been only too happy to oblige and they had ended up doing it all the time. Maybe that was why he had spanked Shayna Matthews, he thought. Because even though that other relationship had ended years ago, it just seemed natural to spank a sexy girl when she misbehaved.

Madoc had to force thoughts of spanking from his mind, as he realized how heavy the snow had started coming down. There were already six or eight inches on the highway and with no other cars out, it was getting hard to see exactly where the road was. Maybe that old sheriff had been right, he thought. Maybe he should have stayed in town. Madoc had to admit that driving to Billings in this weather hadn't been the brightest decision he'd ever made. Well, it was too late to change his mind now, he thought. But at least he could put chains on the tires. That would definitely help.

Guiding the SUV onto the shoulder, he turned off the engine.

"Why are we stopping?" Shayna asked.

"I have to put on tire chains. Stay put," he told her, and then added, "And don't try anything."

Taking the keys out of the ignition, he grabbed his gloves from the back seat and got out of the truck. Going around to the back of the SUV, he opened the lift gate and took out the tire chains before closing it again. Going back around to the front, he gave Shayna a glance to find her huddled in the front seat watching him. He knew that the truck would get cold quickly without the heater going, but there was no way he was going to leave it running while he put on the tire chains.

It took him at least a half hour to untangle all four sets of chains and get them positioned on the ground in front of the tires. By the time Madoc had finished, he was not only freezing, but covered in snow as well. And he still to drive the truck forward onto the chains, and then tighten everything up, which was going to take at least another fifteen minutes. Deciding to drive to Billings definitely had to be on his top-ten list of stupid decisions, he thought to himself. They'd be lucky if they didn't end up in a ditch!

Swearing under his breath, Madoc brushed the snow from his jacket with his gloved hands as he walked back around to the driver's side. The windows were so frosted up and covered with snow that he couldn't even see inside.

Yanking the door open, he was just about to climb inside when he noticed that the passenger seat was empty. *Shit*, he thought.

CHAPTER THREE

Though Shayna had been planning to escape all along, she was surprised when the opportunity had presented itself so soon after the Marshal had arrested her. But knowing she might not get another chance, she'd taken it. The Marshal had been so focused on the tire chains that he hadn't even noticed when she'd slipped out of the truck, quietly closed the door, and disappeared into the wooded area along the highway. Of course, he would discover that she had run soon enough, and when he did, he would immediately come after her. That thought made her quicken her step.

Once she had gotten away, her strategy had become simple. She would go back the way they had come, staying to the wooded area, but still traveling parallel to the highway until she got back to Flint Rock. It might take a while, but once there, she would implement her original getaway plan and hitch a ride with a trucker. But in her hurry to get away from the Marshal, Shayna had gone deeper into the forest than she'd intended and before she knew it, she was lost. Too afraid to retrace her steps for fear of running into the Marshal, she pushed ahead. The highway had to be somewhere close, she told herself.

It was snowing even harder than it had been when they had left Flint Rock, the wind blowing the snow sideways even in the depths of the forest. Wishing she had gloves, Shayna stuck her hands in pockets in an effort to warm them up, but it didn't help. Having grown up in Colorado, she knew she should be used to this type of weather, but she was frozen to the core. It didn't help that she had not only tripped over a fallen tree and landed face first in a pile of deep snow in her haste to get away, but she'd slipped a little while after that and fallen on her butt, too. Now, her clothes were full of snow and soaking wet.

Sure she must have been walking for hours, she took her hands out of her pockets just long enough to push up the sleeve of her coat so that she could see her watch. She was surprised to discover that it had barely been thirty minutes since she'd slipped out of the Marshal's SUV. How could she have gotten herself so lost in that amount of time? At this rate, she'd freeze to death before she ever got back to Flint Rock.

Shayna stood where she was for a moment, wondering if she should continue in the same direction she'd been heading for the past half hour in the hopes that she would eventually get to Flint Rock, or if she should retrace her steps back to the Marshal's SUV. As much as she didn't want to go back the way she'd come, she liked the idea of dying of hypothermia even less. Which could happen if she didn't get someplace warm, and soon.

Her mind made up, Shayna started back the way she had come, but within a dozen feet, she realized that her tracks had been completely covered by the falling snow. Tears welled in her eyes and she resolutely blinked them back. What was she going to do now?

Telling herself she couldn't just stand there or she really would die of hypothermia, Shayna began to trudge through the snow in the direction she hoped led to the Marshal's SUV. After another thirty minutes of walking, however, she was just about to give up and head in another direction when she stumbled out of the trees and into a clearing.

Shayna blinked, wondering if the small cabin in front of her were a hallucination. What would a cabin be doing out there in the middle of nowhere? Did people hallucinate when they went into hypothermia? she wondered. She didn't know and right then, she was too cold to really care. If she were just imagining the cabin, maybe she could pretend to get warm if she went inside. Shivering, she eagerly hurried through the snow to the building.

Not bothering to consider whether it was occupied or not, Shayna automatically grabbed the doorknob and gave it a turn, only to frown when she realized the door was locked. That was actually good, she thought. If the door was locked, then that probably meant the cabin was real and not a hallucination. Balling her other hand into a fist, she banged loudly on the door.

"Hello?" she called. "Is anyone in there?"

When she didn't get an answer, Shayna leaned forward to look through the window in the door. Though she couldn't see much inside the darkened cabin, she saw enough to know that it was empty. She chewed on her lower lip, wondering if she should break into the cabin or not, but then told herself that she had no choice. It was either that or freeze to death.

Taking a step back, she looked around for something she could use to break the window. Spotting the stack of logs on the porch beside the door, she quickly picked one up and gripping it as tightly as she could in her numb fingers, she smashed it against the glass. Dropping the log back onto the porch, she carefully reached her arm through the opening and unlocked the door. Pushing it open, she went inside, and then closed it behind her.

She felt warmer already, Shayna thought. Grateful she had finally found shelter from the storm, she leaned back against the door for a moment and took in her surroundings. It was sparsely furnished, with a small bed against one wall, a table and chairs, and a row of tiny cabinets with a countertop beneath them. But it was the pot-belly stove on the opposite side of the room that caught her attention. Thank God, she thought. A fire was exactly what she needed. She was so cold that she could barely keep her teeth from chattering.

Eager to get a fire going, Shayna stumbled over to the stove. She almost cried with happiness when she spied the big box of matches on the shelf behind the stove. Though there were no logs, there was a box with smaller pieces of wood, as well as stacks of old newspapers she could use to get the fire going. Once she did, she would go back out to the porch for some logs. The thought of going back out into the snow again made her shiver even more and she had to fight to control the shaking that threatened to overwhelm her. Telling herself that she would be warm soon enough, she bent over to open the door of the stove. There was a pile of old ash right in the middle that would have to be moved before she could start a fire. Picking up the small fire poker from where it rested against the wall, she was just about to use it to scrape out the charred bits of wood when the door to the cabin burst open.

Startled by both the noise and the gust of freezing cold wind that swept into the cabin, Shayna whirled around to find the Marshal standing in the doorway. He was covered in snow and looked even madder than when she had tried to hit him with the bookend back at the boarding house. She took a step back, her hand tightening reflexively on the poker.

He advanced on her, his eyes narrowing. "Put down the poker," he ordered.

She shook her head and only gripped it more tightly in her numb hands. "Can't you just go back to Denver and forget you ever saw me?" she pleaded.

The Marshal took another step toward her. "You know I can't do that."

"Can't?" she demanded. "Or won't?"

"Same difference. Either way, you're going back to jail," he reasoned, taking another step toward her. "Now, put down the poker. You're already in enough trouble as it is. Do you really want to add assaulting a Federal Marshal to your list of crimes?"

As he spoke, the Marshal took another step toward her. But though Shayna held on to the poker even more tightly, she knew deep down that she would never be able to hit him with it. Which was why it was almost ridiculously easy for him to take it away from her a moment later.

Though she tried desperately to hold onto it, he wrestled the poker from her grasp within seconds and tossed it

128

onto the floor. The next thing she knew she was face-down over the small table. Damn him, he was going to spank her again! Then again, as frozen as her butt was, she probably wouldn't even feel it, she thought.

"You were already in for one hell of a spanking for making me chase you through the snow," he growled. "But after that little episode with the poker, you'll be lucky if you can sit down by the time I'm done."

Shayna glared at him over her shoulder. "I should have hit you with the damn thing, you bastard!"

Behind her, Madoc ground his jaw. If there was ever a woman that needed a good, hard spanking, it was Shayna Matthews, he thought. And this time, he wasn't stopping until he was sure that all the fight was out of her. Running off into the snow had to be the dumbest thing anyone had even done.

Lifting his hand, he brought it down on her shapely, jean clad ass, only to stop abruptly when he felt how wet her clothes were.

"My God, you're soaking wet!" he exclaimed. "What the hell did you do, go for a swim somewhere?"

The look she gave him this time wasn't nearly as defiant as before. "I t-tripped and f-fell in the s-snow," she stammered, her teeth chattering.

Madoc stared at her in disbelief. Tripped and fell? It looked like she had been rolling around in the snow for an hour! He'd been so angry before that he hadn't noticed, but now he could see that her lips were blue and she was shivering uncontrollably. Why the hell hadn't she said something to him before? Because she had been more interested in whacking him with the fire poker, he reminded himself wryly.

Even though Shayna really did deserve a spanking, Madoc wasn't about to give her one while she was on the verge of hypothermia. As furious as he was with her for trying to escape, he definitely didn't want her to freeze to death, especially now that he had her back in custody again. He would have to get her warmed up, and fast!

The spanking forgotten for the moment, Madoc took Shayna's arm and gently pulled her to her feet. "We need to get you out of these wet clothes before you freeze to death," he told her.

Without waiting for a reply, Madoc unzipped Shayna's coat and tugged it off her shoulders. She didn't even bother to resist, but simply stood there. That only made him more worried. All the fire that had shone in her eyes as she'd tried to hold him at bay with the poker was gone now. Tossing the wet coat onto a chair, he turned back and slid his hands beneath the hem of her shirt.

Shayna's head jerked up in surprise. "What do you think you're doing?!" she cried, trying to push his hands away.

Madoc paused, but didn't take his hands away. "I'm trying to get you out of these wet clothes and into bed before you freeze to death," he explained. "Now stop being such a pain and let me help you."

She looked at him in confusion, but after a moment, she slowly nodded her head.

Madoc wasted no more time getting the rest of Shayna's wet clothes off. Lifting her shirt over her head, he tossed it on top of her coat, and then quickly went to work on her jeans. As he unbuttoned them, however, he couldn't help but notice how round and perfect her breasts were beneath the sexy lace bra she wore, or the way his body responded to the sight.

Stop it! he chided himself. Now was not the time to be ogling his prisoner. She was standing there freezing to death, for heaven's sake! But even as he told himself that, he knew he would have to be a monk not to see how hot she was, especially when those long, shapely legs of hers came into view as he pulled off her sodden jeans.

Trying hard not to look at his half-naked prisoner, Madoc led her over to the bed, sat her down, and wrapped the blanket around her shivering form.

"I'm going to make a fire," he said.

130

Going over to the pot-belly stove, Madoc grabbed several pieces of newspaper from the stack and crumpling them up, shoved them inside along with some kindling. Reaching for the box of long-handled matches on the shelf above the stove, he lit one and held the flame to the newspaper. Needing to go outside for some logs now that he'd gotten the fire going, he closed the door to the stove and turned to head for the door, only to pause in mid-step when he caught sight of Shayna.

She was huddled beneath the blanket, shivering and watching him with a glazed expression. Fool woman, he thought. She was lucky she hadn't ended up dead running out in the middle of a snowstorm like that. Shaking his head, Madoc opened the door and stepped out onto the porch.

Outside, the snow was coming down even harder and didn't look like it was going to let up any time soon. Which meant that he and Shayna were probably going to be stuck in the cabin until it stopped. *Great*, he thought.

Of course, he wouldn't be in this position right now if he had just left Shayna Matthews cuffed, Madoc told himself angrily as he stacked logs into his arms.

He'd gone after her as soon as he realized she was missing, but when he hadn't caught up with her right away, it quickly became apparent that she'd had more of a head start than he'd first thought. Furious with himself for letting a prisoner in his custody escape, he'd spent the next half hour trying to find her. But the snow had been falling hard and fast, and it was just by luck that he'd come across Shayna's trail at all. Even then, it had taken a while to find her. If she hadn't stumbled across the cabin, they might both be in trouble by now.

His arms full, Madoc turned and went back inside the cabin with the logs. Though Shayna was still wrapped up in the blanket, she didn't look like she was shivering anymore, he noticed. Setting the logs down beside the stove, he added a couple to the fire, and then turned his attention to the cabinets. While he wasn't all that hungry after the big meal he'd had at the diner, he had no doubt that Shayna could do with something warm. He just hoped there was something in the cabin to eat.

Though the first two cabinets were empty, he was relieved to find that the third held a jar of instant coffee, as well as half a dozen cans of soup and several cans of fruit. It wasn't much, but it would do, he thought. Grabbing one of the cans of soup, he opened it and poured the contents into a pot. He gave it a sniff test, decide it was still good, and then set it on the stove to heat.

While he waited for the soup to warm up, Madoc took Shayna's wet shirt and jeans, and draped them over the backs of the chairs closest to the stove so that they would be able to dry. When that was done, he checked the soup and found that it was already bubbling. Taking two mugs from the shelf, he wiped them out with his shirt and poured a generous amount of soup into both of them.

Mugs in hand, he walked over to where Shayna was sitting on the bed and held one out to her. "Drink this," he said.

As Shayna reached out to take the mug, the blanket slipped from one shoulder, and Madoc caught a glimpse of the tops of her breasts before she pulled it back up. "Thank you," she said softly.

Madoc said nothing in reply, only watched while she drank the soup. When she had finished, he took the mug from her and set in down on the table alongside his own.

"Are you feeling warmer now?" he asked, turning back to her.

She nodded. "A little," she said quietly, but he could see that she was getting back to her normal self. "You still look like you're cold, though," she added after a moment.

Madoc frowned at her observation. He hadn't realized it, but now that Shayna had mentioned it, he had to admit that he was a little cold. But he wasn't about to let her know that. He knew it was silly, but he just couldn't let on that he was cold. Men didn't do that, not where he came from. And definitely not in front of a woman, especially one who was a prisoner.

"I'm fine," he said.

She lifted a brow, clearly not believing him. "You were outside just as long as I was, which means you're probably just as cold as I am," she pointed out. "Why don't you get into bed and we can share the blanket?"

Madoc lifted a brow at her words. Though the invitation to crawl into a warm bed with a half-naked woman was tempting, he had no doubt Shayna Matthews was trying to play him again. Just like she had when she'd convinced him to take off the cuffs. Well, not this time. "I said, I'm fine," he told her gruffly.

She shrugged. "If you say so," she said. "But you're obviously freezing."

Madoc made no reply, hoping she would let the matter drop, but to his annoyance, she continued.

"What is it with you men, anyway?" she said. "You think that if you admit you're cold, we'll think less of you or something. Well, you don't have to worry about that with me. I couldn't possibly think any less of you than I already do. So, stand over there and freeze if you'd rather."

He ground his jaw, refusing to rise to the bait. "I will," he said.

When Shayna made no comment, he thought she had finally given up on trying to cajole him, but then she spoke again.

"You're starting to shiver," she said. "Not only is it really blowing your whole tough-guy image, but it's making me cold again."

Madoc scowled at that. He knew she was trying to embarrass him into admitting that he was cold. Then, once she got him into bed, she would try to use her feminine charms on him. And unfortunately, while he didn't want to fall for her scheme, she was right about him being cold.

He thought about it for a moment. *Aw, the hell with it,* he decided. He wasn't going to fall prey to her charms, so why did he care what she was up to? And since that was true, there was no reason to stand there freezing. Shaking his head, he motioned for her to move over.

"All right," he said. "But only because you're being such a pain in the ass about the whole thing."

As he sat on the edge of the bed to take off his boots, Shayna scooted over to make room for him, but the bed was small, so it did little good. There was no way he was going to fit his large frame on there with her comfortably unless they cuddled up close together. As he moved closer to her sexy, curvy body a few minutes later, Madoc told himself once again that he wasn't going to allow her feminine charms have any effect on him.

CHAPTER FOUR

Shayna tried to give the Marshal as much room as she could on the bed while still trying to find a comfortable position. This had to be the smallest bed she'd ever seen, she thought to herself. Or maybe it just seemed smaller because the man in it with her was so big. Then again, maybe it was because it had been a long time since she'd been in bed with a man at all. It hadn't exactly been at the top of her list of things to do since going on the run. And she had to admit that the Marshal was gorgeous.

Stealing a glance at him from beneath her lashes, Shayna almost laughed at the effort he was making to keep his distance. It was obvious he hadn't wanted to get into bed with her. It had probably been a blow to his manly ego to admit he was even freezing in the first place, she thought. But she really had hated to see him standing there shivering. Of course, just because she hadn't wanted him to freeze didn't mean she was completely comfortable with the idea of being in bed half naked with him, either. But sharing body heat made sense. Moreover, it had gotten him to stop hovering over her like a guard dog. She might be his prisoner, but it didn't mean she wanted to be reminded of it.

Shayna studied the Marshal in silence. He was lying on his back, his arm pillowed behind his head, his expression unreadable as he stared up at the ceiling. She was going to stuck in this cabin with him for at least a day or two, she thought, which made him a captive audience of sorts. Perhaps she could find a way to turn that to her advantage. But as much as wanted to jump right in with both feet and plead her case with him, she knew he wouldn't be very receptive if she did. Which meant that she would have take it slowly.

"What's your name?" she asked after a moment.

He gave her a sidelong glance, his golden brown eyes narrowing suspiciously. "My name?"

She shrugged. "Call me old fashioned, but I like to know a guy's name when I climb into bed with him," she said dryly.

Though his mouth quirked slightly at her lame attempt at humor, he made no reply. She was starting to think he wasn't going to answer her question at all when he finally spoke.

"It's Madoc," he said. "Madoc Cutler."

Madoc. It was an unusual name, but strong sounding, like a hero in a romance book might have, she thought. Somehow, it fit a guy who hunted down fugitives for a living.

Deciding that talking about the weather would be non-productive, Shayna fell silent again. Despite the fact that she knew she had to take her time with him and get him to slowly let down his guard, she couldn't think of a single thing to talk about that wasn't related to her being a fugitive.

"So," she said, trying to sound nonchalant. "How did you find me?"

His jaw tightened at her question. "It wasn't that difficult once I picked up your trail in the snow."

Her brow furrowed when she realized he thought she meant how he'd found her at the cabin. "No, I meant how did you find me in Flint Rock?" she clarified.

"Oh," he said. "I remembered seeing you on a wanted poster, and recognized you."

Shayna's frown deepened at his words. "So, you really were just passing through town and decided to stop for something to eat at the diner?" she asked incredulously. "I thought you had come there specifically to arrest me."

The Marshal turned his head to look at her. "I'm actually supposed to be on vacation. I just happened to be in

136

the right place at the right time," he said. When she scowled, he added, "Or not, I guess, depending on your point of view. You know, you really should have dyed your hair or something. The glasses aren't much of a disguise."

"I'll remember that the next time," she said sarcastically, only to realize that there wasn't going to be a next time. Not unless she could manage to escape from Madoc Cutler.

She rested her head on her hand and gazed down at the handsome Marshal. "I didn't steal that money, you know," she said softly. "And I certainly didn't murder anyone."

"The police back in Denver think you did," he said.

"Well, they're wrong," she insisted. "I'm innocent. I was framed."

Shayna held her breath, waiting for him to tell her once again that he wasn't interested, and that he didn't want to hear her going on and on about how innocent she was. But to her surprise, the Marshal simply said, "Then why did you run?"

"Because even my lawyer thought I was guilty. He told me that we would never win with the evidence they had against me, and that I was going to go to prison for a very long time," she said. "He advised me to take the deal the district attorney offered, but I couldn't. Not only would I have gone to jail for ten years for something I didn't do, but part of the plea bargain was that I would have to return the money. I didn't have it, so I couldn't very well accept the plea bargain."

Shayna waited for Madoc to say something, but when he didn't, she knew she was going to have to make herself more sympathetic in his eyes. "Even my family told me that I should run," she said. "They knew I hadn't done what the police said and that the way things were going, I could end up in jail for the rest of my life."

Again, she waited for the Marshal to say something, but instead, he just stared up at the ceiling.

"Even with my family urging me to flee, it wasn't an easy decision to go on the run," she continued. "I've always been really close with my parents and my younger sister. I was afraid of what becoming a fugitive would do to them. I didn't want them hounded by the cops or the media. But what could I do? I didn't want to go to jail for something I didn't do. I know I probably shouldn't be telling you this, but my sister helped me get away. I've been on the run ever since."

Beside her, Madoc seemed to be considering her words. "The warrant said you were wanted for suspected murder, which means that no body was found," he said. "What's that about?"

Shayna was a little surprised the Marshal didn't already know the story, especially since it had been all over the news. But she imagined that after a while, all the crimes he read about just blurred together. She was just happy that he was actually finally willing to listen to her side of it.

"It'll probably be easier if I start at the beginning," she said. "I worked at a big manufacturing company back in Denver. For the past several years, I worked directly for the Chief Financial Officer, Evan Mercer. My job was to oversee the employee retirement funds," she explained. "The company has a lot of employees and the funds are worth a lot of money. A couple of weeks before everything happened, some computer programs I had running brought up several red flags indicating some irregularities in the funds. It was nothing drastic, but more money than usual was going out, and though I checked and double-checked, I couldn't figure out where it was going."

She reached up to tuck her hair behind her ear. "I started to get a really funny feeling and decided I'd better mention it to Evan," she continued. "But that night, he called me at home and asked me to meet him at the office. He said he needed to talk to me about something important and that it couldn't wait until morning. When I asked what he wanted to talk to me about, he said he didn't want to discuss it over the phone."

138

"So, what did he want to talk to you about?" the Marshal prompted.

"I don't know," Shayna replied. "When I got to the office, he wasn't there. I thought that maybe he was just late, so I waited for a while, but he never showed, so I finally left and went home. I figured I'd talk to him the next morning, but he didn't come in to work." She paused. "Later that day, the police came by with a warrant to seize all of our records. Apparently, they'd received an anonymous tip that half-a-million dollars had been stolen from the retirement fund. Before I even knew what was going on, they came back to arrest me for embezzlement."

Shayna swallowed hard at the memory of how humiliating it had been to be handcuffed and led out of her office while her co-workers had watched.

"I thought it was all just a big mistake, but then the police started showing me all the evidence they had against me," she said. "They had numbers for Cayman bank accounts that I never opened, reservations for a plane flight out of the country that I never made, and emails to my boss that I never sent discussing the best way to go about moving the money I had supposedly stolen."

She sighed. "I thought Evan would show up and straighten everything out, but then the nightmare got even worse. My lawyer told me that with the amount of evidence the cops had against me, they would have no problem making the embezzlement charges stick. But the cops wanted me for more than that. They started trying to get me to confess to killing Evan. It was their theory that we had embezzled the money together, but that I had gotten greedy and decided to kill him so I could have it all for myself."

"And they were sure he'd been murdered?" Madoc asked when she finished.

She shrugged. "They seemed convinced of it," she said. "They found blood at his house and my fingerprints were all over the place. I tried to tell them that I didn't know anything about the blood, and that my fingerprints were there because I'd been to his house dozens of times. But they weren't really interested in hearing my explanations."

"Didn't your lawyer ever suggest that maybe this Evan Mercer had actually stolen the money and set you up?" Madoc said.

"He brought it up," Shayna admitted. "But with all the physical evidence against me, the cops weren't going to even look into the possibility that I'd been framed. It would just make their case weaker."

Madoc was silent a moment. "So, what do you think?" he finally asked. "Could Evan Mercer have set you up?"

Shayna considered that for a moment. "I don't know, but I hope not," she said honestly. Of course, if her boss wasn't behind it, then that probably meant he actually had been murdered, she thought grimly. "Evan and I have been friends since I started working at the company. He'd always been like a father-figure to me. I can't imagine him framing me for embezzlement and murder."

Beside her, Madoc shrugged his broad shoulders. "If not him, then who?"

Shayna shook her head. "I don't know."

In her heart, she really didn't think her boss was the one behind this, but she had no other suspect to offer. She wished she could think of something else to say, something that might sway the Marshal into believing her, but she had already told him the whole story.

Shayna chewed on her lower lip. At least the Marshal had been willing to listen to her this time, which had surprised her. Not that it meant much, she supposed. But it was the best she could hope for at this point. Maybe if she had a chance to keep working him, he might actually start to believe her.

She would have to take it slowly, though. If she pushed too hard, he might get suspicious and realize she was trying to play him. That would only get her turned over to the cops that much faster. Or get her put over his knee again. She blushed at the thought.

She had been lucky the Marshal had taken pity on her when he had found her at the cabin. What was it with him and spanking, anyway? she thought. Didn't he know he was in the twenty-first century? She didn't even think people still did that.

The first time he'd spanked her she had been so shocked by it that she hadn't really realized what was going on. But that second time – when she had tried to hit him with the clock – she had definitely felt every smack. Even now, she could almost feel the sting of his hand coming down on her bottom. Oh God, was her bottom actually tingling? she wondered.

She shook her head, trying to clear it. *Get those thought out of your head right now*, she told herself. *Focus on the important stuff, like figuring out what you're going to say to the Marshal tomorrow.* She needed to continue to try to get him on her side. But she would have to be subtle, she warned herself.

At the sound of his deep breathing, she realized the Marshal had fallen asleep. Turning her head, she studied him again. Wow, he was really gorgeous, she thought. And not nearly as tough-looking when he was asleep.

Shayna rolled over onto her other side and tried to fall asleep, too, but she found herself looking back over her shoulder at Madoc again and again. It was just her luck, she thought. Here she was in bed with the best looking guy she'd ever seen and he was bound and determined to put her in prison. How unfair was that?

Madoc slowly awoke the next morning to the sleepy realization that the stove had apparently gone out sometime in the night. Not in any rush to face the cold of the cabin, he instinctively burrowed closer to the warm woman next to him. As he did so, he couldn't help but notice how perfectly they fit to together as they lay spoon-like in the small bed. Or how wonderful her hair smelled as he buried his face in it. Or that apparently his little soldier was standing at attention and quite content to nestle against her very soft and well-shaped bottom. Without even realizing what he was doing, he found his arm sliding around her waist to gently pull her even more tightly against the hard wall of his chest.

As his cock awoke more fully, however, so did he. Madoc stifled a groan as he slowly took his arm from around Shayna's slender waist and shifted to put some distance between his morning hard-on and her ass. *Shit!* He knew it had been a mistake to get in bed with her last night! What the hell had he been thinking?

Moving carefully so as not to disturb her, Madoc slipped out of bed and grabbing his boots, sat down on one of the chairs to put them on. He had just finished lacing them up when the rustle of blankets caught his attention. He looked up to find his prisoner pushing herself into a sitting position on the bed. His first thought was, damn, she looked good in the morning. His second was to wonder if she had been awake enough to feel his arousal pressing up against her bottom. But as she pushed her long hair back from her face and blinked at him sleepily, he decided that she hadn't.

Madoc got to his feet. "Your clothes are dry if you want to get dressed," he told her. "I'm going to go see what it's doing outside."

All he had to do was look out the window to know that it was still snowing, but the truth was that he wanted to put some distance between himself and his prisoner. Grabbing his coat from the back of the chair, he shrugged into it as he strode to the door.

Once outside, Madoc stood on the porch, staring out at the falling snow and trying not to think about the fact that Shayna Matthews was half naked on the other side of the door. His cock went hard again at the image and he swore under his breath. What was it about Shayna Matthews that had him

142

responding like this? Coming on to her back at the diner had been permissible when he'd thought she was a waitress. But she was a wanted fugitive. More than that, she was his prisoner, dammit!

Reaching into the pocket of his jeans, he pulled out his cell phone. He should call his boss, Madoc thought, and let the man know that he'd run into some bad weather and wouldn't be able to get back to Denver until the roads were passable. He flipped open his phone, only to scowl.

"No signal," Madoc muttered. "That's just great."

Snapping the phone closed, he shoved it back into his pocket and turned to go back inside. Shayna was just getting dressed when he walked into the cabin and he came to an abrupt halt at the sight of her wiggling into her tight jeans. Damn, she had a great ass, he thought. The image of Shayna Matthews draped over his knee while he spanked her tight, little derriere immediately came to mind and he had to stifle a groan.

As if just realizing that he had come back in, Shayna whirled around to face him. Her face coloring, she hastily did up the buttons on her jeans.

Closing the door, he took off his coat and put it on the back of a chair. "It's still snowing just as hard as it was yesterday, so we're stuck here," he told her.

Shayna made no reply, but he saw the relief on her face. And why wouldn't she be relieved? Madoc thought. It meant another day of freedom for her.

Abruptly the conversation he'd had with Shayna the night before came back to him and he frowned. If she was to be believed, then it sounded like she had gotten a raw deal. If her attorney was worth the money he'd been getting paid, then the man would have looked into her story and mounted a defense instead of advising her to take a deal. But that wasn't his problem, Madoc told himself. Regardless of whether she was innocent or not, she had jumped bond and it was his job was to bring her in.

Aware of Shayna's gaze on him, Madoc crossed the room to the stove and began to make a fire. Once that was done, he opened a can of soup and poured it into a pot, then set it on the stove to heat. As he stood there waiting, he spotted movement from the corner of his eye and turned his head to see Shayna standing beside him. She didn't say anything, but merely held out her hands to warm them by the stove.

Though Madoc did his best to ignore her, it was difficult, and he was glad when the soup started to bubble. Grabbing two mugs off the shelf, he poured soup into each and carried them over to the table. Though she looked reluctant to do so, Shayna left her post by the stove and sat down opposite him.

They ate in silence, which suited Madoc just fine. The less interaction he had with his prisoner, the better. Shayna, however, didn't seem to feel the same way, because after a few moments, she spoke.

"So," she said. "Where did you go on vacation?"

Madoc frowned, caught off guard by the question. "What?" he said.

"Last night, you said that you had been on vacation," she reminded him. "I just wondered where you went."

Madoc said nothing for a moment. He didn't usually discuss his personal life with prisoners when he was transporting them. Then again, he'd never gotten snowbound with one before. "I went out to Seattle for my brother's wedding," he said finally.

Across from him, Shayna smiled. "That must have been nice."

From the expectant look on her face, Madoc knew she was waiting for him to say something in reply to her comment, and when he didn't, she prompted him with another question.

"Are you originally from the Seattle area?" she said.

He shook his head. "Texas."

She nodded. "Have you lived in Denver long?"

144

"A while," he said, and he saw her frown at his noncommittal answer.

"Do you like it?" she asked.

"Yes."

It was obvious from her expression that Shayna expected him to elaborate, but again, he didn't, and Madoc hoped that would put an end to the conversation. But to his annoyance, she took his reluctance to talk about himself as her cue to tell him about herself instead.

At first, Madoc didn't pay much attention to what Shayna was saying, but as the morning wore on, he found himself not only starting to listen to her, but actually joining in the conversation. To his surprise, he and Shayna had a lot more in common than he would have thought, including their love of cheesy horror flicks. Madoc almost fell off the chair when she admitted that she loved zombie movies.

"And I have the DVD collection to prove it," she added with a grin.

That prompted a lively debate about the best zombie movie ever made, and though they agreed to disagree, the conversation had Madoc wondering where a woman like Shayna Matthews had been all his life. When he had suggested to any of the other women he'd gone out with that they spend the night in front of the television watching *Night of the Living Dead* instead of going out to a dance club, they had looked at him like he'd lost his mind.

From there, the conversation turned to Madoc and his life growing up in Texas. To his surprise, he found himself telling her not only about the close relationship he had with his family, but also about his job as a U.S. Marshal.

Sitting back in his chair, Madoc glanced out the cabin's one small window and was stunned to see that it was getting dark outside. He couldn't believe that he and Shayna had spent the whole day sitting and talking, but quite obviously, they had.

"I should go get some more wood before it gets dark," he said, pushing his chair back and getting to his feet.

Shayna pushed her chair back from the table as well. "I'll go with you," she said. "We need more snow to melt so that we have some water."

It wasn't snowing nearly as hard outside as it had been earlier, Madoc noticed as they stepped onto the porch. Pulling on his gloves, he walked over to the stack of logs while Shayna went to fill the pot with fresh snow.

Madoc was just leaning down to pick up the first log when a huge pile of snow slid off the roof of the cabin and fell directly on top of him. Swearing under his breath as freezing cold snow went down the collar of his coat, he reached up to brush it off when he heard the sound of feminine laughter coming from behind him.

Still brushing the snow from his coat, he turned to give Shayna a scowl. "You thought that was funny, did you?"

She was trying hard not to laugh as she shook her head. "No," she said, and then giggled. "Well, maybe just a little."

"Really?" Madoc drawled, scooping up a handful of snow and forming it into a ball. "Let's see how funny you think it is now."

Shayna's dark eyes went wide as she realized exactly what he intended to do with the handful of snow. With a squeal, she sidestepped wildly to avoid the snowball he threw her way, laughing when it missed her and fell harmlessly to the ground.

With a grin, Madoc immediately bent down to scoop up another handful of snow, only to get smacked squarely in the chest with one himself when he straightened.

"That's a point for me!" Shayna shouted triumphantly even as she tried to sidestep the second snowball he threw at her. She wasn't fast enough to avoid the projectile this time, however, and she squealed as it made a splat on her coat.

Madoc chuckled. "Guess that means we're tied!"

Apparently taking that as a challenge, Shayna quickly bent to make another snowball. Madoc did the same, and they spent the next ten minutes laughing and hurling snowballs at

146

each other like two kids. Having grown up in Texas, Madoc had never taken part in a snowball fight before and he had to admit that it was fun. Or maybe it was just Shayna that made it fun, he thought.

Which was why he agreed rather reluctantly to a truce when she called for one. Once back inside the warmth of the cabin, she turned to him with a laugh.

"I haven't had a snowball fight in years," she said. "I forgot how much fun they are."

Shayna's face was aglow and flushed from being outside, and almost against his will, Madoc found his gaze drawn to her mouth. Her lips were full and pink and slightly parted, as if they were waiting to be kissed. And God help him, for some reason he couldn't explain, he wanted to kiss her. Hell, he'd wanted to taste her lips since he'd first seen her behind the counter at that diner.

Don't do it, he warned himself. But it was too late; he had already bent his head to kiss her.

CHAPTER FIVE

He really, really shouldn't be doing this, Madoc thought. But while his head was telling him to do one thing, his body was telling him to do another, and as Shayna's soft, luscious lips parted beneath his, he felt himself listening less and less to what his head was telling him to do, and more and more to what his body was saying.

With a low groan, he slid his hand into her long, dark hair and pulled her closer, deepening the kiss. God, her mouth tasted so sweet. Like fresh peaches, he thought. He told himself that it was probably because they had eaten some fruit earlier, but he knew that almost all of that sweetness was Shayna herself.

She melted against him with a sigh, her hands sliding up his chest to grip the edges of his coat so that she could pull him even closer, and in that moment, he knew he was lost. Even so, a very small voice in the back of his head whispered again that he should stop before things went too far, but Madoc thrust the thought aside. After being trapped in a cabin with a woman as sexy as Shayna, he knew there was no way he was going to listen to reason. He wanted Shayna Matthews, and he wanted her now!

Still kissing her, Madoc pushed Shayna's coat off her shoulders and down her arms. Tossing it aside, he found the hem of her shirt and began to push it up, taking his mouth from hers only long enough to lift the garment over her head. He went to work on her jeans next, hastily undoing the buttons so that he could push them down her long, shapely legs.

Despite his eagerness to see Shayna completely naked, however, Madoc couldn't resist pausing for a moment to gaze down at her. Though he had seen her in a bra and panties the night before, he'd been too focused on getting her warmed up to allow himself more than a quick look, but now, he stood there breathing hard as he drank in the sight of her.

He would have loved to have taken his time removing her bra and teasing the nipples that were already hardening beneath his gaze, but he was too aroused for that. He moved to take off her lacy bra, but she was already pushing his coat from his shoulders and down his arms. There was something very sexy about Shayna undressing him, he decided, especially when she pushed his hands away as he tried to help. She was so eager that she almost ripped the buttons from his shirt as she took it off. Man, was that hot!

Tossing the garment aside, Shayna let her gaze run over his bare chest admiringly for a long moment before reaching for his belt. Pulling him closer, she used one hand to tug him down for a kiss while she undid his belt with the other. He decided she was quite talented to still keep kissing him while being able to get his jeans down at the same time. As he stepped out of them, he felt her hand close around his hard cock and caress him firmly as she moved her mouth passionately over his.

Eager for Shayna to be as naked as he now was, Madoc stripped off her bra and panties with the same urgency as he had the rest of her clothing. Pulling her into his arms, he trailed hot kisses over her jaw and down her neck until he came to her breasts. Cupping the sweetly curved mounds in his hands, he took one turgid nipple into his mouth to suckle on it before going to her other breast and lavishing the same attention on the hardened peak he found there. Still cupping her creamy breasts in his hands, he slowly kissed his way back up to her ear.

Shayna's head fell back, giving him easy access to her neck, and Madoc took that as an invitation to kiss and nibble at the sensitive spot just below her ear. She moaned softly, only to gasp out loud a moment later as he took the pale pink buds of her nipples between his fingers and firmly squeezed them.

150

Madoc was about to bend his head to take one of those hard, little peaks into his mouth again when he felt Shayna's hands on his arms, tugging him toward the bed. He went willingly, letting his gaze run over her naked form appreciatively as she lay back on the bed. He took in her pink-tipped breasts, slender waist, and long, shapely legs. She was perfect, he thought.

"God, you're absolutely gorgeous," he breathed.

Shayna blushed at his words, but before she could say anything in reply, Madoc leaned down and slowly began kissing his way from one slender ankle all the way up her leg to her inner thigh. As he neared her pussy, he heard her moan, and he couldn't help but grin at the urgency in the sound. She was just as excited as he was. He lifted his head to meet her gaze as he reached the downy hair at the juncture of her thighs. Holding Shayna's eyes with his own, he ran his tongue teasingly over her plump, little clit. She threw her head back with a moan and lifted her hips, begging him for more, and he gave her more, lapping at her clit in a way he knew would drive her wild.

But as he ran his tongue up and down the slick folds of her pussy, she grew more and more excited, and the urge to be inside her became uncontrollable. With a low growl, he climbed onto the bed and settling himself between her legs, he entered her fully in one deep thrust.

Shayna wrapped her long legs around him, taking him even deeper, and Madoc groaned at how incredibly hot and tight she felt around him. It was like their bodies had been made to fit together, he thought.

Lowering himself onto his forearms, Madoc covered Shayna's mouth with his own, his tongue finding hers as he slowly began to move inside her. Beneath him, Shayna lifted her hips to meet his thrusts and together, they found the perfect rhythm.

A part of him wanted to go slowly, but he was so turned on that he knew that wouldn't be possible. And from the way

Shayna was digging her nails into his shoulders, it was likely that she was already close to the pinnacle as well. With a groan, he began to thrust even harder, driving into her more deeply each time. She met him thrust for thrust, her legs squeezing even more tightly around him.

Madoc had never felt so out of control with a woman in his life, but Shayna made him feel as if he were about to explode as any moment. Somehow, he managed to keep his orgasm at bay until Shayna threw back her head and screamed out with her own pleasure. Only then, did he let go, exploding inside of her in a soul-shattering release.

Afterward, as they lay together gently kissing and caressing each other, Madoc was surprised to feel himself begin to harden again. He would have thought that it would take hours to recover from such an intense orgasm, but apparently, Shayna had that kind of effect on him. He couldn't seem to get enough of her. But as he began to trail kisses down her neck to her breasts again, he decided that this time, they would go slower.

Much later, as he lay in bed with Shayna curled up asleep in his arms, Madoc tried to tell himself that it had been a mistake to sleep with her, but he couldn't, not when it had felt so incredibly right.

Shayna awoke the next morning to find herself alone in the small bed. Sleepily brushing her hair back from her face, she pushed herself up on her elbow and looked around for Madoc, but the cabin was empty. He had probably just gone outside for more wood, she told herself. Then again, she thought wryly, maybe the sex with her had been so good that the Marshal had changed his mind about bringing her in and decided to go back to Denver and forget he'd ever seen her. No, she couldn't be that lucky, she thought as she lay back down. Besides, he wouldn't have just left her stranded in the middle of nowhere.

Thinking of the sex they'd had brought all the memories of last night rushing back to her. Amazing was the only word she could think of to describe it. And unexpected.

To say she had been stunned when Madoc had kissed her was an understatement. Shayna had been just as surprised to find herself kissing him back. But at the first touch of his mouth on hers, all reason and doubt had fled her mind. She had never lost herself to passion like that before.

But now in the light of day, a small part of her wondered if she had slept with him in the hopes that he would let her go. Just as quickly, however, she realized that though it would be nice if he did let her go because of it, that hadn't been the reason at all. The passion that had erupted between them had been real. And it had been magical as well. The Marshal had awakened something in her that she hadn't known existed.

But what about Madoc? What was his reason for making love to her? Back at the diner, he had made it no secret that he was attracted to her. Had he finally just acted on that attraction or was there more to it than that? Part of her wanted to believe it had been more. She couldn't deny she and Madoc definitely had chemistry together. God, why couldn't she have met him before this whole mess?

Shayna was just daydreaming about how things might have been between her and the Marshal had they met under different circumstances when the door to the cabin opened. Holding the blanket to her breasts, she pushed herself up on her elbow as Madoc came in. Not sure exactly what to say to him after their romp in bed last night, she nervously chewed on her lower lip and waited for him to take the lead.

To her dismay, Madoc didn't say anything right away, however, but just stood there, his expression unreadable, and as the silence between them lengthened, Shayna grew more and more uncomfortable. Maybe last night had been a mistake, she thought. She was just about speak when Madoc cleared his throat.

"It's stopped snowing and I can hear plows off in the distance. We're not that far from the highway," he told her stiffly. "We can leave as soon as you get dressed."

Shayna told herself that she shouldn't be surprised by Madoc's words. She hadn't honestly expected him to let her go simply because they had slept together. And if she hadn't been so caught up her own thoughts when he'd walked in, then she would have realized that the man she had made love with last night was gone, and in his place was the no-nonsense U.S. Marshal who had taken her into custody. But she had at least expected him to acknowledge that they had slept together. Then again, maybe he was already regretting it.

Swallowing hard, Shayna started to push back the blanket, only to pause when she noticed Madoc turn away so that his back was to her. Considering she and the Marshal had just spent the night together, what he probably perceived as a gentlemanly gesture actually hurt her for some reason, and she found herself blinking back tears as she reached for her clothes.

It didn't take Shayna very long to get dressed, since they didn't have any bags to pack, they were ready to leave within minutes. Madoc left some money on the table to pay for the damage to the window as well as the food they had eaten. And then, without a backward glance, they left the small cabin.

They made the walk back to Madoc's truck in silence. Shayna had been surprised that he hadn't handcuffed her before they'd left the cabin. Maybe he figured that after she'd nearly frozen to death the last time she'd tried to escape, she wouldn't be foolish enough to do it again, she thought. That didn't stop him from taking her arm once they got back to his truck, she noticed. What did he think, that she was going to try to flag down a passing trucker? she wondered. But then she saw the Montana State Trooper's car parked behind Madoc's SUV, and her stomach knotted.

"You folks need some help?" the officer asked as they trudged through the snow to the SUV.

Shayna held her breath as she waited for Madoc to identify himself and explain to the other man that she was a wanted fugitive he had captured. Since Madoc had wanted to dump her off with the locals in the first place, he was probably going to ask the state trooper to escort her the rest of the way to Billings, she thought.

Madoc gave her a sidelong glance before turning his attention back to the trooper. "My wife and I were caught in the snow," he told the other man. "We had to hole up in a cabin about a mile in."

Shayna blinked, sure she hadn't heard Madoc right.

But the state trooper was nodding. "You two were lucky you found a cabin," he said. "You would have frozen to death if you'd been out here in your truck. You need any help getting back out on the road?"

Madoc shook his head. "I don't think so, but if you wouldn't mind waiting for just a few until we get started, I'd appreciate it."

Shayna's head was spinning as Madoc helped her into the passenger seat. She sat there trying to understand what had just happened while he cleaned the rest of the truck off. Was he going to let her go after all? she wondered. Or did he just want to turn her in himself? If that were the case, then why had he told the state trooper she was his wife?

Desperately wanting to know the answer to that, but afraid to come right out and ask for fear of what Madoc would say, Shayna was silent as he got into the SUV and they pulled onto the highway. With a wave of thanks to the trooper, they were on their way with Shayna feeling more confused than ever. She didn't want to get her hopes up, but as they were driving down the highway toward Billings, however, her curiosity finally got the better of her.

"Why didn't you turn me over to that state trooper back there?" she asked quietly. It was the first time either of them had spoken since they'd left the cabin.

The muscle in Madoc's jaw flexed, but he didn't look at her. "Because it's just as easy for me to take you back to Denver," he said.

Shayna felt her heart sink at his words, the small hope she had been holding onto collapsing. Blinking back tears, she turned to stare blindly out the side window.

After last night, and then with what he had said to the trooper, she had truly begun to think Madoc might actually let her go. But apparently the fact that they'd slept together didn't mean anything to him. She didn't know what hurt more. That he didn't believe she was innocent, or that he could still turn her in after they had had such amazing sex. Maybe it hadn't been as good for him as it had for her, she thought bitterly.

They made the rest of the drive in silence. Shayna found herself wishing Madoc would turn on the radio or something. Anything to distract her from thoughts of what awaited her back in Denver. In a couple of hours, she would be back in jail. The one night she'd spent there after she had been arrested had been awful enough, and the thought of going back made fresh tears well in her eyes. Especially because this time, she didn't think she would be getting back out.

As they reached the outskirts of Denver, Shayna glanced at the handsome man beside her, wondering if she should try to plead her case with him again, but then decided against it. She had spent the past two days working on him. If she hadn't swayed him during that time, there was really nothing left to say. Besides, she didn't want to spend the remaining freedom she had left arguing with Madoc. With a sigh, she tore her gaze away from the Marshal to gaze out the window again.

Shayna was so lost in her own thoughts that she didn't realize Madoc had turned into a parking garage until he pulled the SUV into a space. Her brow furrowing, she gave him a curious look.

"Where are we?" she asked.

He turned to look at her with those incredible golden eyes of his. "My apartment building," he said. "I've decided not to turn you in. At least not until I can check out your story."

Shayna blinked in surprise, unable to believe what she'd just heard. "What made you change your mind?" she said softly.

Madoc said nothing for a moment, and Shayna held her breath as she waited for him to answer.

"I didn't say I changed my mind. I just said that I was going to check into it before I turn you in, that's all," he said gruffly.

Shayna made no reply, but she knew from the way he said the words that it was more than that. If he were just interested in checking into her story, he could have done it while she was in jail. He must really think she was innocent for him to put himself at risk like this. Of course, some part of her was also hoping that his reasons might be a little more personal than that. That maybe last night had meant something to him after all. She tried to control it, but her heart began to beat wildly at the thought that not only might she finally have found a way to get out of this mess, but that Madoc might actually care for her.

CHAPTER SIX

What the hell was he doing? Madoc asked himself as he let Shayna into his apartment. He was risking his career, his reputation, even his freedom, all for a woman he had just met! And for what? Maybe going to his brother's wedding had infected him with some kind of mental disorder or something, he thought. What else could explain such a serious lack in judgment?

But no matter how much he tried to tell himself that he was being crazy, and that he should just drop Shayna off at the Denver PD, he couldn't. She was innocent; he knew that deep down in his gut. And while he hadn't said anything to Shayna until they had gotten back to Denver, he had actually made the decision not to turn her in while they had been in bed that morning. She had looked so vulnerable lying there sleeping that he couldn't bear the thought of her spending even one night in a jail cell much less going to prison for the rest of her life. Especially for something she didn't do.

And if he hadn't slept with her, would he still be so willing to help her clear her name? he wondered. Of course he would be, he told himself. The fact that he had just spent the night having the most incredible sex of his life with her hadn't factored into his decision at all.

Madoc ground his jaw. *Yeah, right!* Who the hell was he kidding? He had criticized his brother for getting involved with a protectee in the Witness Protection Program, and here he was falling for a fugitive! That thought stopped him cold. He was definitely not falling for Shayna Matthews! He was helping her in the interest of justice, that was all.

His hand tightening on the handle of the overnight bag he held, Madoc cleared his throat. "I'm going to grab a quick shower and a change of clothes, then head over to the office and see what I can dig up," he announced. "Make yourself at home."

Before Shayna could reply, Madoc walked down the hallway and into his bedroom. Stripping off his clothes, he took a shower, and then pulled on a fresh pair of jeans and a clean shirt. When he went back into the living room, it was to find Shayna standing at the window, gazing out at the snow-covered mountains in the distance.

"I'll be back as soon as I can," he said, pulling on his coat. "Don't answer the phone or open the door to anyone. And whatever you do, don't go anywhere."

A small smile curved her lips. "I won't," she said.

Digging into his pocket for his keys, Madoc started for the door.

"Madoc?"

His hand on the doorknob, Madoc turned to see Shayna chewing on her lower lip and looking at him gratefully.

"Thank you," she said softly.

Madoc wanted to tell Shayna that she shouldn't be thanking him yet. That if he didn't succeed in finding something to clear her name soon, then she'd very likely end up going to prison anyway. But she looked so worried standing there that it was all he could do not to stride across the room and take her in his arms. Not trusting himself to speak, he merely gave her a nod and walked out.

The building that housed the U.S. Marshals offices was across town from his apartment, but the traffic was surprisingly light, so it took less than a half hour to get there. Once inside, Madoc went directly to his boss's office. Since he knew he wouldn't get much investigating done with the workload that was sure to be waiting for him, Madoc had decided to take a couple more days off. Though Deputy Chief Evans wasn't thrilled with the idea of Madoc taking more time off, the other man agreed. Of course, it helped that Madoc went into great detail about the two "miserable" days he'd had to spend holed up in the cabin.

Deciding the best way to check out Shayna's story was to find what the Denver police had on the case, Madoc went over to the precinct where she had been arrested. Fortunately, he had a friend who worked as a detective there, so getting a look at the file wasn't as difficult as it might have been if he'd had to go through normal channels. That didn't mean his friend didn't wonder why Madoc was interested in a case that had already been solved.

"It might be connected to another case I'm working on," Madoc told the other man with a shrug.

Opening the folder, Madoc read through the file. Though everything had been done by the book, it was clear that the police hadn't wanted to investigate anyone else after finding the evidence on Shayna. Though Madoc supposed he couldn't really blame the cops. The evidence against Shayna was solid and if he had been working the case, he probably would have come to the same conclusion.

With a sigh, he began to read through the file again, more slowly this time. Things had unfolded just like Shayna had told him. According to the lead detective who had investigated the case, the police had received an anonymous tip from someone saying that Shayna had embezzled the money. Of course, the call had come from a pay phone so there was no way of knowing who had actually made it, but the caller had to be the person who had framed Shayna. As for the emails she had supposedly sent to her boss, Evan Mercer, they had all come from her work email address. While that wasn't as bad as being sent from her personal computer, it would be almost impossible to prove she hadn't been the one who wrote them. Which left the bank account in the Caymans, but since there was no way to find out who actually opened it, that was another dead end.

Madoc picked up the crime-scene photos from Evan Mercer's house. When Shayna had told him the police said they had found some blood, Madoc had assumed there would be more than the half dozen droplets on the carpet in the picture. After seeing that, Madoc was even more inclined to think Shayna's boss had set her up. Now, they just needed to prove it. But how?

Madoc thought a moment. The next logical step was to search Mercer's place. While the police had probably already done that, there might be something they overlooked, especially if they were only looking for evidence against Shayna, he told himself. At least, he hoped they had.

Wondering whether to go straight there or back to his apartment first, Madoc opted for the latter. Since he was going to have to break into Mercer's place, it made more sense to do it after dark. Besides, he hadn't eaten anything since that morning and he was starving. Figuring that Shayna was probably just as hungry, especially since there wasn't much in the way of food back at his apartment, he decided to pick up some Chinese food on the way home.

As he left the police station, Madoc realized he was looking forward to seeing Shayna. Hopefully, she hadn't done anything foolish while he'd been out, like call her family to let them know she was back in Denver, he thought. He could just imagine her telling them the whole story.

Shayna stared at the door in disbelief. She couldn't believe Madoc had gone out and left her alone in his apartment. If she wanted to, she could make a run for it, she told herself. But she wasn't going to. Outside of her family, Madoc was the only other person who believed she was innocent and that meant a lot to her. She trusted him to help her, and she wasn't going to let him down.

With a sigh, Shayna put her hands on her hips and surveyed the apartment. It was nice, she thought, taking in the roomy living area and modern kitchen. Very masculine, but then had she really expected any less from a man like the Marshal. Her lips curving into a smile, she decided she liked

162

it. Then again, she had been living in the boarding house for so long that she probably would have liked his apartment if he'd had shag carpeting on the floor, a lava lamp on the coffee table, and a disco ball hanging from the ceiling. Well, maybe not, she conceded.

Abruptly, she remembered Madoc's invitation to make herself at home. While raiding his refrigerator was tempting, Shayna decided she needed a shower first. After being in the same clothes for the past two days, she felt totally grimy. Making her way through the living room, she walked down the hall toward the room the Marshal had disappeared into earlier.

Madoc's bedroom was as masculine-looking as the rest of his apartment, and there was something equally inviting about it, Shayna thought. As she took in the huge four-poster bed with its navy blue comforter, she blushed hotly as she pictured Madoc making love to her there. An image of her beneath him, her legs wrapped tightly around his waist while he plunged deeply into her, played over and over in her mind. That thought, as well as all of the other ways the gorgeous Marshal would pleasure her with his body had her pussy practically purring, and she let out a little moan as she walked into the adjoining bathroom.

Thirty minutes later, Shayna had showered and dried her hair, and was standing in front of the mirror, wearing only her bra and panties. The thought of putting on her jeans and long-sleeved shirt again after she'd just gotten all nice and clean wasn't very appealing, but neither could she walk around Madoc's apartment in her underwear.

She chewed on her lower lip, wondering whether Madoc would mind if she borrowed a shirt to wear. While he had told her to make herself at home, she wasn't sure that extended to borrowing his clothes. But it was either that or put hers back on, she told herself. With a shrug, she padded back into the bedroom and over to the closet.

Madoc had a variety of shirts to pick from, including several white dress-shirts. Choosing one of those, Shayna slipped her arms into the sleeves and buttoned it up. It was big on her, coming to mid-thigh, and it reminded her of wearing her boyfriend's shirt, something she'd always kind of liked. She knew it was improbable since the shirt was obviously clean, but she could have sworn she still smelled Madoc's masculine scent on it. Regardless, it made wearing the Marshal's shirt extremely comforting.

Going back out into the living room, Shayna started to make her way to the kitchen, but then stopped at the sound of a knock on the door. Remembering Madoc's warning not to open the door to anyone, she ignored whoever it was and continued on her way to the kitchen, only to stop when the knock came again.

"It's Mrs. Murray from across the hall, dear," a woman's voice called. "Are you in there?"

Her brow furrowing, Shayna walked over to the door and looked out the peephole to see an elderly woman standing there. As if somehow sensing that Shayna had looked out to verify the identity of her visitor, the woman smiled and lifted the plate of cookies she was holding in offering. Shayna knew she should probably ignore the older woman, but she couldn't. When Madoc had warned her not to open the door to anyone, he obviously hadn't meant his sweet, elderly neighbor. Besides, with her gray hair back in a bun and that warm smile, she reminded Shayna of her grandmother.

Running her hands over her long, dark hair, Shayna fixed a smile on her face and pulled open the door. "Can I help you?" she asked.

The elderly woman's smile broadened. "I'm Mrs. Murray from across the hall," she explained again. "I heard you and Madoc coming in earlier, and I thought I'd bring over some chocolate chip cookies. They're homemade," she added, holding out the plate.

Automatically taken in by the other woman's sweet manner, Shayna couldn't help but reach out to take the plate of cookies from her. It would have been rude not to, Shayna told herself. Besides, they smelled so delicious. It was all she could do not to grab one off the plate and bite into it right then.

"Thank you," she said. "That was very sweet of you, Mrs. Murray."

Mrs. Murray waved her hand. "'Twas no trouble at all, my dear," she said, and then glanced over Shayna's shoulder. "I couldn't help but notice Madoc leave earlier, so I thought you might like to sit down and have a little girl talk."

Shayna didn't know what to say at first. Madoc had told her not to let anyone into the apartment, but the sweet woman had gone to all the trouble of making cookies for her. Shayna didn't know how well Madoc was acquainted with the older woman, so she wasn't even sure if he would want her in his apartment. But what was Shayna going to do, slam the door in Mrs. Murray's face?

"Actually, Madoc just went into work for a little while," Shayna said. "He'll probably be back any minute."

Mrs. Murray made a tsking noise. "I've lived next door to that boy for years now, and one thing I know. When he goes into work, he's never right back," she said. "So, since he's probably going to be a while, what do you say we girls get some coffee to go with these cookies, dear? You can tell me all about the wedding."

If the woman knew about his brother's wedding, then she must know the Marshal fairly well, Shayna thought. She supposed it wouldn't hurt to let the woman in for a little while. Besides, it had been a long time since Shayna had been able to sit down and just chat with someone about everyday things. Smiling again, she took a step back to let the other woman into the apartment. With her sweet, take-charge demeanor, Mrs. Murray was beginning to remind Shayna more and more of her grandmother.

"Why don't you sit down and I'll make some coffee," Shayna suggested as she set the plate of cookies down on the coffee table.

"I don't think you told me your name, dear," the older woman said as she took a seat on the couch.

"It's Shayna," she said, giving the woman her real name without thinking.

Shayna cringed inwardly. Oh God, what if Mrs. Murray remembered hearing her name on the news? It wasn't a common name, after all.

But Mrs. Murray merely smiled. "What a lovely name," she said. "Is it Irish?"

Shayna breathed a sigh of relief. "You know, I'm not really sure," she said, and then quickly added, "Why don't I go make that coffee?"

Still chiding herself for tripping up like that, Shayna hurried into the kitchen before the other woman could stop her. However, since Madoc's apartment had an open floor-plan, Mrs. Murray was able to continue their conversation while Shayna made coffee. To her relief, the older woman had let the subject of Shayna's name drop and had moved onto Madoc's brother's wedding, wanting to know how it was. Though that wasn't necessarily any better, Shayna thought as she got the coffee going. While Madoc had opened up quite a bit to her at the cabin the day before – something which still surprised her – he hadn't really said all that much about his brother's wedding. She needn't have worried, though, because the sweet, elderly Mrs. Murray didn't let her get a word in edgewise. All Shayna had to do was smile and nod her head in agreement at the appropriate times.

Walking back into the living room, Shayna set the mugs she'd been carrying down on the table and joined Mrs. Murray on the couch.

"Thank you, dear," the older woman said. Picking up her mug, she sipped her coffee. "You're so much nicer than the other girls that Madoc has brought home. And much prettier, too, I don't mind telling you."

While Shayna blushed at the compliment, she also felt a ridiculous little stab of jealousy at the other woman's words.

166

Just because she had let Mrs. Murray think she was Madoc's girlfriend didn't mean she had any right to be jealous of how many other girls the Marshal had brought back to his apartment. He was an attractive man, after all. Certainly, he'd had lots of girlfriends. Besides, she had no claim to him. Still, that didn't mean she couldn't ask Mrs. Murray about them.

Shayna reached for a cookie. "Really?" she said, trying to make her voice sound casual.

Mrs. Murray waved her hand dismissively. "Not that I would ever say that to Madoc, of course, but none of those other women were right for him."

As she ate her cookie, Shayna felt an inexplicable surge of joy at hearing that none of Madoc's previous girlfriends had been right for him. Which was just silly, of course, she told herself.

"So, how long have you and Madoc been seeing each other, dear?" the older woman asked.

Shayna sipped her coffee again. "Not long," she said. Wow, was that an understatement! she thought.

Mrs. Murray smiled. "Well, you're just what he needs in his life, dear," she said. "Someone to make an honest man of him."

Shayna almost laughed at that. She wasn't exactly making an honest man out of Madoc. If anything, she was turning him into a criminal. She probably didn't want to mention that to the older woman, though. Before she could say anything, however, the apartment door opened. At the sound, both Shayna and the other woman looked toward the entryway to see Madoc standing there, a grocery bag in the crook of one arm. For a moment, he just stood where he was, staring at the two of them, but then his eyes narrowed.

Having come to recognize that look on the Marshal's face, Shayna shifted uncomfortably in her seat. Mrs. Murray, however, gave him a warm smile as she got to her feet. Shayna set her mug down on the table and stood as well.

"Madoc, dear boy," his elderly neighbor said. "I was just having the most pleasant conversation with your lovely girlfriend."

Shayna saw Madoc's mouth tighten at the words. "Really?" he drawled, his gaze going from the older woman to her.

"Oh, yes!" Mrs. Murray told him. "Shayna was telling me all about how beautiful your brother's wedding was, weren't you, dear?"

Mrs. Murray turned to give Shayna a smile, which she somehow managed to return, despite the fact that Madoc was still glowering at her.

"Well, I'm going to go back to my own apartment and leave you two lovebirds alone," the older woman announced. Reaching out, she took Shayna's hand in both of hers. "Shayna, dear, it was so lovely meeting you. Do come by sometime, won't you? I'm sure you'll be spending lots of time over here."

Ignoring the glare Madoc was sending her way, Shayna nodded and told the woman that she would indeed stop by to see her.

Still smiling, Mrs. Murray carefully made her way around the coffee table and walked over to where Madoc stood. Giving Shayna another smile over her shoulder, the tiny woman turned back to the Marshal and put a hand on his arm.

"Don't let her get away, dear boy," she said, her voice a loud whisper. "This one is a keeper, I tell you."

Madoc glanced at Shayna, his expression unreadable. "I'd have to agree with that," he said. "Someone definitely needs to lock her up."

As Madoc showed the older woman out, Shayna took the opportunity to make her escape. Picking up the mugs in one hand and the plate of cookies in the other, she carried them into the kitchen. Maybe if she acted like nothing had happened, then Madoc would do the same. *Yeah, right*, she thought.

168

"What the hell didn't you understand about don't let anyone into the apartment?" the Marshal demanded as he followed her into the kitchen.

Shayna let out a sigh as she turned away from the sink. Madoc had set the grocery bag down on the table and was now standing there with his arms folded across his broad chest while he glowered at her.

Telling herself that engaging the Marshal in a shouting match would probably only get her into more trouble, she gave him a shrug. "Mrs. Murray knocked on the door and said she was your neighbor," Shayna said as she walked past him into the living room. "She saw us come in together, so I couldn't very well ignore her. It would have been rude."

Shayna heard Madoc swear under his breath as he followed her into the living room. "What if she had recognized you?" he said.

She waved her hand dismissively. "I seriously doubt that sweet, old woman spends her days staring at wanted posters," she said sarcastically, and then added, "In fact, I'm pretty sure no one does that, but you."

The muscle in the side of Madoc's jaw flexed. "This isn't a game, dammit! I'm putting my life on the line for you, Shayna," he ground out. "If you don't start using your head, you're going to get us both thrown in jail."

Shayna didn't need to be reminded how important it was for her to keep a low profile; she'd been doing it for months without Madoc's help. "Lighten up, already, will you?" she snapped. "Mrs. Murray didn't recognize me, so there's no harm done. Sheesh!"

Madoc's golden brown eyes narrowed warningly. "Maybe another trip over my knee would make you start to take this more seriously," he said softly.

She automatically took a step back, her eyes going wide at the mention of another spanking. "There's no way I'm letting you spank me again!"

His mouth quirked. "I wasn't giving you a choice."

Madoc was starting toward her even as he spoke, and Shayna quickly darted to the side, putting the low-slung coffee table between her and the Marshal. They stood like that for a moment, each eyeing the other warily. Knowing the only way she was probably going to avoid the spanking would be if she locked herself in the bedroom for the rest of the night, Shayna made a run for it.

But Madoc was faster. Cutting Shayna off, he grabbed her arm and, in one swift motion, sat down on the couch and threw her over his knee. Outraged, Shayna immediately tried to push herself off his lap, but Madoc merely shoved her back down with a hand. A moment later, he wrapped an arm around her waist and began to pepper her upturned bottom with hard, stinging smacks.

"*Owwww!*" she cried. "Let me up, damn you!"

But like he'd done the other two times he had spanked her, Madoc ignored her protests and continued to bring his hand down over and over on her bottom.

"Not until you learn to start listening to me," he growled.

Shayna struggled against his hold, squirming this way and that, but much to her horror, all her wiggling and kicking did was cause the shirt she was wearing to ride up and expose her skimpy, bikini panties.

Red-faced, Shayna immediately stopped squirming, hoping that if she lay there submissively, Madoc would think she had been spanked enough and stop. But to her dismay, he continued to spank her, delivering a sharp smack to first one half-naked asscheek, and then the other. If anything, he seemed to be spanking her harder now. Or maybe it only felt that way because her cheeks were exposed.

Shayna was too mortified to care about how much the spanks were stinging now, though. It didn't matter that Madoc had seen her naked the night before. This was completely different. Being draped over his lap with her panty-covered ass

170

exposed for his viewing pleasure while he spanked her was too embarrassing for words.

Her face colored even more as she thought of Madoc looking at her rapidly reddening bottom. Though she hadn't gotten a look at her derriere after the other times he'd spanked her, she was sure that after this spanking, it was going to be positively glowing! The idea of the handsome Marshal's gaze fixed on her ass had her squirming all over again, but for a completely different reason. This time, it wasn't to protest the spanking he was giving her, but because the thought of him gazing at her bottom was making her pussy start to tingle.

Shayna's eyes flew wide. Oh, God! She could not be getting turned on! Not while he was spanking her! But there was no mistaking her arousal. And the more she focused on the tingling between her legs, the more excited she became. To her shock, she realized that her pussy was actually getting wet! This could not be happening!

A thought even more horrifying came to her then. What if she got so wet that it soaked through her panties? Then Madoc would be able to tell that she was excited. She couldn't let that happen!

Blushing hotly, Shayna renewed her struggles to free herself. "Madoc, please..." she begged. "That really...*owwww!*...stings!"

Shayna wasn't sure whether her words would have any effect on the Marshal this time, especially since they hadn't the other times she'd tried it, but much to her relief, after giving her one more hard smack to each cheek, Madoc stood her back on her feet.

Automatically, Shayna reached back to cup her freshly-spanked asscheeks with both hands, only to gasp at how hot they felt. If anything, her bottom seemed to be throbbing even more now that the spanking was over. She had to bite her lip to keep from crying out when she squeezed her cheeks with her hands. He had really done a number on her this time.

She gave Madoc a sullen look. "That spanking really stung, you know."

He shrugged. "Well, I only did it in the hopes that you might actually be a little bit more careful. It was for your own good, you know," he said, and then added more softly, "Come here."

Taking her hand, he pulled her closer so that she was standing between his legs. Reaching around, he cupped her tender asscheeks in both of his strong hands and began to gently massage them. Shayna instinctively opened her mouth to protest, but found herself sighing with pleasure instead. Wow, she hadn't expected that! Just a moment ago, she was kicking and squealing at the feel of his hand on her bottom, and now she couldn't get enough of his touch. She didn't know how that could be possible after the spanking he'd just given her, but right then, she wasn't interested in giving it much thought. Instead, she closed her eyes and let herself enjoy the sensation.

Madoc must have noticed her reaction to what he was doing because he chuckled. "Did I tell you that I couldn't help but notice how great you look in that shirt," he said. "In fact, I wouldn't mind seeing you in it all the time."

Shayna felt her heart leap with joy at his off-handed comment. *Careful,* she warned herself. *Don't read more into it than you should.*

Taking her hand again, Madoc suddenly pulled her down to sit on his lap. The rough material of his jeans against her tender bottom made her gasp, but the sound was swiftly muffled as he captured her mouth in a long, drugging kiss. And while the feel of his lips on hers didn't make her completely forget about how sore her poor bottom still was, it did make her think a whole heck of a lot less about it. God, the man was a good kisser!

He deepened the kiss, his tongue making slow, swirling motions inside her mouth, and she melted against him with a small sigh of pleasure, her arms automatically going around his neck. His kiss alone was enough to almost make her go dizzy, but then he started to lightly trail the fingers of one hand up her bare leg, and she knew right then that it was only going to get better.

Madoc broke the kiss to give her a long, soulful look as his hand slowly continued up her leg and toward her inner thigh. Shayna felt her pulse quicken as his hand slipped beneath the tail of the dress shirt and found its way to the edge of her bikini panties. She waited breathlessly for him to slide his fingers underneath her panties and touch her, but instead, he dipped his hand between her legs and caressed her tingling pussy through her panties. Even with the material in the way, his touch was enough to make her moan and she clutched his shoulders for support. The way he slid his fingers up and down her wet groove made her think he truly intended to tease her to orgasm before he ever got her panties off.

Just when it seemed like she might actually come, he paused long enough to slide his fingers into the waistband of her panties and yank them effortlessly down her legs. She wondered how he could possibly have gotten them off so easily given their positions, but then she forgot about the logistics of the maneuver as his fingers delved into the wetness waiting between her legs. It seemed to Shayna that Madoc knew her body better than she did, and she began to moan softly as he found her clit and caressed it gently.

Sliding his other hand loosely into her hair, Madoc gently tilted her head to the side as he nibbled his way along her jaw line and over to her ear. Shayna shivered, gooseflesh pebbling her skin as he trailed hot kisses down her neck. That part of her body had always been an erogenous zone and the Marshal seemed to know exactly how she liked to be touched there.

Between her legs, he had begun making slow circles round and around her clit, and the two sensations had her crying out as spasms of pleasure rippled through her body. Madoc moved his fingers in time with her undulating hips, stretching her pleasure out longer and longer until she thought she couldn't take any more. Only as her orgasm gradually began to subside, did his fingers on her clit begin to slow.

Letting out a soft, little sigh of pleasure, Shayna tipped her head forward and opened her eyes to find a grin tugging at the corner of Madoc's mouth.

"It seemed like you enjoyed that," he observed teasingly.

She smiled. "*Mmm-hmm*," she breathed, and then as a naughty idea popped into her head, she added in a husky voice, "In fact, I think I should show you exactly how much."

Giving him a sexy look, Shayna slid off his lap and dropped to her knees in front of him. Leaning forward, she kissed him lingeringly on the mouth before tracing a path along his hair-roughened jaw and down his neck as she began to unbutton his shirt. She ran her hands over the hard wall of his muscled chest and down to his taut, flat abs, marveling to herself as how well-built he was. Sliding her hands back up his chest to his broad shoulders, she pushed his shirt off. Then, with his help, she made quick work of his jeans, taking them off as well.

Sitting back on her heels, Shayna let her gaze run over Madoc's naked body. Damn, he was hot! In fact, she could just sit there and look at him all night, she decided. When they had made love at the cabin, it had been so frenzied that she hadn't had a chance to really appreciate how truly gorgeous he was, but now she wanted to take him all in. God, there wasn't a part of his magnificent body that wasn't perfect!

But no matter how good the rest of him looked, her attention kept coming back to his extremely hard cock, standing proud and erect between his muscular legs. Unable to resist temptation any longer, she decided to give in to it. Leaning forward, she wrapped her hand around his throbbing erection, and then giving him a naughty look, she took him in her mouth. She wasn't sure which of them groaned more

174

loudly, Madoc because it felt so good, or her because he tasted so wonderful.

Shayna took her time pleasuring him, slowing running her tongue first over the head of his cock, and then up and down the length of him. As she lowered her head to do it all over again, she gently cupped his balls with her other hand, lovingly caressing them, then ran her tongue up his cock as if he were a delicious treat. Which he was, she decided as she swiped her tongue over the glistening bead of precum she found on the head of his cock. *Mmmm*, she thought. He tasted so good!

She continued to tease him like that for a while longer, slowly running her tongue all over him before she changed tactics and took his entire cock deep in mouth. As she felt him slide all the way to the back of her throat, she couldn't help but let out a little moan. Madoc was obviously enjoying it, too, because he groaned as well.

Shayna could tell that he was getting close to coming and she had to argue with herself about what she should do next. A part of her wanted to feel his come shooting into her mouth, but the other part of her decided that would have to wait. Right now, she wanted to feel that glorious cock of his inside her!

As she got to her feet a moment later, she couldn't help but smile at the disappointed look on Madoc's face. But just as quickly, his expression changed to one of eagerness as she climbed onto his lap and slowly eased herself down onto him.

He was so big that it was a wonder she could take him all in, but take him all she did, and Shayna caught her breath as she felt him fill her completely. For a moment, she sat there unmoving, just enjoying the feel of him deep inside of her. But then she began to rotate her hips in slow, insistent circles. Madoc reached out to grasp her hips, clearly wanting her to move faster, but she playfully smacked his hands away.

"Hands off," she ordered. "I'm in charge of this ride."

Madoc held up his hands in a placating gesture. "Whatever you say," he agreed, a grin tugging at the corners of his mouth.

Despite his words, however, it clearly wasn't in Madoc's nature to sit back and do nothing, because soon after, he reached out and began to undo the buttons on her shirt. A moment later, he pushed it off her shoulders and tossed it onto the cushion beside them. Her bra quickly followed, and then he was cupping a breast in each hand. Capturing each of her nipples between a thumb and forefinger, he began to roll them gently back and forth with his fingers.

As much as Shayna wanted to take things slowly, she couldn't. Within moments, she found it impossible to sit still and began to move up and down in time with his caresses. But just because he had gotten her moving didn't mean she couldn't be the one to set the pace, she told herself with a little smile. With that in mind, she rode him slowly, grinding herself hard against him each time she came down.

But Madoc only let her torture him like that for so long before he took charge. Giving her nipples a firm squeeze, he slid his hands down her waist and over her hips to cup her asscheeks. Her breath caught in her throat as he began to massage her bottom. While her ass didn't sting as much as it had right after the spanking, it still tingled just enough to make what he was doing with his hands feel even more incredible than if she hadn't gotten spanked at all. Who knew that a good spanking could make sex so incredible?

Without realizing it, Shayna discovered that she had started to ride him faster and faster, and before she knew it, she was already approaching orgasm. For one, wild moment, she wondered if she should try to hold off or not, but that decision was made for her as Madoc gripped her hips tightly and began to pull her down even harder and faster against him.

Shayna closed her eyes and threw her head back as the first ripples of ecstasy coursed through her. They started somewhere deep inside of her, and then began to spiral

176

outward, and by the time the pulsating waves of pleasure crested over her, she realized she was already screaming in ecstasy. And yet, despite how loudly she was crying out, she still managed to hear Madoc's groans of satisfaction, and knowing that he was coming with her only made her own orgasm that much more intense.

Much later, as she lay draped against his shoulder, she heard Madoc whisper in her ear.

"You know," he said softly. "I could really get used to this."

Shayna smiled against his neck. "Me, too."

As she cuddled up against him, Shayna couldn't help but wonder what Madoc had meant by that comment. Had he just been referring to the sex? While it was amazing, Shayna realized that she was starting to hope for something more between them. And yet, at the same time, she was amazed she could even be thinking such a thing. She had just met Madoc days ago. Was she really falling for him, or was she just confusing gratitude for love?

Deciding she didn't have an answer to that question right then, Shayna closed her eyes and snuggled closer to the wonderful man beside her.

CHAPTER SEVEN

By the time he and Shayna roused themselves from the couch, the food Madoc had picked up from the Chinese restaurant earlier was cold, so they had to reheat it in the microwave. Rather than sit at the kitchen table to eat, though, they carried their plates into the living room and settled back down on the couch. Despite how hungry he was, however, it was difficult to focus on eating with Shayna sitting so close to him. She had pulled up her knees, which made the shirt slip down and expose the tantalizing skin of her thigh and hip. It also didn't help that she kept letting out these sexy, little sighs of pleasure as she ate, either. They reminded him of the passionate noises she had made while they had been making love earlier. And all that did was make him want her again.

"I feel like I haven't eaten in days," Shayna said as she used her chopsticks to pick up another piece of chicken. "You don't know how tempted I was to eat every one of those cookies Mrs. Murray brought over."

Madoc scowled. He still couldn't believe that his sweet, nosy neighbor had been sitting there on the couch drinking coffee with Shayna when he'd come in. "You shouldn't have let her in," he said. "And you definitely shouldn't have given her your real name."

Shayna gave him an embarrassed look. "It just kind of came out. Mrs. Murray is so friendly that I just didn't think, I guess," she said, and then added, "You don't think she'll remember seeing me in the newspapers or anything, do you?"

From everything he knew about his elderly neighbor, the woman was probably more inclined to watch *Dr. Phil* than *America's Most Wanted*, and even if by chance she had seen Shayna's picture on the local news all those months ago, she probably wouldn't remember. At least Madoc hoped she wouldn't.

Realizing that Shayna was looking at him expectantly, he shook his head. "I doubt it," he said, and then gave her a stern look. "But that doesn't mean you don't have to be more careful."

Beside him, Shayna nodded. "I will. I promise," she told him, and then as if she were afraid he would scold her some more, she hurried on. "So, were you able to find out anything that might help me?"

Madoc helped himself to more rice before answering. "I read through the police reports, but there wasn't much to go on," he said. "I'm thinking our best bet is going to be to take a look around your boss' apartment."

Her brow furrowed at that. "But if he had left anything incriminating around, wouldn't the police have found it when they searched his place."

Madoc shrugged. "Not necessarily," he said. "When the cops were at his place, they were looking for evidence against you, not him, which means they could have missed something that would incriminate him."

Though Shayna said nothing, Madoc could see the flicker of hope in her eyes. While he knew finding evidence linking Evan Mercer to the embezzlement was probably going to be a long shot, especially since the man had been so careful about covering his tracks up to that point, Madoc didn't say that to Shayna. Instead, he told her that they could go check it out as soon as they were finished eating.

"You want me to go with you?" Shayna asked, looking at him in surprise.

Madoc nodded. "You'd be more likely to recognize something of a financial nature faster than I would," he said. "Besides, if I leave you here alone, you'll probably just invite the rest of my neighbors over."

Shayna made a face at him, but said nothing. In all honesty, she was thrilled that Madoc wanted her to go with him to check out Evan's apartment. It was difficult to believe that two days ago he had been determined to toss her back in jail, she thought. Now, he wanted her to help him prove her innocence.

Finishing up with dinner, Shayna went into the bedroom to get dressed while Madoc took their plates into the kitchen. Ten minutes later, they were on their way to Evan Mercer's apartment.

Shayna hadn't given much thought to how they would get into the man's apartment once they got there, and she was surprised when Madoc knelt down to pick the lock. Oh God, she thought, she really had turned the upstanding Marshal into a criminal. That made her frown. While she knew she would be too selfish to turn down his help now that he had agreed to give it, she would feel absolutely awful if Madoc got into trouble because of her.

She was still worrying about that when Madoc opened the door and ushered her inside the apartment. Closing the door behind them, he turned on the light.

Shayna whirled around to look at him. "Shouldn't we be doing this with flashlights?" she whispered.

Madoc looked at her in confusion. "Why would we use flashlights?"

She shrugged. "I don't know," she said. "They always do that in the movies."

His mouth quirked. "Yeah, well, a flashlight flickering around in a dark room looks way more suspicious than turning on the light," he told her. "Now, you said he has a home office, right?"

She nodded.

"Then let's start in there," he said.

Having been to her boss's apartment several times, Shayna knew exactly where Evan Mercer's home office was, so she led Madoc directly down the hall and into a small room off to the right. Unfortunately, her boss wasn't the most organized person on the planet, so searching through the stacks of books and papers on his desk took awhile. It didn't help that Shayna had no idea what she was even supposed to be looking

181

for. But when she asked Madoc, all he said was, "something incriminating."

"That's a big help," she muttered as she pulled open another one of the desk drawers.

Like the others, this drawer was stuffed with stacks of old paperwork, both personal and business related. Letting out a sigh, Shayna took out a handful of papers and began to skim through them. She was just nearing the bottom of the stack when she saw something that caught her attention.

"I think I may have found something!" she said excitedly.

Across the room, Madoc looked up from the folders he'd been rifling through. "What is it?"

"Account numbers for an offshore bank," she said.

Pushing the drawer of the file cabinet closed, Madoc came over to stand beside her chair. Resting one hand on the back of it, he leaned over to read the paper on the desk in front of her.

"Lawrence Mulrooney is the CEO of the company where I worked," she explained, pointing to the man's name at the top of the paper. "And these," she added, pointing to the column of seemingly-meaningless numbers, "are overseas bank accounts."

Madoc's brow furrowed. "And what does that mean?"

Shayna tilted her head to the side to look at him. "It means that Evan Mercer wasn't the one who framed me," she said. "Mulrooney wouldn't need to have all of these offshore accounts if he weren't trying to hide something. He must have been the one moving money out of the retirement funds and Evan must have found out about it. Isn't this what we were looking for? A list of overseas bank accounts is suspicious enough to get the cops to take a look at Mulrooney, right?"

Madoc shook his head. "Unfortunately, no. Not by itself," he said. "The DA wouldn't want to muddy up his case by looking at someone like Mulrooney. Not based on something like this. Especially when they already have the case wrapped up against you."

Shayna felt her heart sink. What good was having proof if they couldn't use it to get her out of this mess?

Beside her, Madoc was frowning thoughtfully. "Can you type up an official looking bank document showing money being transferred into these accounts from the retirement funds?" he asked after a moment.

She looked at him in confusion. "I suppose so," she said. "But they wouldn't stand up to any scrutiny. I don't have any of the dates or routing numbers for the transactions, so what good would it do?"

The Marshal shrugged. "I'm not trying to use it as evidence for the DA," he said. "But if I can convince this Mulrooney guy that I have more evidence than I do, I might be able to get him to incriminate himself."

Shayna' brow furrowed. "But why would he admit anything to a U.S. Marshal?"

Madoc flashed her a grin. "Because he's not going to know I'm a U.S. Marshal."

Some of Shayna's excitement at the prospect of finding out who had framed her waned once she had heard the rest of Madoc's plan, however. When he'd first outlined his plan on the way back to his apartment the night before, it had seemed so simple. Madoc would get Mulrooney to admit on tape that he had embezzled the money and framed her. But as she listened to Madoc set up a meeting with the CEO on the phone the next morning, she realized how much risk the Marshal was taking to help clear her name. Madoc couldn't tell any of his coworkers what he was doing, which meant that he was going to be completely on his own. That worried her. If they assumed Mulrooney had embezzled the money and framed her, then he had most likely murdered her boss as well. That meant he was dangerous and she wasn't quite sure she liked the idea of Madoc confronting him alone. While she was incredibly

183

grateful to him for helping her, she was also getting more and more worried about something happening to him because of it.

She had spent the whole morning trying to figure out how to tell him about her fears, but for some ridiculous reason, she couldn't seem to get the words out. And then after lunch, Madoc had announced he was going out to pick up some surveillance equipment for his meeting with Mulrooney that night.

While he was out, Shayna chided herself for not saying something to him. She would bring it up the moment he got back, she told herself. Of course, she didn't really expect him to pay much attention to her concerns. He had way too much testosterone to let his girlfriend's worries get in the way.

That thought made her stop in her tracks. Girlfriend? Had their relationship already gotten to the point where she thought of herself as his girlfriend? She couldn't help but wonder if Madoc thought of her the same way. Obviously, he was attracted to her, but would he want to pursue anything long-term with her after they had cleared her name? She hoped so, but she had no way of knowing for sure.

Shayna was still mulling that over when Madoc returned with a bag full of surveillance gear. Remembering her earlier promise to talk to him about her fears, she brought up the subject while he unloaded the bag.

"I don't know if this whole thing is such a good idea, Madoc," she said as she watched him pull a small cylinder-shaped item out of the bag and pin it inside his coat.

He glanced at her. "Sure it is. We need evidence and this is the best way to get it."

She hugged her arms around her middle and chewed on her lower lip. "I know and I really appreciate it, but shouldn't you have back-up with you for this kind of stuff?"

Madoc's mouth quirked as he shrugged into his coat and checked the position of the item he had pinned inside it. It must be some kind of microphone or something, she thought.

184

"Mulrooney is a petty, white-collar criminal," he told her. "I think I can handle him."

Shayna sighed inwardly. What was it with guys and their egos? she wondered. "You're forgetting that Mulrooney probably murdered Evan Mercer."

"Based on what we know, I'd say that Mulrooney went over to talk to Mercer and panicked when he found out Mercer was on to him," Madoc said. "It wasn't like he planned to murder Mercer, so I don't see him as the cold-blooded killer. Besides, I don't plan on confronting him by myself. Once I get the evidence I need, I'll call in the local PD and let them take care of him."

Madoc made it sound so simple, she thought. "Well, I'd still feel better if you had back-up with you," Shayna insisted, and then added, "In case things don't go as planned."

Madoc reached out to gently brush her hair back from her face. "I can't bring anyone else in on this, Shayna," he said. "Not without them finding out about you. Besides, everything will go just fine."

She chewed on her lower lip again. "Maybe it would be a good idea if I went with you."

"Absolutely not," he said firmly. "It's too dangerous."

She frowned up at him. "You just said that it wasn't dangerous."

His mouth tightened. "I didn't say that at all," he corrected. "What I said was that I could handle him. But if you come with me, I'll be worrying about you when I should be focusing on Mulrooney and that would definitely make things dangerous."

"But what if something goes wrong, and you need back-up?" she persisted.

Madoc sighed. "I'll be fine. If I need help, I have my cell. I'll call for backup."

"But..."

He gently cupped her cheek with his hand. "I'll be fine, Shayna. Really," he told her. "I'm trained for this kind of thing, remember?"

She swallowed hard. "You'll be careful, right?"

The corner of his mouth edged up. "Always," he said. Lowering his head, he kissed her gently. "I'll be back soon. And if everything goes as planned, we'll have all the evidence we need to clear you by morning."

As the door closed behind Madoc, everything suddenly became perfectly clear to her. There was no denying it anymore. This was more than just wanting to be Madoc's girlfriend. She was completely head-over-heels in love with the man. How else could she explain the fact that she suddenly couldn't care less about him proving her innocence? She'd gladly go on the run for the rest of her life if it meant he would be safe. She wouldn't be willing to do that for him if she weren't in love, she told herself.

And now that she finally recognized her feelings for what they were, she wasn't going to just sit back and do nothing while he risked his life for her. Regardless of how glib he was being about the whole thing, Madoc was putting himself into serious danger. And she wasn't going to let him do that on his own! Grabbing her coat, she headed for the door. Madoc needed her help, whether he wanted to admit it or not. And she wasn't going to let him down!

The park had already emptied out by this time of day, and in the gathering dusk, Madoc glanced at his watch. Damn, Mulrooney was late. Madoc hoped that didn't mean the other man had decided not to show. This was their only chance to get the evidence necessary to clear Shayna's name. If the CEO didn't bite, then they were screwed.

And if their plan didn't work? How far was he prepared to go for Shayna? Madoc wondered. He had already decided on the way back from Denver that turning Shayna in was out of the question. Was it really that much more of a stretch to assume he would help her flee the country if they couldn't clear her name? But how could he just let her go off without him? After everything he had done for her – deciding not to turn her in, hiding her in his own apartment, and now conducting an undercover sting operation all by himself – it was obvious he had completely lost his mind over this woman. So, why not just run off to Mexico with her?

Madoc couldn't even believe he was even thinking of doing that, but he was. Now he could see how his brother, Cade, had fallen in love so quickly. When you met the right woman, it was like a big, ol' truck had just run you over all at once, he thought. There was nothing he could do now, but go along for the ride. His mouth edged up. After the way he'd berated his brother for getting married, Cade was really going to enjoy rubbing this in.

The headlights of an approaching car interrupted his musings and Madoc sat up straighter as the vehicle slowed to a stop. Finally, he thought. Reaching inside his coat, Madoc checked the positioning of the wireless mic again before doing the same to the receiver. Designed to look like a wallet, the receiver was shoved in his back pocket, so it was doubtful Mulrooney would even notice it. Opening the door, Madoc stepped out of the SUV. *Showtime*, he told himself.

A tall man in a suit and tie got out of the car and slowly walked toward him. Even if he hadn't already seen a picture of Lawrence Mulrooney on the company website, Madoc would have known he was the guy he'd been waiting for. He might look like a businessman with the glasses and the graying hair, but he moved like a criminal.

Mulrooney stopped several feet from where Madoc stood. "You Cutler?" he asked.

Madoc inclined his head. "Is that the money?" he asked, gesturing to the briefcase in the man's hand.

Mulrooney nodded. "How do I know this isn't some kind of trap? You could be wearing a wire or something."

Madoc shrugged, trying to appear nonchalant. "Go ahead and frisk me if you want. I don't have anything to hide."

Putting on a bored expression, Madoc held his arms out to the side while Mulrooney patted him down. He had anticipated the man searching him, which was why he had chosen to wear a small back-up pistol strapped to his ankle. He doubted Mulrooney was experienced enough to look for it. And since the wireless mic was just as well hidden, he wasn't too concerned about the other man finding that, either. Even so, he was relieved when Mulrooney finally finished his search and stepped back.

"So, let's see this evidence you have," the CEO said.

Madoc jerked his chin toward the briefcase. If he didn't do this right, Mulrooney was sure to suspect something. "Let me see the color of your money first."

Mulrooney's mouth tightened, but he opened the case and held it up to show the money. Only when Madoc nodded did he snap the briefcase shut again.

Madoc reached into the inside pocket of his coat and took out the envelope with the fake bank paperwork. He pulled the papers out and held them up in front of Mulrooney. When the man reached for them, Madoc pulled them out of his reach.

"Uh-uh," he said. "You can look, but you can't touch. Not until I get the money."

Mulrooney swore under his breath. "You don't expect me to pay for something that I haven't seen?"

Madoc's mouth quirked. "You see with your eyes, not with your hands," he said. "Feel free to take a look, but I'll hold onto it."

Swearing under his breath again, the other man leaned closer to get a better look. "Turn it to the light," he grumbled impatiently. "I can't see it."

After Madoc had adjusted his position so that the light from the streetlamp shone on the paper, the CEO leaned forward again to study it intently.

188

"Damn," Mulrooney muttered. "These are bank transaction codes to my private accounts." He slanted Madoc an accusing look. "Where the hell did you get these?"

"The DA had me go through Mercer's files from his home, just to make sure we had everything against the Matthews woman," Madoc replied. "I came across these and realized they might be of some value to you. I figured you'd be willing to pay a lot of money to keep them out of the wrong hands. I'm always looking to pad my retirement account."

Mulrooney gave him a contemptuous look. "Greedy bastard," he sneered. "It's people like you that give cops a bad name."

"If I'm greedy, then what does that make you?" Madoc shot back. "You're the one stealing from your own company's retirement funds."

"So what if I am?" Mulrooney said as he held out the briefcase. "Like you, I'm always looking to pad my retirement account."

Madoc shook his head. "Looks like you had a sweet deal going, too," he said as he handed Mulrooney the papers in exchange for the briefcase. "So, what went wrong?"

The other man leafed furiously through the pieces of paper, reading them over again. "That idiot, Mercer, started putting his nose in where it didn't belong. Everything was fine until he called and told me that he knew what I was up to. That's when everything started going to crap."

I got you now, you bastard, Madoc thought. He already had enough on Mulrooney to provide reasonable doubt to Shayna's attorney. Now it was time to go in for the kill and get the CEO to admit that he had framed her for everything.

Dammit! Shayna couldn't hear a thing from her hiding place behind one of the trees on the edge of the clearing. She thought about moving closer, but didn't want to be seen. Madoc would be furious if he knew she had come to the park. Besides, she was only there in case something went wrong.

And she could see well enough for that. Not that she had any clue what she would do if Mulrooney tried anything. Heck, she didn't even have a cell phone! She was starting to think Madoc had been right. It was foolish for her to be there.

In the clearing, Madoc had just handed the papers to Mulrooney in exchange for a briefcase. She started to let out a sigh of relief, but then immediately tensed again as the two men continued to talk. What the heck could they have to chat about for so long? she wondered. It wasn't like they were old friends or anything. Madoc was just supposed to get the information he needed, and then leave. This was taking way too long, she thought. Maybe something had gone wrong.

As she watched, Mulrooney reached behind him to adjust his trousers. The move pushed aside his suit jacket and in the half-light, Shayna could see a dark glint right above his belt. Oh God, she thought. He had a gun!

Without thought to her own safety, Shayna burst out from behind the tree. "Madoc, he's got a gun!" she screamed. "Watch out!"

Madoc stared in disbelief. *Shayna?* What the hell was that dang woman doing there?

Mulrooney jerked his head around at the shout. "What the hell's going on?" he demanded, swinging back around to face Madoc. "This was a trap!"

Reaching behind him, Mulrooney pulled out the gun Shayna had mentioned and began to level it at Madoc.

Madoc swore under his breath. Not having time to go for the gun he had strapped to his ankle, he took a quick step forward and grabbed Mulrooney's arm before the man could get the gun pointed in his direction. Balling his free hand into a fist, Madoc threw a series of punches at the other man's face. Of course, Mulrooney was doing his best to block them, and Madoc was so focused on the pistol in the man's hand that he couldn't get in a well-aimed blow. But at least it kept Mulrooney from taking a shot at him.

190

He and Mulrooney were still locked like that when Shayna ran up to them. To Madoc's consternation, she took up a position behind the CEO and began to pound the man on the back with her fists. The blows weren't very effective, but they distracted Mulrooney enough so that Madoc could finally get in a solid punch to the man's jaw.

Mulrooney went down like a sack of potatoes, releasing his hold on the pistol. Ripping it out of the man's hand, Madoc automatically reached for his cell phone so that he could call the police, but stopped when he realized Shayna was standing there shaking and looking altogether terrified. Madoc glanced down at Mulrooney. The guy was out cold and wouldn't be a threat. Calling the police could wait, he decided. Reaching out, he pulled Shayna into his arms.

"Shhh," he said softly. "It's okay, sweetheart. We got him."

Shayna held him tightly. "He had a gun, Madoc. I had to warn you," she said, her voice muffled against his coat.

"I know," Madoc said. "It's okay now."

She lifted her head to look up at him. "Did we get what we needed?" she asked.

Madoc nodded. "Yeah, we did," he said. "Mulrooney confessed to everything."

Still holding onto her with one arm, Madoc pulled out his cell phone and called the police. When he was done, he put the phone away and gave Shayna a tender kiss on the lips.

"Shayna, we're going to have to talk about what you were doing here, but right now, you need to go back to my apartment," he said when he lifted his head. "The cops will be here any minute and they can't find you here. Can you get home okay?"

She nodded. "I'm okay," she said, and then gave him a tremulous smile. "Now that I know you're safe."

Reaching on tiptoe, she kissed him again, and then turned to leave.

But his voice stopped her. "Wait a minute," he said. "How did you get here?"

She gave him a sheepish look. "I borrowed Mrs. Murray's car," she said. "I told her it was important."

Madoc shook his head. "We really do have to talk," he muttered. "I'll be home in a couple of hours. Now go before the cops get here. And drive safe."

He shook his head again as he watched her go. Shayna was completely unbelievable. The woman had no fear. She had seen the gun and come running over to whack on the guy anyway. On one hand, he couldn't help but admire her spunk. But on the other, he couldn't help but be furious that she had once again refused to listen to him. If anything had happened to her...

When he got home, he was definitely going to have that talk with her, Madoc promised himself. Actually, there wasn't going to be a whole lot of talking going on, unless he counted the communicating his hand was going to be doing with her bottom!

It was well after midnight when Madoc finally got home. Though the Denver police had taken Mulrooney off his hands quickly enough, Madoc had spent the better part of the night talking with the district attorney about the case. The DA had found it difficult to believe Madoc had just stumbled onto the information that blew the case wide open. That had led to Madoc's boss being called in. But Madoc had played it cool and stuck to a simple story about being given some information from an anonymous source. Madoc claimed he hadn't wanted to bother anyone with it until he had checked it out himself since it seemed like such a long shot. Though his boss had looked skeptical, too, there wasn't much either man could say, not when Madoc had Mulrooney confessing everything on tape.

Letting himself into his apartment, he closed the door, and looked around for Shayna. Though the lights were on, both the living room and kitchen were empty, but the coat thrown carelessly over the arm of the couch told him that she was there. Thinking she had probably gone to bed, he shut off the lights and headed for his bedroom.

The sight of Shayna asleep in his bed made him catch his breath. She was curled up into a ball, the blanket tucked under her chin. She looked so cute and innocent laying there that he could have stood there all night just watching her. But then he reminded himself that they did have to have a talk.

Sitting down on the edge bed, Madoc reached out and gently brushed Shayna's hair back from her face. She immediately stirred at his touch, her eyes fluttering open. She blinked at him sleepily for a moment, but then as if suddenly remembering the night's events, she came more fully awake. Pushing her hair back from her face, she pushed herself up into a sitting position. The blanket slipped down, and he saw that she was once again wearing his white dress shirt.

"Did you just come in?" she asked, her voice husky with sleep.

He nodded. "A couple of minutes ago."

"Did everything go okay?" she said.

Again, he nodded. "The DA has the tape of Mulrooney confessing to everything. He'll be formally dropping all the charges against you in the morning," he told her. "You're a free woman."

For a moment, Shayna just stared at him, but then she smiled brightly. With a laugh, she threw her arms around his neck and hugged him tightly. "Oh God, Madoc! I don't know how to thank you!"

Chuckling, Madoc wrapped his arms around her. "I'm sure I'll think of something," he said, and then pulled away to look at her. "But first, we need to talk about what you did tonight."

Shayna blinked up at him. "What I did?" she asked innocently.

He frowned. "I told you to stay here and wait for me, but instead, you decided to follow me to the park."

"Oh, that," she said softly, only to lift her chin a moment later. "It was a good thing I did, otherwise you wouldn't have known Mulrooney had a gun."

Madoc's jaw tightened. "Shayna, he would never have pulled his gun if you hadn't jumped out from behind a tree shouting like that."

"You don't know that," she said. "He could have planned on shooting you all along."

"I doubt it," Madoc said. "Besides, I had everything I needed at that point and was about to take the money and leave. You could have gotten both of us killed tonight."

She flushed. "I'm sorry. I saw the gun and I got worried. I just didn't want you to get hurt," she said, and then added, "I was only trying to help. I won't do anything like that again."

Madoc's mouth quirked at that. "Somehow, I doubt that, sweetheart," he said. "I think it's in your nature to act before you think."

Shayna gasped. "That's not true!" she protested.

"Yes, it is," he said. "But it doesn't mean I have to put up with it. After the spanking I have in mind for you, I think you'll be a lot less likely to do anything so foolish for quite a while."

Her eyes went wide at the mention of a spanking. "You're not serious!"

But Shayna could see from the expression on his face that Madoc was definitely serious. She would have put up more of a fuss, but she was still sort of fuzzy from sleep and before she could even attempt to put up a serious protest, she found herself being pulled over his knee. Even though past experience told her that struggling against him wouldn't do any good, she found herself fighting to push herself off his lap anyway. But his firm hand on her lower back held her easily in place as he pushed up the dress shirt she had worn to bed.

194

"Ah, no panties," he observed. "Good. That'll make it easier."

Shayna groaned. She really loved Madoc, but these spankings of his were a real pain in the butt. Literally.

"*Owwwww!*" she yelped as the first smack came down on her bare bottom. "Do you have to start out so hard?"

"If I don't spank you hard, you won't think I'm serious," Madoc said, giving her another sharp smack on the ass. "And I wouldn't want you to think that."

Oh, yeah, he was serious, all right, Shayna thought as he began to methodically apply his strong hand to first one cheek, and then the other. Without the benefit of panties, the spanks had her ass blazing right from the very start, and even though she told herself it would do no good, she still struggled all the same, wiggling and squirming around on his lap.

All that did was cause Madoc to wrap his arm tightly around her waist and spank her even harder.

"What you did tonight was beyond foolish, Shayna," Madoc said, punctuating each word with a stinging slap. "When you ran into the clearing, Mulrooney could easily have tried to shoot you instead of me."

"But he...*owwwww!*...didn't!" she pointed out.

"And then, as if that weren't enough," he continued, "you decide to join the fight."

"I had to!" she told him in between yelps. "You needed help!"

"I needed you to be safe!" Madoc told her.

"But..."

"Oh, and let's not forget about borrowing Mrs. Murray's car," he added, giving her a hard spank to each of her sit-spots.

"*Owwwww!*" she cried. "Okay, okay, I get it! You've made your point! I promise to not do anything that foolish ever again!"

At her words, Madoc paused for a moment to rest his hand on her tender bottom, and she let out a sigh of relief. "Once again, I really doubt that," he said.

She craned her neck to look at him over her shoulder. "But I promise I really will try to be better," she said softly, and then added, "Besides, it's not like I'm going to get involved with a murderer again any time soon, right?"

From the scowl Madoc gave her, Shayna immediately realized she had said the wrong thing, but before she could explain, he had lifted his hand and was bringing it down on her ass again. The smacks seemed even harder than they had before and all she could do was press her face into the covers and kick her legs. To her relief, however, he didn't give her much more than another dozen or so before he flipped her over and cuddled her on his lap.

"You really scared me out there tonight, Shayna," he told her, his voice rough with emotion. "I know you were only trying to help, but you could have gotten yourself killed. I don't ever want you doing anything like that again." He drew in a ragged breath. "I couldn't stand it if anything happened to you."

Shayna felt herself melt at his words. If she had any doubt as to what his feelings were for her, they disappeared in that moment. Ignoring the way the rough material of his jeans rubbed against her freshly-spanked bottom, she leaned forward and kissed him hard on the mouth. He returned her kiss just as passionately, his mouth moving over hers with an eagerness that left her breathless.

When Madoc lifted his head several long minutes later, it was to set her gently on the bed so that he could take off his clothes. Once he was naked, he stood beside the bed and gazed down at her. "I love you, Shayna Matthews," he told her hoarsely.

Even though she knew how he felt about her, hearing him say the words out loud made her heart leap for joy. Tears of happiness welling in her eyes, she smiled up at him. "I love you, too," she said, and then added, "Now, get that gorgeous body of yours into this bed and make love to me."

Madoc promptly obeyed, his mouth finding hers in a kiss as he settled himself between her legs.

Afterward, as they lay together in the huge bed, a thought occurred to Shayna and she smiled. "You know," she said softly as she idly trailed her fingers up and down his muscular chest. "If you hadn't come into that diner in Flint Rock, I'd still be living my life on the run and we never would have found each other."

Madoc chuckled, the sound a deep rumble beneath her ear. "If I hadn't gone in there," he told her. "I would never have met the woman I want to spend the rest of my life with."

Her pulse fluttering, Shayna pushed herself up on her elbow to look down at him. "Are you saying what I think you're saying?"

Madoc grinned. "Yup," he drawled, and then added, "You know, since that diner holds such special meaning for both of us, maybe we should have our reception there."

Laughing, Shayna snuggled up beside him. Now, that was a romantic thought, especially since that diner would always be special to them. Even so, she couldn't really see them having their wedding reception there. Thank God, Madoc wasn't serious, she thought. Then she frowned. He had been joking, hadn't he?

THE CUTLER BROTHERS SERIES

BOOK 3

THE CUTLER BRIDES

CHAPTER ONE

Riley Cutler usually hated flying and everything that went with it, including the tiny seats with no leg room, the crappy food, and the stale, dry air. But cuddling closer to her handsome husband, Cade, she found that she didn't mind those things nearly as much. Maybe the airlines should provide everyone with a sexy seatmate, she thought with a little smile. It certainly made the flight go faster.

Officially, they were going down to Texas for Cade's parents' fortieth wedding anniversary, but that was really just an excuse to get everyone together again. When she and Cade had gotten married, Riley hadn't seen his parents for more than a few days, hardly enough time to get to know them. Of course, she'd seen them again several months ago at Madoc and Shayna's wedding, but again, it had been just for a long weekend. She was really looking forward to spending some relaxing time with not only Cade's parents, but also with Madoc and his new bride as well. Riley had the feeling she and Shayna were going to hit it off great.

Thinking about Madoc and Shayna's wedding made Riley think about her own. It was hard to believe she and Cade had been married almost a year already. It seemed like just yesterday that the U.S. Marshal had shown up on her doorstep. They had met while she'd been in the Witness Protection Program and though their relationship had started out rather rocky, it hadn't taken her long at all to fall completely in love with him. She couldn't believe how lucky she was. Not only had she met and married a wonderful guy, but she had also been able to drop out of the Witness Protection Program because the organized crime boss she'd been hiding from had turned state's evidence and gone into the program himself. The Marshals had no longer believed she was in danger and she'd been able to return to her old life. Of course, her old life was even better now that Cade was in it.

Flipping through the fashion magazine she'd brought with her, Riley stopped when she came to an advertisement for a pair of sexy, high-heeled sandals. "Aren't these cute?" she said, holding the magazine at an angle so that Cade could see, too. "Wouldn't they look great on me?"

Her husband looked up from his outdoor magazine to glance at hers. Upon seeing the shoes however, he lifted a brow. "I'm sure they would, but I don't think you need any more shoes, do you, honey?"

Riley looked up at him from beneath lowered lashes. Though even she had to admit she had more pairs than the average woman, shoes were definitely her weakness and she couldn't resist buying the newest style in footwear when it came out. "Well, actually, I do," she said. "It completely slipped my mind until now, but we were in such a rush to leave that I think I forgot to pack the shoes I was going to wear to your parents' anniversary party."

Cade gave her a dubious look. "Did you really forget or did you deliberately decide not bring them just so you could buy new ones?"

A blush crept into her cheeks. She had made a conscious decision not to pack them, of course, but only because they really didn't go with her dress.

"Of course I forgot!"

Riley tried to sound as truthful as she could, but Cade saw right through her lie. She used to be a really good liar back when she was in the Witness Protection Program, but for some reason, she couldn't ever seem to lie convincingly to her husband.

"That's what I thought." Cade let out a loud, dramatic sigh. "Well, you know what this means, don't you?"

"What?" she asked innocently.

His mouth quirked. "It means you'll be going over my knee for a good, sound spanking when we get to the ranch, sweetheart."

Her pulse still skipped a beat at hearing her husband say the words. It was amazing how much her attitude toward spanking had changed over the past year, she thought. When Cade had put her over his knee to give her a spanking that first time at her apartment, she had put up a terrible fuss, kicking and squealing for all she was worth. Actually, she had made a fuss the first half dozen times he had spanked her. After they'd gotten engaged, however, something had happened to change all that and she'd started looking forward to getting spanked. But knowing she could never come right out and tell her fiancé that, she'd started to do little things to get him to spank her. Perceptive as he was, Cade had quickly figured it out. So now whenever she wanted a spanking, all she had to do was just act a little naughty. Almost anything would do, like buying yet another pair of shoes. It wasn't that Cade really cared whether she bought a new pair; it was just simply a signal to him that she wanted to get spanked.

"Don't you think your parents might notice if you dragged me off to the bedroom the minute we got to their ranch?" she pointed out.

Cade frowned slightly as he considered that. "You're probably right," he agreed after a moment. "I guess I'd better spank you now then."

She gasped. "Now? Are you crazy? On the plane?"

But her husband had already taken her hand and was pulling her to her feet.

"Honey..." she began, but the words trailed off as he led her toward the back of the plane.

Since it was an evening flight, the interior of the cabin was dimly lit, something a blushing Riley was grateful for as they made their way to the restroom. She needn't have worried, though, because none of the other passengers were paying any attention to them.

While Riley couldn't deny that the thought of her gorgeous, dark-haired husband spanking her thirty-thousand feet in the air was rather thrilling, it also made her a little nervous, and she stopped outside the door to the restroom to voice her concerns to Cade.

"Honey, we can't," she protested. "Someone could hear."

His mouth quirked. "Then we'll have to make sure we're quiet."

As Cade opened the door and urged her inside, Riley could only wonder what had gotten into her husband. He was always up for adventure, especially when it came to sex, but they'd never done anything this daring. Not that she was complaining really. The whole thing was a major turn-on!

The small bathroom seemed even tinier with her tall, broad-shouldered husband in it with her, but Riley found herself forgetting all about her dislike of tight spaces when Cade ordered her to turn around and put her hands on the wall in that soft, sexy voice of his. Eager for her spanking, Riley obediently placed her palms on the wall, bending over just enough to thrust out her bottom.

Instead of placing his hand on her back like he usually did when she was draped over his knee, though, Cade wrapped his arm around her middle. Holding her close against him, he ran his other hand over her short skirt.

"If we were home, I'd give you a warm-up over your skirt," he said in her ear. "But in the interest of time, I think it'd be best if I just get straight to the main event."

As he spoke, her husband lifted her skirt to reveal a skimpy pair of bikini panties. Her pulse fluttering, Riley slanted him a look in the mirror on the adjacent wall, watching in fascination as Cade slipped his fingers beneath the waistband of her panties and slowly pushed them down to the middle of her thighs. There was something very delicious about watching him do that in the mirror, she decided.

Riley held her breath as she waited for the spanking to begin and was surprised when Cade reached out to gently caress her bottom. Though it was something he always did before giving her a spanking, she didn't think he would take the time since they were only having a quickie.

Cade must have remembered where they were because all of a sudden, he lifted his hand and brought it down on her right cheek with a resounding *smack!*

Riley gasped at the sting his hand had left, but then quickly bit her lip to stifle a tiny yelp as he smacked her on the other cheek. Though she was pretty sure the spanks couldn't be heard over the loud noise of the plane's engines, she didn't know about her cries of protest, so she kept her lip firmly held between her teeth just in case.

Transfixed, she stared at their reflection in the mirror, watching as her husband lifted his hand again. This time, however, he brought it down on her ass in a flurry of rapid-fire spanks that had her dancing from foot to foot within seconds. He moved from one cheek to the other with a rhythmic precision that had her bottom coloring in no time, and she watched with fascination as her creamy skin turned a rosy pink color. Wow, she really loved this mirror. Maybe they should put one up right beside the bed at home! Her pussy tingled at the thought, and she had to resist the urge to slide her hand down to touch herself.

As if reading her mind, Cade stopped spanking her to slide his hand between her legs. Riley moaned as his finger found her wet pussy and dipped inside. Just as quickly, though, Cade withdrew his finger. Dismayed, Riley opened her mouth to protest, only to close it again when she saw her husband undoing his belt.

Riley watched hungrily as Cade pushed down his jeans to free his cock. Hard and throbbing, it stood at attention, and when he rubbed the head along her pink asscheeks, she impatiently reached back to wrap her hand around him and help guide him inside her pussy. To her relief, Cade didn't need any more urging. Grasping her hips in his hands, he slid his cock deep into her pussy in one smooth motion.

Unable to stifle her moan of pleasure, Riley closed her eyes and allowed it to escape her lips. But then Cade's grip tightened on her hips, and as he started to move in and out of her, she was forced to bite her lip again to keep from crying out. She could tell by the way Cade was thrusting that he was just as excited as she was. Oh yeah, this was definitely going to be a quickie! Wanting to make sure she was able to come as quickly as possible, Riley slid her hand between her legs and began to finger her plump clit with quick, little motions.

Suddenly remembering they were in front of a mirror, Riley turned her head to gaze at their reflection. The sight that met her eyes was so unbelievably sexy that all she could do was watch in fascination as Cade took her from behind. Oh yeah, she was definitely getting a mirror put up in the bedroom!

Cade grasped her hips more firmly, thrusting into her harder and faster, and Riley had to bite her lips to stifle her cries of pleasure as her orgasm coursed through her. Just then, Cade held himself completely still inside of her, and she heard his own muffled groan in her ear as he found his own release. God, she loved it when they came together like that!

Smoothing her skirt over her hips afterward, Riley looped her arms around Cade's neck and gave him a lingering kiss on the mouth. "Now, why didn't we do that when we flew to Hawaii for our honeymoon? It would've made the flight a whole heck of a lot faster, not to mention more fun."

Cade chuckled. "It definitely would have," he agreed. "But as I tend to remember, you were on your best behavior, so I didn't have a reason to spank you."

Riley considered that as she and Cade settled back in their seats several minutes later. Well, she supposed if she wanted any spankings while they were down in Texas, she was just going to have to see about getting herself into trouble as frequently as possible!

206

Shayna was glad she and Madoc had decided to drive down to Texas instead of fly. While flying would have been faster than the two day drive from Denver to Dallas, she was sure it wouldn't have been as much fun. This way, she and Madoc had been able to take their time and enjoy each other's company. They had stopped along the way at any and every tourist attraction that caught their eye, something which was quite different than their last road trip five months ago, she thought with a smile. Back then she had been a fugitive and the handsome U.S. Marshal had arrested her and been dragging her off to jail. Or he would have if they hadn't gotten caught in a snowstorm and had had to hole up in a deserted cabin. There, she had not only finally gotten him to listen to her story about being framed for a crime she didn't commit, but had also fallen in love with him.

After they had cleared her name, she and Madoc had been inseparable, getting married five months later. While their wedding had been perfect, everything had been so hectic that she hadn't had much of a chance to spend time with Madoc's family. But she was going to make up for that now because she and Madoc would be spending two weeks at his parents' ranch outside of Fort Worth. She really looked forward to getting to know them better, especially his brother, Cade, and his wife, Riley. She just intuitively knew she and the other girl were going to hit it off great.

"There's a rest area coming up. Want to stop and take a break?" Madoc asked.

Shayna pulled herself away from her thoughts to glance at her husband. "Sure."

After using the facilities, she and Madoc still didn't feel like getting back in the SUV right away, so they walked up to the small picnic area situated on a grassy hill just behind the main buildings. When they got to the top, Shayna was surprised by how far she could see. Even though the hill wasn't very high, it still towered above most of the nearby

Texas countryside, and the view was beautiful. Slow, rolling hills, covered in waving grass, spread out as far as the eye could see. Here and there, a cow or an oil well dotted the landscape, but mostly it was uninterrupted and pristine. She wished they had thought to grab a bite to eat and bring it up here. It would have been nice to sit and have lunch at one of the small tables while they enjoyed the view.

She turned to give Madoc a smile. He was sitting down on the bench-style seat, his arms lazily outstretched to either side of him on the picnic table. "It's beautiful, isn't it, hon?"

His golden brown eyes traveled up and down the length of her body to take in the tank top and shorts she wore, lingering on her bare legs.

"Not as beautiful as you," he said, his mouth curving into a sexy grin.

Shayna felt herself blush at her husband's compliment. She'd never blushed so much until she'd met Madoc. He just had a way of looking at her that made her think he was always visualizing her completely naked.

Reaching for her hand, he gently pulled her closer until she was standing between his legs. As his arms circled her waist, Shayna automatically looped hers around his neck. With a little laugh, she bent her head to kiss him on the mouth. The kiss wasn't some quick peck on the lips, but instead, it was slow and passionate, leaving Shayna breathless. When she lifted her head, she couldn't suppress the sigh of pleasure that escaped her lips.

"Too bad we're not someplace a little more private," she said huskily.

Madoc made a show of looking around the deserted rest area before lifting his gaze to hers again. "I don't know. It seems pretty private to me."

Her eyes widened. "You can't be serious?"

"Why not?" He slid his hands up to cup her breasts through the thin tank top.

208

Shayna caught her breath as she felt her nipples immediately harden in response. It had always been a secret fantasy of hers to make love outdoors, but she didn't think she could ever be bold enough to act it out.

"Madoc..." she began.

But her husband was already unbuttoning her khaki shorts and pushing them down her legs. As he gently ran his hands up her bare legs, Shayna felt the last of her resolve disappear, along with her shyness. Surely, they could have a quickie without getting caught, she told herself.

Shayna waited breathlessly for Madoc to take down her panties, but instead he surprised her by taking her hand and guiding her over one of his muscular legs. Though she went willingly, she couldn't help but give him a confused look over her shoulder.

"I thought we were going to booty," she said.

The corner of his mouth edged up. "We are," he said, lightly resting his hand on the curve of her bottom. "But since I don't know how much spanking we'll be able to do while were at my parents' ranch, I thought I'd give you one now to tide you over until we get home."

Shayna hadn't thought about that. But she supposed Madoc was right. They wouldn't have much privacy at the ranch. Which would mean she would have to wait two weeks for another spanking.

She gave her dark-haired husband a naughty smile. "Well, when you put it that way, I definitely think you're right. I do think you should give me a spanking."

Shayna couldn't help but smile at Madoc's deep, sexy chuckle. It wasn't so long ago that she hated to get spanked. Or at least she had the first half dozen times or so that her husband had put her over his knee. But then one evening after they'd gotten engaged, he had playfully smacked her bottom a couple of times while they'd been having sex in the doggy-style position, and it had been a huge turn-on, much to her surprise. As they'd been cuddling together afterward, she had shyly admitted to him that she'd liked the spanking, and then asked if they could do it again sometime. Well, sometime turned out to be the very next night when Madoc treated her to her very first erotic spanking. It came complete with lots of rubbing and caressing in between some very pleasurable spanks, which weren't too hard or too soft, but just perfect. Shayna couldn't remember ever being so turned on!

She let out a little sigh of pleasure as Madoc slowly caressed each panty-covered cheek with his strong hand for one long delicious moment before he slipped his fingers inside the waistband and pulled them down to the middle of her thighs. When he rubbed his hand over her bare bottom, she sighed again, only to let out a startled, little, *"Oh!"* as he lifted his hand and gave her a sharp smack on each cheek. The sound echoed around them, making it seem louder than it probably really was, but before Shayna could mention it, her husband brought his hand down again, this time a little harder.

"Owwww!" she yelped. "Honey, that stings! Don't I get a warm-up?"

Madoc chuckled again. "Since anyone could pull into the rest area at any time, I think we're going to have to skip the warm-up. Besides, how else will it tide you over until we get home if it doesn't sting at least a little, babe?"

He didn't wait for an answer, but lifted his hand and gave her ass a series of firm, deliberate smacks that had Shayna wiggling and squirming around on his lap almost from the start. But her protests were all part of the game, and she knew Madoc knew it. She loved each and ever spank he meted out, even if her bottom was usually a rosy shade of pink and stinging like crazy by the time he was done.

But while she loved the feel of Madoc's hand coming down over and over on her bottom, she loved it even more when he stopped in between to caress her freshly-spanked asscheeks, just like he was doing right now. Shayna let out a moan and spread her legs as far as the panties banded around her thighs would allow. It was her little way of telling Madoc

210

that she wanted him to touch her pussy. Lucky for her, he was very good at knowing what she wanted in bed – or wherever else they happened to make love – and this time was no different. Slipping his hand between her legs, he gently ran his finger along the slick outer folds before sliding deep into her pussy.

"You're very wet," he said. "Do you know that?"

Shayna moaned softly, unable to do more than that as her husband slowly moved his finger in and out of her pussy.

Then, all at once, Madoc slid his finger out. Dismayed, Shayna opened her mouth to complain, but her husband gently took her arm and stood her on her feet before she could get the words out. Any desire to protest disappeared when she saw him start to unbuckle his belt. While she wouldn't have minded some more foreplay, she was definitely ready to have him inside of her. She was as aroused as she could possibly get.

Her pulse fluttering in anticipation, Shayna quickly pushed her panties down the rest of the way, and then stepping out of her sandals, climbed astride her husband where he sat on the bench, and slowly lowered herself onto Madoc's hard cock.

He slid into her in one, smooth motion, and Shayna couldn't stifle the moan of pleasure that escaped her lips even if she'd wanted to. But as unbelievably good as his cock felt nestled deep within her, she knew it would be even better when she started to ride him. With that in mind, she lowered her head to kiss him as she slowly and methodically began to rotate her hips.

Madoc slid his hands down her back and over her hips to cup her freshly-spanked ass. Shayna gasped as he squeezed her cheeks, and then sighed against his mouth with pleasure as he began lifting her up and down.

Shayna began moaning out loud, not caring if anyone heard her. She didn't think it could get any better, but then Madoc tipped his head forward and began nuzzling her neck.

She hadn't discovered it until after they'd gotten married, but her neck was one of her favorite erogenous zones.

She slid her hand into his hair, keeping him focused on her neck while she began to ride him like a wild woman. The bench was a little hard on her knees, but she couldn't care less as she felt the tip of his throbbing cock reaching into the very depths of her pussy. Every time she came down on him, she swore she had a little mini-orgasm.

All at once, Madoc stopped nibbling on her neck and threw back his head to let loose his own groans of pleasure.

Obeying the urging of his hands on her hips, Shayna began to ride him even harder, completely exhilarated to be living out her wildest fantasy with the man she loved.

Shayna's orgasm coursed through her then and as she screamed out her pleasure, she felt Madoc's cum explode hot and pulsing inside of her. She continued to ride him until every last tremor of her climax had subsided. Only then did she look around, checking to make sure that no one had pulled into the rest area while she and Madoc had been distracted. Luckily, no one was around.

Sliding his hand into her long hair, Madoc pulled her down for a kiss. "You're completely amazing, do you know that?" he said against her mouth as he kissed her again.

All Shayna could do was laugh, giddy at what they had just done.

As she and Madoc walked hand-in-hand down to the parking lot afterward, Shayna found herself hoping the Cutler ranch was as big as her husband said, because there was no way she could go two weeks without another spanking. Surely there had to be someplace she and Madoc could slip off to so they could get in a spanking now and then.

CHAPTER TWO

About an hour outside of Fort Worth, the ranch was even bigger than Shayna had imagined, with acres and acres of land, a huge barn, and a beautiful two-story house. Since Riley and Cade had flown down from Seattle the night before, the couple had already settled in by the time Shayna and Madoc arrived that evening, and they immediately came out to greet them when she and Madoc pulled into the driveway. Madoc's parents, Arlene and John Cutler, were right behind their son and daughter-in-law, and as soon as Shayna got out of the SUV, she immediately found herself enveloped in a welcoming hug from each of her in-laws.

"It's so good to see you again, my dear," Arlene Cutler said, pulling away to gaze down at Shayna. Dressed in jeans and a western shirt, she was tall and slender with graying hair that she wore in a smart-looking bob. She also had the same intriguing golden brown eyes as her sons, Shayna noted. "How was the trip? You're not too sore from such a long drive, I hope."

Over by his brother, Madoc chuckled and Shayna felt herself blush, knowing exactly what he found so amusing. While she definitely wasn't sore from the drive, her bottom was still a little tender from that very thorough spanking her husband had given her at the rest area. She always felt the effects of a good, firm spanking more when Madoc didn't give her a warm-up first, she thought. Not that she was complaining, of course. It had been an incredibly sexy spanking and she would definitely remember it as one of her favorites for a long time to come. She had to stifle a giggle as a naughty, little thought suddenly popped into her head. Maybe she should tell them that it wasn't the drive that had her

213

sore, but the spanking Madoc had given her that still had her bottom tender four-hundred miles later! Then again, maybe not.

"Nope, not sore at all. The drive was great," she said, giving the older woman a smile. "Though it's good to finally be here. The ranch is absolutely beautiful. I can see why Madoc loves it so much."

"Just wait until the boys show you girls around," John Cutler said. "You're going to love it here as much as they do."

Though in his sixties, the retired U.S. Marshal stood as straight and tall as his sons, and with his angular jaw and handsome features, it was easy to see where Madoc and Cade got their rugged good looks.

"Why don't we go inside so you and Madoc can get settled into your room," Arlene suggested. "Dinner's just about ready to be put on the table, and we can all sit down and catch up."

Cade and John offered to help Madoc with the luggage while Shayna and the other two women started toward the house.

"Whoa," she heard Cade remark as Madoc opened up the back of their SUV. "Think you and Shayna could have brought any more luggage? You're only staying for two weeks, you know."

Madoc chuckled, but his reply was lost as he leaned into the SUV to begin unloading the bags. Whatever he'd said, it must have been funny though, Shayna thought, because both Cade and his father laughed.

"Men," Arlene scoffed as she led the way onto the big wrap around porch and into the house. "They think that just because they can get by on a change of underwear and a toothbrush, we women can too!"

Shayna and Riley both laughed. That was definitely true, Shayna thought. But while Madoc liked to complain about all her clothes, he certainly didn't seem to mind when she came to bed wearing all kinds of sexy lingerie and super

214

high-heels. Not that she kept any of it on for very long, she thought with a smile.

"I would have brought more myself," Riley said. "I think the real reason Cade wanted to fly instead of drive is because the airlines limit how much luggage you can take."

"I heard that!" Cade called, as he, Madoc, and their father started up the walk, suitcases in hand.

Inside, the big ranch house was just as beautiful and inviting as the outside, and Shayna immediately felt at home as she stepped into the huge entryway. Off to the left was a spacious living room, while on the other side was a formal dining room and eat-in kitchen. There was also a hallway straight ahead that looked like it led to a family room, and Shayna was just able to catch a glimpse of the pool through the French doors. The water looked so tempting that she almost wished she could take a dip before dinner.

The upstairs guest rooms were beautifully decorated in the same southwest style as the rest of the house, Shayna noted as she and Madoc dropped their bags off. The room was dominated by the big, four-poster bed and she could already imagine the fun she and Madoc were going to have in it. The bed was so high off the floor that she could probably bend over it and have her bottom be at the perfect height for a spanking, she thought. Too bad they didn't have time before dinner to try it out now!

As they made their way back downstairs a moment later, her husband gave the hand he was holding a tug, pulling her closer to his side.

"That spanking I gave you back at the rest area might not have to tide you over until we go home after all," he said softly. "My parents' room is way at the other end of the hallway from ours."

Shayna felt her pulse skip a beat at the mention of a spanking. Had he read her mind? "What about Riley and Cade? Aren't they right down the hall?"

Madoc shrugged. "Yeah, but I wouldn't worry too much about that. The walls are too thick for my brother and Riley would hear anything coming from our room."

That was probably true, Shayna thought. And anyway, she was sure she and Madoc could improvise if they had to. After all, the ranch was huge. They weren't limited to the bedroom. There had to be lots of different places where her husband could spank her that were more private. Just thinking about the possibilities had her tingling all over.

When they went back downstairs, Madoc's parents gave them a tour of the house before leading them outside to the patio. Riley and Cade were already seated at the big, round table near the pool and Shayna's eyes widened a little at the array of food on the table. There was easily enough to feed a small army. Her mother-in-law must have spent the better part of the day in the kitchen!

As they filled their plates a few minutes later, Madoc asked his father how things had been going on the ranch. Never having actually been on a ranch before, Shayna was amazed as her father-in-law described all the work that went into one. She had just naturally assumed the ranch was more of a hobby for the retired Marshal, but she discovered that it was a full-time working cattle ranch.

"Dad was telling me earlier that none of this season's calves have been branded yet," Cade said, looking at Madoc. "I told him we'd give him a hand."

Madoc helped himself to another baked potato. "Sounds good," he said, and then glanced at Shayna. "What do you think, babe? Want to help?"

Shayna eyed him over the rim of her water glass. "You're kidding, right? Why would I want to help hurt those poor baby cows?"

Her husband chuckled. "It doesn't really hurt them. Besides, I'm sure Riley's going to help, right?" he said, glancing at the other girl.

Shayna looked at Riley to see the other girl shaking her head, obviously as disgusted by the idea as she was. Beside his wife, Cade looked amused, as did his father.

"Okay, you two," Arlene said. "Stop teasing your poor wives." She looked at the two girls. "We don't brand cattle like that anymore. We put tags in their ears with something that looks a lot like the tool used to pierce your ears. Of course, the guys still like to call it branding because they think it sounds more manly than admitting that they're out piercing ears like an eighteen-year-old girl at the mall."

"It's still manly," Cade insisted. "It's tough to hold down a two-hundred pound calf while you poke a hole in his ear."

Riley was still shaking her head. "I don't care either way. I don't want to see it."

"Aw, come on," Cade cajoled. "It'll be fun."

"Yeah," Madoc added. "We'll even teach you how to rope the calves yourselves."

Arlene scowled at the men. "That's enough, you two. I'm sure Shayna and Riley would much rather go into town and do some sightseeing than stay here and brand a couple hundred cattle. Wouldn't you, girls?"

At the relieved look on both of their faces, Arlene smiled. "That's what I thought," she said, and then proceeded to tell them about all the things they could see in the area.

While some of the tourist attractions sounded like fun, Shayna had to admit she was more interested in doing some shopping. Across the table from her, Riley agreed, saying she heard there were some excellent shops in the historic Fort Worth Stockyards. Arlene agreed, telling them how the old stockyards had been converted into a shopping and entertainment district.

Mention of the stockyards got the men's attention and John suggested they should all go see a rodeo down there while they were in town. Shayna had never been to a rodeo before, but she agreed that it sounded like fun, as did Riley.

"I read that you can watch them herd longhorn cattle down the main street of the stockyards every day," the blond girl said. "Is that true?"

"Sure is," John said. "In the early days, Fort Worth used to be a stopover point for the cattle herds as the drovers moved them north towards Kansas and the railroads. Later, as Fort Worth continued to grow, the stockyards changed from being just a stopover to being the actual destination for people bringing livestock in from all over the west. Cattle and other livestock were bought and sold and transported right out of the stockyards. They do the cattle drive through the main street just to show people what Fort Worth looked like in the 1800's."

Shayna stirred cream and sugar in her coffee. "How interesting. I didn't realize Fort Worth was quite that historic."

"This area has quite a lot of history behind it," her father-in-law explained. "There're all kinds of small museums and historic landmarks that talk about everything from agricultural inventions to fights with the local Indian tribes. And of course, there's the legend of the Confederate gold."

Madoc and Cade both let out a groan at that.

"Dad, not that story again," the younger Cutler brother said. "Please."

"What story?" Riley said, eagerly leaning forward in her chair.

Madoc sipped his coffee. "Supposedly, there was a shipment of payroll gold headed north toward the end of the Civil War. Unfortunately for the men transporting the gold, the Confederates surrendered before delivery could be made. The men had no choice but to turn around and try to bring the gold back. However, no one knew what to do with it, so folklore says that in a desperate move to keep the Union forces from getting their hands on it, the men buried it somewhere near here. The theory was that the gold would be needed when the South rose up again, but that never happened and everyone apparently lost track of where the gold was buried."

"Of course, it's all a complete crock," Cade added. "People have been searching for that gold for a hundred years and no one's found even a clue."

"Just because no one's ever found it doesn't mean it isn't there, son," Arlene said.

Cade snorted. "Don't you think someone would have found it by now if it did exist? Hell, Madoc and I spent practically every summer looking for it when we were kids."

Shayna looked at her husband in surprise. "You did? That must have been fun."

Madoc's mouth quirked. "More like a waste of time."

"Do the stores in Riverville still sell those phony treasure maps claiming to be able to lead you to the gold like they did back when we were kids?" Cade asked, pouring more coffee for both Riley and himself before asking if anyone else wanted some more.

His father nodded. "Of course. You can find them everywhere. Even at the general store."

"We should get one," Riley said, her blue eyes bright with excitement.

Cade sipped his coffee. "You'll only be wasting your time."

Riley shrugged. "So what? It sounds like fun." She turned her attention to Shayna. "What do you think? Are you up for a little exploring?"

Shayna couldn't help but smile at the other girl's enthusiasm. Hunting for buried treasure actually did sound like fun, no matter what the guys thought. "I'm in," she said.

"It's settled then," Riley said. "We'll go into town tomorrow and get one of those maps."

Madoc leaned forward to rest his forearms on the table. "Just make sure you girls take some time to look at a real map first. There are a few areas to the north of here you need to stay away from," he warned. "They're not always marked on those silly treasure maps, but they're federal property that's been leased out to various corporations for the purpose of strip mining. Those companies can be more than a little territorial when it comes to their leased property and they definitely don't appreciate trespassers."

Both Shayna and Riley agreed that they would be careful and stay away from those areas. Even so, Shayna couldn't help but think that looking for the gold was actually going to be a lot of fun.

CHAPTER THREE

While Riley and Shayna didn't have any intention of helping tag the calves, neither of them minded sitting on the fence and watching their sexy husbands work up a sweat as they herded the animals into the corral the next morning. While Cade usually wore jeans and a button-up shirt on his days off, Riley had never seen him in a cowboy hat before, but just seeing him in the Stetson with his shirt off had her temperature rising in a way that had nothing to do with the Texas heat. Beside her, Riley noticed Shayna was eyeing Madoc with the same lusty look, and she couldn't help but smile. Who knew jeans and a cowboy hat could be so darn sexy? Then again, Riley thought, the brothers would probably look sexy in anything.

After getting the first group of calves into the corral, Cade and Madoc made their way over to where Riley and Shayna were perched on the fence.

"You sure you girls don't want to stay and help us with the tagging instead of going into Fort Worth today?" Cade asked, giving Riley a teasing grin.

Riley exchanged a look with her sister-in-law. "We're sure," she laughed.

"Okay, but you're going to miss out on all the fun," Madoc told them.

"Yeah, after we get done with the tagging, we thought we'd go out and do a few fence repairs, then come back and shoe some horses," Cade added.

Shayna laughed. "That sounds like so much fun, but I think we'll pass. Thanks anyway."

Cade and Madoc both chuckled at that, making Riley think the two men had been teasing them. Before she could call her husband on it, however, he closed his mouth over hers in a kiss.

"Have fun shopping," he told her when he finally lifted his head. "And be careful."

"We will," Riley promised even as Shayna told Madoc the same thing.

After another lingering kiss from their husbands, Riley and Shayna hopped down from the fence and walked back to the house to grab their purses. They had asked Arlene over breakfast if she wanted to join them, but the older woman had declined, saying she was going to be busy all day.

It took about an hour to drive to Fort Worth, but it seemed much less than that, Riley thought, mainly because she and Shayna spent the whole time talking. Though she and the other girl had grown up in different parts of the country, they were close enough in age to have a lot in common, and as Riley had suspected, they hit it off great.

Of course, most of their conversation centered on Cade and Madoc. It was amazing how alike the two men were, Riley thought. The brothers didn't realize it, but they were almost carbon copies of each other. Besides both of them being U.S. Marshals, they both also loved the outdoors, liked the same kind of movies, ate the same kind of foods, and had even fallen for the same type of independent, outgoing girl.

Since their husbands wanted to take them sightseeing, Riley and Shayna concentrated their focus on shopping, something they knew neither of the men would care to do anyway. Their main priority was finding shoes for Riley to wear to the anniversary party, so they made sure to stop at every shoe store in the popular shopping area of University Village. As it turned out, Riley quickly found a cute pair of strappy high-heeled sandals that would go perfectly with her dress. But she also found the most gorgeous pair of cowboy boots, and though they were a bit on the pricey side even on sale, once she tried them on, she couldn't resist buying them. It just didn't seem right to come to Texas and not buy a pair of cowboy boots, she told herself. Shayna apparently agreed because she bought a pair as well.

After a light lunch, the two women did some more shopping in Fort Worth before deciding to head back to the ranch. On the way, they stopped in Riverville, the small town near the ranch that John Cutler had mentioned to them the night before at dinner.

Finding parking on the main street was easy and Riley and Shayna took their time wandering around the small town. Though nowhere near as big as Fort Worth, Riverville had quite a few quaint, little shops that piqued both their interests.

Remembering the general store Cade had talked about, she and Shayna made it a point to stop there. Though designed to resemble the general stores of the old west, it sold modern goods, including the usual tourist stuff like magnets, shot glasses, and T-shirts. While Shayna looked for a magnet to add to her collection, Riley browsed through the other things for sale up at the counter. Her gaze immediately fell on the stack of treasure maps and she eagerly picked one up.

"Look what I found," she said, holding it up so that her sister-in-law could see. "Want to get it?"

Shayna glanced up from the magnets, her eyes lighting up when she saw the map. "Definitely!"

Thrilled that the other girl was up for an adventure, Riley handed it over to the elderly Mexican man behind the counter just as Shayna came over with her magnet.

"So," he said in slightly accented English as he regarded them with kind, dark eyes. "You are going to hunt for the treasure."

Riley smiled. "Yes."

The old Mexican ran his boney fingers over the piece of vellum, smoothing the edge that had curled. "This map was taken from the original," he said. "It is authentic."

Riley doubted that, but she smiled at the old man nonetheless. Though she knew Cade and Madoc were probably right and there was no gold to be found, Riley also knew she and Shayna would have tons of fun looking for it anyway. Hunting for treasure was just a good reason to get out and go horseback riding.

When they got back to the ranch that evening, Madoc was just coming in from the barn and he offered to help carry their shopping bags into the house.

"Where's Cade?" Riley asked as they stepped into the entryway.

"Still outside in the barn," her brother-in-law answered and then glanced at Shayna. "Do all these go upstairs?" he asked, referring to the shopping bags in his hands.

Shayna nodded. "Yes, but I want to show your mother what I bought before we take them up." She looked at Riley. "Are you going to come show Arlene what you bought?"

Riley thought a moment, her lips curving into a smile as an idea came to her. "Actually, I think I'll go put on my boots so I can model them for Cade first."

While she really did think that was the best way to show off her new cowboy boots, Riley had an ulterior motive as well. When Cade saw she had bought a pair of boots in addition to the shoes she'd specifically went to the store to buy, he would surely think a spanking was called for. At least, she hoped he would. And the barn would be a perfect place to get one!

Her pulse fluttering at the possibility of getting a spanking, Riley hurried upstairs to the guest room to change. Kicking off her sandals, she shimmied out of the shorts she was wearing and into the flirty suede mini-skirt she'd bought. Pulling on her new boots, she ran a brush through her long, blond hair, then surveyed her reflection in the full-length mirror, turning first one way and then the other. Paired with the tank top she wore, the skirt and cowboy boots showed off her long legs perfectly. Cade would take one look at her and be unable to resist putting her over his knee, she thought with a smile.

224

Cade was in one of the empty stalls when she walked into the barn a few minutes later. At her entrance, he glanced up from what he was doing, only to do a double take when he saw how she was dressed. He let out a low whistle.

"Wow, do you look hot," he said. "How come I've never seen you in those boots before?"

She walked over to where he stood, adding a little extra wiggle to her hips as she did so. "Because I just bought them today."

Cade lifted a brow. "I thought you went shopping for shoes."

Riley shrugged. "Oh, I did, but then I saw these boots and I just couldn't resist. And they go so great with this new skirt, don't you think?"

His golden brown eyes lingered on her legs for a moment. "They do," he agreed. "But that doesn't mean you should have bought them. I guess you didn't learn anything from that spanking I gave you on the plane, did you?"

Riley's pulse quickened at the mention of a spanking. Her husband was so good at playing this game, she thought. "But honey," she protested. "I can't come all the way to Texas and not buy a pair of cowboy boots."

Cade set the hay fork he'd been holding aside. "That's fine. As long as you realize it's going to get you another spanking."

She formed her lips into a pout, but before she could say anything, her husband took her hand and led her over to the stack of hay bales in one of the other stalls.

"You can't spank me here!" she complained, knowing her protests were all part of the game.

He turned to face her, an amused expression on his handsome face. "Why not? All the hands have already left for the day and we have much more privacy here than we would up at the house."

Riley almost smiled. That was exactly what she had been thinking. But still while the barn provided privacy, there was also the possibility of someone walking in and catching them. For some reason, that only made the whole idea of getting spanked there even more arousing. The thought of the spanking she was about to get already had her pussy purring!

"Okay," she agreed. "But don't spank me too hard."

Her husband chuckled. "No harder than you deserve, sweetheart."

She gave Cade another pout, but didn't protest when he sat down on a bale of hay and gently guided her over his knee. While it certainly wasn't the best part of the spanking, there was something very exciting about being put over her husband's knee. Maybe it was the feel of his firm hand on the small her back, she thought. Or maybe it was the way he rested his other hand on her upturned bottom. Or maybe it was simply the anticipation of that first spank. Whatever it was, it always made her pulse flutter wildly.

Thinking this would be a quickie spanking like the one he'd given her on the plane, Riley expected Cade to lift her skirt, pull down her panties, and start right in on her bare bottom, but she was surprised when he caressed her bottom through her skirt instead.

"This is the second time this week I've had to spank you for buying a pair of shoes without permission, sweetheart," he said. "I think your shoe habit is getting a little out of control, don't you?"

Riley squirmed on his lap; the mock scolding Cade was giving her was as much of a turn-on as the spanking that would soon accompany it.

Without warning, his hand suddenly came down on her ass with a sharp, resounding smack. She jumped, letting out a startled, little yelp.

"Don't you?" he prompted again, giving her another smack.

"*Owwww!*" she squealed. "Not really, no. As I tend to remember, I never agreed to that whole ask-you-for-permission-to-buy-shoes thing."

226

That earned her another half dozen spanks. "Oh, really? You don't remember the conversation we had where you asked me to help you get control of your shoe buying fetish? I agreed because your side of the closet is already filled to capacity." He paused long enough to administer several more firm smacks to each cheek. "I'm not sure you even have room for these boots."

She shrugged, as much as she could shrug while hanging upside down over her husband's knee. Even though the spanks stung, she couldn't resist provoking him further. "I'll just put them on your side of the closet then."

Above her, Cade chuckled. "Ten extra for being so saucy," he told her.

Riley looked over her shoulder to stick her tongue out at him.

"Make it twenty," he said.

Though she gave him a pout, Riley couldn't help but smile at their light banter as she turned back around to focus her gaze on the hay-strewn floor. The hand that came down on her bottom was anything but light, however, and she squirmed and yelped as he applied a series of stinging smacks to her entire bottom.

"*Owwwww!*" she protested. "Honey, what about my warm-up."

"This is your warm-up," he replied, pushing up her skirt. "I'm just getting started."

A moment later, his hand was coming down on her panty-covered bottom. He moved with a steady rhythm, smacking first one cheek, and then the other until her asscheeks felt hot all over. Only then did he pull down her panties.

Riley held her breath in anticipation as she waited for the spanking to continue, but again Cade surprised her by cupping her ass and giving it a firm squeeze. Her skin tingled where his hand touched and Riley moaned.

"So, how much did these boots cost, sweetheart?" Cade asked softly.

Riley was so caught up in what he was doing with his hand that she barely heard him speak. She lifted her head to look at him over her shoulder. "Wh-what?"

Cade regarded her with an amused expression. "How much did you pay for the boots?"

The question took her by surprise and she had to think before answering. "A hundred-and-twenty-five dollars," she said.

If her husband was surprised at the dollar amount, he gave no indication of it. Instead, he simply nodded. "Then I think a hundred-and-twenty-five spanks would be fair, don't you?"

Riley blinked at the number. Though it sounded high, she was sure Cade gave her that many and much more whenever he spanked her, but still....

Before she could reply, however, Cade lifted his hand and brought it down hard on her right cheek.

"One," he announced.

Was he really going to count out each and every spank? Riley wondered even as his hand connected with the opposite cheek.

"Two," he said.

Cade continued spanking her like that, counting each smack as his hand came down on first one cheek and then the other. And while Riley loved every minute of the spanking, she still squirmed and squealed, not to mention kicked her booted feet liked crazy whenever his hand connected with the tender area of her sit-spots. *Ouch!*

"One-hundred-twenty-four and one-hundred-twenty-five," Cade announced, finishing up with two very hard smacks on her bare bottom.

Riley lay limply across her husband's strong thighs. Thank goodness the boots had been on sale, she thought as he gently rubbed her throbbing asscheeks, because she wasn't sure if her poor bottom could have taken it if she'd had to pay full price. God, she loved sales!

228

But even if her bottom was throbbing, she had to admit that she'd just gotten an absolutely wonderful spanking! She was just about to tell Cade as much when he took her arm and gently stood her on her feet. Riley immediately began to reach back to cup her bottom, but before she could, her husband scooped her up in his arms and deposited her on the bales of hay stacked beside the one on which he'd been sitting. Riley squealed in protest as her freshly-spanked asscheeks made contact with the rough, scratchy hay, but she quickly forgot all about her tender bottom when she saw her husband unbuckling his belt.

Her blue eyes went wide. "Honey, we can't! Someone could come in!"

Cade grinned down at her. "No they won't," he said as he went to work on the buttons of his jeans. "There's this unwritten rule on a ranch. If the barn's rockin', then don't come knockin'."

Riley couldn't help but laugh. "You're making that up," she said.

"Maybe," he chuckled.

As he spoke, Cade pushed down his jeans and Riley barely had a chance to catch a glimpse of his hard cock before he put a hand beneath each of her legs and gently raised them in the air so that she was in a V-position. A moment later he was sliding into her wet pussy.

Riley gasped as she felt him fill her, only to let out a little moan as her tender asscheeks rubbed against the scratchy hay when he began to thrust. But as much as her bottom might want to protest, having Cade's hard cock moving inside her was so good that she couldn't concentrate on anything but how wonderful it felt. If anything, the tingling in her bottom seemed to add to her pleasure!

She leaned back against the hay bale behind her as Cade spread her legs wider and began to thrust even more deeply. The position allowed the tip of his cock to come into contact with her G-spot on every thrust and she couldn't control the moans that escaped from her lips. God, this felt so good! It definitely didn't hurt that Cade's thrusts were making her tender bottom press against the rough hay bale each time he drove into her; it almost made it feel like she was still getting spanked!

Riley could only imagine that the position was just as good for Cade. Not only did having her legs stretched out like this make her pussy extremely tight, but she also suspected that the view of his cock sliding in and out of her was incredibly arousing, too.

She would have liked the sex to have gone on and on forever, but the combination of so many sexual sensations was too much for her. Fulfilling the fantasy of having sex in the barn, the feel of the hay on her tender bottom, not to mention what his cock was doing to her all served to push her over the edge within moments. Riley couldn't have held back her orgasm even if she'd wanted to and she screamed out with pleasure as she came harder than she thought she'd ever had. Just as her orgasm was starting to diminish, Cade threw back his head back and groaned as his own climax surged through him. His extra-hard thrusts only served to catapult her into a second orgasm and she relished the sensation of coming along with him.

Afterward, Cade let her legs relax and Riley automatically wrapped them around him, pulling him in close even as he leaned forward to claim her lips in a searing kiss.

"My bottom is terribly tender, you know," she complained softly as she smoothed her skirt over her panties a few minutes later.

Cade's mouth quirked. "Then maybe you'll think twice before you buy another new pair of shoes," he said as he buttoned his jeans.

When Riley gave him a pout, he pulled her into his arms and kissed her again. "These boots really do look sexy on you, you know."

230

Riley laughed as she felt a blush rise to her face. While her new cowboy boots did have the desired effect, she thought as they walked back to the house, her bottom was so sore that she didn't know how she was going to manage to sit through dinner.

CHAPTER FOUR

"Do you think your brother spanks Riley?" Shayna asked Madoc as they were getting dressed the next morning.

Her husband stopped in the act of buttoning his shirt to look at her in surprise. "Cade? You're kidding right?"

She shrugged. "Riley was fidgeting around in her seat the whole time we were having dinner last night," she pointed out as she pulled her long, dark hair up into a ponytail and secured it with a cloth-covered elastic. "And I'm sure she got into trouble for buying those expensive boots."

Madoc shook his head. "No way would my brother ever give his wife a spanking. He's too uptight. The closest he probably comes to being adventurous in the bedroom is leaving the lights on."

Though Shayna doubted Riley and Cade's sex life was as boring as her husband made it out to be, she couldn't help but laugh anyway. Having been spanked quite often since meeting Madoc, Shayna recognized the signs of a tender bottom when she saw one, and Riley looked like hers had definitely been tender last night. But since Shayna couldn't very well come out and ask her sister-in-law if Cade spanked her, she supposed she would just have to continue to wonder.

Over breakfast, Arlene asked what everyone planned on doing that day. Madoc said that since Shayna and Riley wanted to start searching for the Confederate gold, he and Cade were going to ride down to the southern end of the property and help the ranch hands mend some of the fences there.

"Just remember, stay away from that mining property we told you about," Cade warned.

"We will," Riley promised.

After taking a closer look at the map with Riley after breakfast, however, Shayna saw that there was a big X just to the north of the Cutler ranch, specifically in the area that both men had told them to stay away from. When she pointed it out to Riley, though, the other girl just shrugged.

"What they don't know won't hurt them," she said. "Besides, we'll stay away from anything marked private property."

Shayna supposed her sister-in-law was right. Madoc and Cade had no interest in looking for the buried treasure, and therefore no interest in the map, she reasoned. The only way their husbands would find out what they'd been up to was if she or Riley told them, which they wouldn't. Unless they found the Confederate gold, of course. Shayna couldn't help but smile at that. *Yeah, right.*

Madoc and Cade already had horses saddled and waiting for them when she and Riley walked out to the barn a little while later. Shayna hadn't ridden for years, but she'd taken riding lessons when she was a kid, and she climbed into the saddle eagerly. Of course, the guys had picked out really sweet horses for them to ride. She and Riley wouldn't have any problem at all.

"Be careful," Madoc told her.

"We will," she said, leaning down to give him a kiss.

Even though the map didn't have any modern landmarks on it, it would still be easy to get to the location of the supposed treasure. If she and Riley kept an eye on the land formations as they rode north, they should have no problem. According to the map, there was a big river that split into two smaller streams right near the location where the treasure was thought to be. All they had to do was find the river, and then follow it until they came to the part where it branched off.

Even if the treasure hunt was a wild goose chase, the ride was certainly worth it. The Texas countryside was beautiful, Shayna thought. In fact, it reminded her a lot of the area where she'd grown up in Colorado.

"I think we're supposed to head in that direction," Riley said, urging her mare alongside Shayna's to show her the map.

Shayna studied the map for a moment before lifting her gaze to survey their surroundings. According to the map, the big river should be somewhere on the other side of that hill up ahead.

Urging their horses forward, she and Riley rode in that direction. When they got to the top of the hill, however, they found that the river was a whole lot bigger than it looked on the map. Shayna realized they would have to cross over it at some point to get to the X on the map, but they sure as heck couldn't do it here.

"What's that?" Riley asked.

Shayna turned her attention away from the river to look in the direction her friend was pointing. In the distance on the other side of the river, she could see a big cloud of dust being kicked up. She was just able to make out several trucks and a bulldozer, as well as a lot of men moving around. She and Riley were too far away to see what the men were doing, however.

"They must be doing some mining," she told Riley.

Riley agreed that there was no way they could traverse the river right there, especially since they didn't want to attract the attention of the men working on the mining property. With that in mind, they decided it would be better to ride parallel to it until they found the fork in the river. Hopefully, it would be shallow enough to cross there, Shayna thought.

They had been riding for ten minutes or so when Shayna spotted something wedged in the branches of a fallen tree on the far side of the river. A quick glance in Riley's direction told her the blond girl had seen it, too. Something about the shape made Shayna think it was definitely out of place.

"What is that, do you think?" Shayna asked.

Riley shook her head. "I don't know. Let's go see."

Curious, they urged their horses forward toward the riverbank, only to both come to an abrupt halt.

"Oh God," Shayna breathed. "Is that what I think it is?"

Beside her, Riley was standing up in her stirrups, trying to get a better look. "I think you're right," she said after a moment. "It's a person."

Shayna swallowed hard. "Do you think he's alive?"

Riley sat down in her saddle, but said nothing for a moment. Then she shook her head. "I don't think so. He's facedown and that looks like blood on the back of his shirt."

Shayna chewed on her lower lip, wondering if they should check anyway, but then decided that the other girl was right. "Do you think we should try to go out there and get him?"

"No way," Riley said. "That river's moving too fast. We'd be risking our own lives trying to get to him."

Shayna silently agreed. "Then we have no choice. We have to go back and tell Madoc and Cade."

She didn't really want to do that, especially considering how much trouble it was going to her and Riley into, but what could they do? They couldn't just leave the guy there.

Abruptly remembering that her husband and brother-in-law had gone to the mend some fences on the opposite side of the ranch, Shayna was afraid Madoc and Cade would still be out, but to her relief, both men were in the barn when she and the other girl rode into the stable. From the looks of it, they'd just gotten back, too.

"Thank God you're here," Shayna said, still breathing hard from the long ride back. Not bothering to dismount, she explained about the body she and Riley had seen floating in the river.

Madoc's brow furrowed as he exchanged a look with his brother. "Are you sure it was a body you saw?" he asked dubiously.

Shayna was taken aback by the question. "Yes, we're sure," she said. "It was a man and he was floating facedown in the river. We even saw the blood."

236

Madoc exchanged a look with his brother again.

"Aren't you going to call the cops or the sheriff or something?" Riley demanded when neither man said anything.

"Why don't we ride up there with you and take a look first before we go calling in the sheriff," Cade suggested.

Madoc and Cade didn't believe them, Shayna realized. What did they think, that she and Riley were making it up? Rather than argue about it though, she and the other girl waited impatiently while their husbands mounted their horses.

By the time they rode back up to the river, however, the body they'd seen floating in it was nowhere to be found, much to Shayna's consternation.

"Well?" Cade asked, looking at the two girls. "Where is it?"

Riley frowned. "I don't know, but he was here. Shayna and I both saw him. He was wedged up against that tree over there."

"Maybe he came loose and floated downstream," Shayna suggested.

The brothers exchanged looks, but said nothing as they urged their mounts in that direction. As she and Riley followed, Shayna expected to come upon the man's body at any moment, but to her surprise, it wasn't anywhere. After half a mile or so, the two men brought their horses to a halt.

"There's nothing here," Cade said. "And a body wouldn't have made it past this part of the river with all of these rocks."

"Well, he couldn't have just disappeared," Riley insisted. "We didn't just make it up, you know."

Cade sighed. "We're not saying that you did. We're just saying that maybe you were confused about what you saw. Things floating in the water can take on all kinds of shapes."

Riley glared at her husband. "We know what we saw, Cade."

Shayna saw Madoc's mouth tighten. "Maybe," he agreed. "But you girls weren't even supposed to be up here anyway. Cade and I specifically told you that you weren't to go near this area."

Shayna glanced at her sister-in-law and saw the other girl's face turn red. "We didn't realize we'd ridden up this far, I guess," she told her husband.

Madoc scowled. "You didn't see the sign back there that said this was a restricted area and to keep out?"

"We must have missed it," Shayna mumbled.

Madoc shook his head. "Let's just go back to the house."

Shayna groaned inwardly. She recognized that look all right. It meant she was in for a spanking. And not the fun kind, either.

They rode back to the ranch in silence. Once in the barn, Shayna took her time getting the mare she'd ridden cooled down and back into her stall. She dawdled over giving the horse fresh food and water, and was just finishing up when Madoc came over.

"In the house," he growled softly in her ear. "Now."

Shayna glared at her husband, but said nothing. As much as she wanted to refuse, she didn't want to make a scene in front of Riley and Cade, or the ranch hands for that matter. Once up in the bedroom, however, she rounded on Madoc as soon as the door was closed.

"I don't know why you're making such a big deal out of this," she said sullenly.

Madoc's brows drew together. "I'm making such a big deal out of it because if you and Riley had gotten caught trespassing on federal property, Cade and I would be bailing you out of jail right now."

She rolled her eyes. "Don't you think you're exaggerating?"

"No, I don't," he said. "Trespassing on federal property is a serious offense around here, Shayna. And considering what a horrible experience being in jail was for you before, I wouldn't think you'd be in any hurry to go back."

238

That gave Shayna pause and she shivered at the reminder. "What if I tell you that Riley and I won't go back up there again?" she asked in a small voice.

"I'd think you were trying to talk me out of giving you a spanking," he growled. "Now, are you going to take your jeans off or should I?"

Shayna didn't move, torn between trying to talk her way out the spanking some more and doing what he'd asked. When her husband had his mind set on spanking her for doing something, there was no talking him out of it, so she might as well just give in and accept her spanking. Besides, she probably did deserve one.

Taking off her boots, she dropped them on the carpeted floor, then unbuttoned her snug-fitting jeans and wiggled out of them. She wondered if she should take off her panties, too, but then decided against it. While she was sure they'd be coming down at some point during the spanking, she wouldn't give him the satisfaction of doing all the work herself.

While she had been undressing, Madoc had taken a seat on the bench at the foot of the bed and was now looking at her expectantly. "Over my knee," he said.

His voice was soft, but still commanding, and Shayna found that she had no choice but to obey. Her pulse fluttering, she slowly walked across the room to where Madoc was sitting, but once she got there, she hesitated. She had draped herself over his knee dozens of times, of course, but there was something so embarrassing about doing it for a bad-girl spanking.

When she continued to stand there, Madoc lifted a brow. "Shayna?"

Her face coloring, Shayna took a deep breath and obediently draped herself over his knee. Madoc immediately placed one hand on the small of her back to hold her there; he rested the other lightly on her panty-covered bottom.

"Ready?" Madoc asked.

Wordlessly, Shayna nodded her head.

A moment later, he lifted his hand and brought it down with a sharp smack on her right cheek. He could at least give her a warm-up first, Shayna thought as she let out a little yelp. Madoc, of course, ignored her protest, delivering a firm smack to the opposite cheek. He went back and forth like that, spanking first one cheek, and then the other until her bottom felt hot all over. And he hadn't even taken down her panties yet!

As if reading her mind, Madoc stopped right then to abruptly pull down her panties.

Shayna lifted her head to look at him over her shoulder. "Couldn't you rub my bottom some in between?" she said, and then added in a small voice, "Please."

Madoc lifted a brow, obviously aware she was trying to use her feminine powers of persuasion on him. "I think you're missing the point of this spanking."

She thrust her lower lip out in a pout. "But honey, it stings."

"It's supposed to," he told her. "How else are you going to remember to behave yourself and do as I tell you?"

Shayna gave him another pout, but turned back around to focus her attention on the floor again. It was useless to argue with her husband about it, especially when she was over his knee.

When his hand came down on her bare ass a moment later Shayna had to bite her lip to stifle a yelp. *Ouch*, that stung, she thought, stifling another protest as he delivered a resounding smack, this time to her very sensitive sit-spot.

Each smack seemed harder than the one before it, and Shayna squirmed and kicked her feet for all she was worth. She desperately tried to stifle her squeals, but every so often one would escape her lips. God, she hoped no one could hear her. She'd be mortified if someone figured out she'd gotten a spanking!

"Honey, please," she begged. "That really...*owwwww!*... stings!"

240

"Good," he told her in between spanks. "That way you won't be tempted to go where you're not supposed to the next time you're out riding. When I give you a warning to stay out of a certain place, I'm doing it for your own good. I want to make sure you remember that."

Shayna bit back another yelp as his hand connected with her ass again. It felt like her poor bottom was on fire! "I promised I wouldn't go up there again," she complained.

Madoc's hand came down again. "Then a couple of more smacks will make sure of that."

A couple of more turned out to be twenty or so, though Shayna couldn't be sure because she didn't keep count. But somewhere in the middle, an unusual, but familiar sound caught her attention. Was that yelping she heard? She strained her ears, stifling her own yelps as she tried to hear over the spanking Madoc was giving her. But before she could figure out what she was hearing, her husband put her back on his feet and pulled her down to sit on his lap.

Shayna gasped as her freshly-spanked asscheeks came into contact with the rough material of his jeans.

Madoc gently brushed her hair back from her face. "I'm serious about not going up there, Shayna," he said softly. "These strip-mining companies have been known to run people off their property with guns and I don't want you getting hurt. Promise me you won't go up there again. Shayna, are you listening to me?"

She dragged her gaze away from the door to look at him. "What? Yes, of course."

But Shayna hadn't been listening. Instead, she'd been trying to figure out what those sounds were that she heard coming from down the hall. If she didn't know better, she'd think Riley was getting a spanking, too!

Madoc gently slipped his fingers beneath her chin. "Shayna, promise me you won't go up there again."

"I won't," she said softly. "Promise."

That seemed to satisfy her husband because he pulled her close for a kiss. Even though Shayna hooked her arms around his neck and returned his kiss, she still couldn't help but wonder what was going on in the next room.

CHAPTER FIVE

Shayna and Madoc were already in the kitchen making lunch by the time Riley and Cade came downstairs a little while later. Since Arlene and John were out for the day, it was just the four of them for lunch and Riley hoped that neither Shayna nor Madoc noticed she was sitting a bit gingerly.

Riley had known from the expression on her husband's face that she would be getting a spanking when they got back to the ranch, but she'd still been a little surprised when Cade had taken her upstairs to their bedroom the minute they had finished cooling down the horses.

"But honey," she'd protested. "Your brother and Shayna are in the next room."

Cade, however, hadn't been dissuaded. "Then you'll have to keep your protests to a minimum, won't you?"

Five minutes later, Riley was over his knee getting her bottom reddened. She had really tried to do as Cade had suggested and keep her protests to a minimum, but she couldn't help letting out the occasional squeal. She only hoped Shayna and Madoc hadn't heard. God, that would be so embarrassing!

After lunch, the two girls decided to go into town to check out some of the shops they hadn't gone into the day before. As Riley pulled out of the driveway and onto the road, she glanced at Shayna.

"Madoc wasn't too angry with you for going up there, was he?" she asked. Though her brother-in-law hadn't seemed upset at lunch, Madoc had looked furious when they'd gotten back to the barn earlier.

Beside her, Shayna shook her head. "No, he was just worried about me," she said. "How about Cade? Was he very mad?"

Riley turned her gaze back to the road, afraid the other girl would see her blush. "A little bit. But he was more concerned than anything."

They rode in silence for a little while before Riley spoke again.

"Contrary to what our husbands think, I know what we saw floating in the stream, Shayna. It was a body," she said.

Shayna shrugged. "I agree with you, but what can we do about it?"

Riley thought a moment. "Maybe we should go see the sheriff," she finally said. "He might be skeptical, but at least he'd be obligated to check it out."

Shayna chewed on her lower lip, but said nothing. Riley supposed it did seem odd to go talk to the sheriff since both of their husbands were in law enforcement, but what could they do when neither Cade nor Madoc believed them? She was just about to point out as much to Shayna when the other girl nodded her head in agreement.

The sheriff's office was easy enough to find since it was across the street from the general store. Finding a parking space, Riley and Shayna walked across the street and went inside. At their entrance, the girl seated at the front desk looked up from her computer. She was pretty with long, dark hair and big, brown eyes. The nameplate on her desk read Rosalinda Sanchez.

She gave them a smile. "Can I help you?"

Riley returned the girl's smile. "We were hoping we could talk to the sheriff," she said.

"Are you here to report a crime?" the girl asked.

Riley glanced at Shayna before answering. "Maybe," she said.

That earned her and Shayna a curious look from the girl behind the desk. "If you'll have a seat, I'll tell him you'd like to speak with him," she said, gesturing to the wooden bench opposite her desk.

Riley and Shayna did as the girl asked, but no sooner had they sat down than the sheriff came out of his office. Neither fat nor thin, he was somewhere in between, with graying hair, a weathered face, and a thick mustache.

"Rosalinda says you wanted to see me," he said, gesturing to the dark-haired girl at the desk. "What can I do for you ladies?"

Riley related what she and Shayna had seen up at the stream that morning, including the fact that they had taken Cade and Madoc up there, but had found nothing.

The sheriff regarded them with amusement. "I see," he said. "I've always thought those Cutler boys were pretty sharp. If they don't think there's anything going on, then they're probably right. Maybe you two ladies should reconsider what you think you saw."

Riley frowned at him. "But we really did see a body."

"Now look, young lady," he said. "We take things like that very seriously around here. If there was a dead body, that means someone would be missing, and since no one reported anyone missing, I really doubt that you saw a body in the river." He held up his hand when Riley started to argue. "Now, I'm not saying that you didn't see something, but things floating in the water can take on all kinds of shapes. It could even have been a dead cow. They bloat up and can look really strange."

Shayna made a face at that. "So, you're not even going to look into it?"

He gave them a placating smile. "That area belongs to Big Sky Mining. I know the head of security up there. If it'll help ease your mind any, I'll give him a call and have him check it out."

Riley frowned again. "But..."

"Now, ladies, I'm very busy, so I'm going to have to ask you to move along," he said soothingly. "I'll let you know what I find out. How does that sound?"

Riley opened her mouth to protest, but found herself and Shayna being ushered out the front door and onto the sidewalk before she could get the words out. Annoyed, Riley was about to say something tart, but forced herself to hold her tongue. If they pushed the sheriff, he might not look into their story at all.

That didn't mean she couldn't vent to Shayna after the sheriff had gotten into his SUV and driven off, though. In fact, she was just about to do so when a female voice interrupted her.

"Excuse me."

Riley and Shayna both turned to see a petite, dark-haired girl hurrying up to them. Riley recognized her as the girl from the sheriff's office, Rosalinda Sanchez.

"Could I talk to you for a minute?" she asked.

Riley exchanged a look with Shayna and both girls nodded. "Of course," Riley said.

Rosalinda tucked her hair behind her ear. "I couldn't help but overhear your conversation with the sheriff, and while he may not believe you, I do."

"You do?" Riley asked in surprise.

The girl nodded. "Whatever you think you saw, you're probably right. Something has been going on up at the Big Sky Mining Corporation for a long time now, but no one will believe it. I know for a fact that over the past several months, quite a few of the people who work for them have disappeared."

Shayna frowned. "But if that's true, then why hasn't the sheriff done anything?"

Rosalinda's mouth tightened. "Because a lot of the people working for him are illegals and no one ever reports them missing," she said grimly. "But I have no doubt that Bill Bingham, the head of security for Big Sky Mining, is behind it. He'd have to be, to keep this covered up so well."

"The guy the sheriff said he was going to talk to?" Riley asked.

The Mexican girl nodded, but before she could say more, a sheriff's vehicle pulled into the parking space nearby, distracting Rosalinda. She gave Riley and Shayna an apologetic smile.

"I've gotta go," she said.

With that, she turned and walked over to the vehicle. Riley had thought it was the sheriff returning, but when the man got out of the truck, she saw he was much younger, probably closer to Cade's age. He was handsome, with dark brown hair and a charming smile, which he flashed at the Mexican girl.

As Rosalinda and the deputy made their way into the sheriff's station, Riley turned to Shayna. "What do you think?" she asked. "Want to check out this Big Sky Mining Corporation and see what Bill Bingham has to say?"

Shayna hesitated for a moment. "Don't you think that's a little risky? This Bingham guy could be dangerous."

"We're not going to do anything foolish," Riley said. "I just want to see if this guy comes across as suspicious. If he does, then we can tell Cade and Madoc."

Then again, Riley thought as they drove out to the Big Sky Mining offices, if she did have to tell Cade, he was going to be really mad. She had promised to drop this, but the spanking she would get would be worth it if it turned out there really was something illegal going on.

The Big Sky Mining offices were made up of several small buildings. Not knowing which one Bill Bingham's office was in, Riley and Shayna decided try the main office first. As it happened, the head of security had his office there. It took some doing to get past the receptionist at the front desk, but eventually, the woman brought them back to Bill Bingham's office.

A big, barrel-chested man, Bill Bingham eyed both girls with interest as they entered his office. "So, what can I do for you?" he asked after Riley and Shayna were seated in front of his desk.

247

Riley and Shayna had decided that rather than come up with a phony story, it would be best to simply tell Big Sky Mining's head of security exactly what they'd seen that morning. At first, Bill Bingham looked stunned when they mentioned seeing a dead body floating in the river, but then his expression darkened.

"I don't know exactly what you two ladies saw floating in the river, but I can assure you it wasn't a dead body," he said firmly. "My men do regular sweeps of the area and they would surely have seen something like that. It was probably just a log or something like that." Pushing back his chair, he got to his feet. "Now, if you'll excuse me, I have a meeting to get to."

Riley's brow furrowed. "Mr. Bingham, with all due respect, I think you might want to have your men take another look. My sister-in-law and I could go with them and show them exactly where we saw the body."

Out of the corner of her eye, Riley saw Shayna shoot her a look of disbelief, but she ignored the other girl, determinedly keeping her gaze trained on Bill Bingham.

Gray eyes narrowed at her. "You've already trespassed on private property once today, Mrs. Cutler. If you do so again, I'll be forced to call in the sheriff. Do I make myself clear?"

Riley felt a shiver run down her back. "Yes."

"Good," he said. "Then if you'll excuse me."

Bill Bingham had already come around the desk and opened the door, giving Riley and Shayna no choice but to leave. Once in the car, though, she couldn't wait to get Shayna's take on the man and what he'd said.

"I think Rosalinda Sanchez is right. Bill Bingham is definitely hiding something," she said, glancing at Shayna. "Don't you think?"

Beside her, Shayna nodded. "Yeah, I do. But that doesn't mean Madoc and Cade are going to think so. Or the sheriff, either." She sighed. "I don't really think there's anything more we can do to convince them, Riley."

248

While Riley knew the other girl was right, it still bothered her that they hadn't been able to get anything out of Bill Bingham. She had been hoping Big Sky Mining's head of security would say something a little more incriminating.

"Oh, and one more thing," Shayna added as Riley turned into the Cutler's driveway. "Let's not mention our little outing to our husbands. I don't think they'd be too understanding if they found out we not only went to see the sheriff, but the head of security for the mining company, too."

Riley wholeheartedly agreed with the other girl about that and quickly promised she wouldn't say anything.

It turned out that she nor Shayna needed to say anything, however, because John Cutler brought the subject up during dinner that evening, much to both girls' chagrin.

"I ran into Sheriff O'Keefe when we were in town today," he said conversationally as he reached for a dinner roll. "He said that you girls had claimed you'd seen a dead body floating in the river on the north end of the ranch. How come none of you mentioned anything about it?"

Beside her, Riley saw Cade glance at her sharply. Across the table from them, Madoc was giving Shayna the same look. So much for their husbands not finding out what they'd been up to, Riley thought.

"Because there was no dead body," Cade said firmly.

"Yes, there was," Riley insisted. "Shayna and I both saw it." She looked at the other girl. "Isn't that right, Shayna?"

Shayna nodded. "It really did look like a body."

Madoc scowled. "Well there was no body when we rode up there with you later."

"We told the girls it was probably just their minds playing tricks," Cade said, giving Riley a pointed look. "It could have been anything in that stream."

Riley opened her mouth to argue, but John was already agreeing with his son, saying that had happened to him on more than one occasion. That led to several of his old Marshal stories, none of which Riley really paid attention to. She was furious that no one would take what she and Shayna were saying seriously.

After the dinner table had been cleared, Madoc excused himself and his wife, saying that since it was such a nice evening, they were going to take a walk. Shayna looked less than thrilled with that idea, which made Riley think her poor sister-in-law was going to be getting a stern lecture in addition to some exercise.

"A walk sounds like a good idea," Cade said after the other couple had left. "Why don't we take one, too, honey?"

Riley blinked in surprise. A walk under the moonlit sky with her handsome husband would be very romantic if it weren't for the fact that it was probably going to culminate in her being put over his knee.

"I really should help your mother in the kitchen," she said.

"Nonsense," Arlene said. "The table's already cleared, so all I need to do is load the dishwasher. You two kids go have fun."

Reluctantly, Riley put her hand in Cade's and allowed him to lead her outside. Normally, she would have been eager to get a spanking, Riley thought as they walked toward the barn, but after getting one last night and then another that morning on top of all the horseback riding, her bottom was a little tender.

When they walked into the barn a few minutes later however, Riley was both surprised and relieved to hear Shayna's voice. Cade couldn't spank her with his brother and sister-in-law there.

"But honey, I..." Shayna was saying to Madoc, her voice trailing off when she noticed Riley and Cade standing there.

As Riley noted the other couple's pose – Madoc standing with his arms crossed over his chest and Shayna looking up at him from beneath lowered lashes – the most

250

ridiculous thought popped into her head. If she didn't know better, she'd say that Shayna was in for a spanking.

"I thought you were going for a walk," Cade said to his brother.

Madoc cleared his throat. "We were, but then we decided to come out to the barn instead so I could show Shayna how to clean the horses' hoofs. What are you and Riley doing out here?"

Cade glanced at her. "We, uh, thought we'd go for a ride."

Riley looked at the other couple eagerly. "Do you and Shayna want to come with us?" she said, ignoring her husband's scowl.

Shayna's eyes lit up at the suggestion, but Madoc answered for both of them, saying they would take a rain check.

As she and Cade saddled their horses, Riley couldn't help but glance over at the other couple occasionally. Did Shayna get spanked, too? she wondered. For some strange reason, the thought that the other girl might get her bottom warmed on a regular basis made Riley's pulse skip a beat.

"Ready?" Cade asked.

Still preoccupied with the idea of her brother-in-law putting his pretty dark-haired wife over his knee, Riley merely nodded and took the hand Cade offered as she climbed onto her horse.

"Where are we going?" she asked Cade as they rode out of the barn.

"Not far," he said noncommittally.

She said nothing for a moment, but then asked, "You're going to give me a spanking, aren't you?"

He gave her a sidelong glance. "Don't you think you deserve one?"

Riley sighed. "Shayna and I just thought telling the sheriff what we saw was the right thing to do."

"It would have been if you had actually seen a body," he said.

It was on the tip of Riley's tongue to tell Cade what Rosalinda Sanchez had said about all the illegal immigrants who had gone missing in the area lately as well as the conversation she and Shayna had had with the shady head of security for Big Sky Mining, but she didn't. If Cade found out she'd gone out there, she'd be lucky if she could even sit down after the spanking he'd give her. Well, maybe that was an exaggeration, she thought, but he would definitely give her a hard spanking.

A few minutes later, Cade slowed his horse to a stop. Dismounting, he came over to offer Riley his hand, and then led her over to a large rock situated beside one of the trees.

"But honey, my bottom is still tender from the spanking you gave me this morning," she protested.

"Well, obviously that spanking I gave you didn't have the desired effect, so you need another reminder," he replied. "Now push down your shorts and climb over my knee."

Riley hesitated for a moment, but then did as he asked. She'd barely unbuttoned her shorts and wiggled them down over her hips when Cade took her hand and guided her over his knee. She automatically placed her hands on the grassy ground to steady herself. Not that she needed to worry; Cade's strong hand on the small of her back held her in place quite effectively.

From her vantage point, Riley had a perfect view of the barn and as she waited for Cade to begin, she found herself wondering if her sister-in-law was getting spanked even now. The thought had Riley's pulse fluttering with excitement just like it had back in the barn. Before she could think on that, however, her musings were interrupted as her husband slowly pulled down her panties. A moment later, his hand came down on her bare bottom with a resounding smack.

"*Owwwww!*" she yelped and looked at him over her shoulder. "Don't I at least get a warm-up first?"

252

His mouth quirked. "I think that spanking I gave you this morning is all the warm-up you need," he drawled. "Besides, I want you to remember this spanking the next time you want to go snooping around."

Riley gave him a pout, but turned around to focus her attention on the ground again. Cade immediately brought his hand down on her bottom again, this time a little harder, and she squealed again. Her husband ignored her protests, of course, bringing his hand down over and over on her bottom until she was squirming and wiggling around all over his lap. Her ass felt like it was on fire! Cade lectured her the entire time he spanked her, too. He seemed determined to get her to understand how important it was to stop poking her nose into places it didn't belong.

"*Owwwww!*" she squealed as he administered a sharp smack to her sit-spot. "Okay, honey! I get it!"

Riley really hadn't been listening to what he was saying. She just hoped if she agreed with him, then he wouldn't spank her as much.

"Somehow, I doubt that," Cade said. "So, I'd better give you a couple more spanks just to be sure."

A couple more turned into a whole lot more, and somewhere in the midst of the smacks, Riley began to protest that she'd learned her lesson, but Cade's hand continued to come down on her asscheeks. He even gave her a few good spanks on the backs of her thighs, right below the curve of her cheeks. Ouch, those really stung!

When he finally stood her back on her feet, Riley immediately reached around with both hand to cup her throbbing bottom. She was always amazed at how hot her asscheeks felt after a spanking.

"That was a really hard spanking!" she complained, sticking her lower lip out at him.

"You deserved it," Cade said, getting to his feet. "I just hope this spanking will help you remember to behave yourself.

Even if it was a body you saw, I don't want you getting yourself involved in stuff like that. It's too dangerous."

Riley knew Cade was just worried about her, and she couldn't be upset with him for that, even if he had just given her a hard spanking. "I know," she said softly. "But my poor bottom is really sore."

He brushed her hair back from her face with gentle fingers. "How about I give your bottom a nice, gentle rub when we get back to the house then? I'll even use some lotion. How does that sound?"

Exquisite, Riley thought as he bent his head to give her a tender kiss on the lips. With some TLC like that to look forward to, she couldn't wait to get back to the house. But then as she considered how sitting in the saddle was going to feel against her freshly-spanked bottom, she decided to suggest they walk the horses back instead.

CHAPTER SIX

Shayna couldn't look at Riley and Cade the next morning without blushing. If the other couple had come into the barn a few minutes later the night before, they would have seen her draped over her husband's knee with her bare bottom on display. Admittedly, Shayna had forgotten all about Riley and Cade once Madoc had started spanking her, though. She had tried to talk her way out of the spanking, of course, but Madoc had been of the opinion she deserved one for what she'd done, and her poor bottom had felt like it was on fire by the time he'd finally let her up. Her ass was fire-engine red all the way from the tops of her cheeks to the backs of her thighs. She hadn't done very well at stifling her protests, either. She had no doubt that anyone standing within fifty feet of the barn would have known exactly what had been going on in there. And afterward, he'd made her sit on a scratchy hay bale while he lectured her! She was just glad he hadn't known about their visit to the mining company, or her bottom would really have been in trouble.

Of course, Shayna couldn't complain too much about the spanking he'd given her. They had both gotten so turned on by doing it in the barn that she and Madoc had run all the way back to the house and up to their room. It might have been a bad-girl spanking, but it was still arousing as hell! She and Madoc hadn't even gotten all of their clothes off before they had fallen into bed and made passionate love for hours. Needless to say, before finally dropping off to sleep, though, Madoc had made her promise again to cut out all the snooping.

Cade must have made Riley promise the same thing because as they were clearing the table of the breakfast dishes a little while later, the other girl mentioned to Shayna that maybe they should just forget about what they'd seen. Shayna was all for that. After all, they were supposed to be there on vacation, not investigating a possible crime. Not that Madoc or Cade were going to give them a chance to do any more snooping anyway. After breakfast, the two men suggested they all go into Fort Worth and do some sightseeing.

Eager to spend some vacation time with their husbands, Shayna and Riley eagerly agreed. Ten minutes later, they were all headed for Fort Worth.

Though they primarily spent the day taking in the tourist attractions, Shayna and Riley managed to drag their husbands into a several shops in both Sundance Square and Traders Village. They went over to the Fort Worth Stockyards later in the day and arrived just in time to catch the longhorn cattle drive down the main thoroughfare. Never having seen longhorn cattle before, Shayna was amazed at how big the animals were.

Since they were going to the rodeo at the stockyards that night, they decided to have dinner at one of the restaurants there, and then browse around the shops before the show. Shayna had been looking forward to the rodeo ever since her father-in-law had mentioned it the first night they'd been at the ranch, but she didn't know how much fun watching barrel racing and bull riding could be. Of course, when she mentioned that to Madoc on the way back to the ranch, he chuckled and told her that she could give it a try herself on the mechanical bulls some of the saloons had. Though Shayna declined, she couldn't resist telling Madoc that she wouldn't mind watching him do it. Just the thought of how he'd look had her pulse fluttering wildly. In the back seat, Riley agreed, saying she'd like to watch Cade ride on a mechanical bull, too.

As she fell asleep in Madoc's arms that night, Shayna had to admit that spending the day sightseeing with her husband, Riley, and Cade had been a lot better than snooping around on federal property.

After breakfast the next morning, Riley asked Shayna if she wanted to go into Riverville for a little while since the guys would be busy shoeing horses. Though Shayna had been considering taking a dip in the pool, she agreed. She could go for a swim when they got back, she decided.

She and Riley were just coming out of the general store later that morning when they ran into Rosalinda Sanchez.

"So, did you find out anything when you went to Big Sky Mining the other day?" she asked eagerly. When both Shayna and Riley looked at her in surprise, she added, "You did go up there, right?"

"Well, yeah," Riley admitted. "But we didn't find anything out. Bill Bingham was less than forthcoming, not to mention a little peeved that we'd been trespassing on private property. He threatened to have us arrested."

The Mexican girl folded her arms. "He's hiding something, I know it," she said. "I was just about to take a run up there and see what I can dig up. Do you want to come with me?"

Shayna exchanged looks with Riley before answering. "I don't know, Rosalinda," she began.

"Everyone calls me Rosie," the other girl said with a grin.

Shayna smiled. "Rosie. Anyway, our husbands weren't too happy when they found out we'd talked to the sheriff the other day. They made us promise we'd stay out of trouble."

Rosie lifted a brow. "Do you two always do what they tell you?"

Shayna saw Riley flush. "Well, no, but..."

"Please," Rosie said before Riley could continue. "Something terrible is happening up there, I know it. People are disappearing and I can't do anything about it on my own. I need your help."

Shayna glanced at Riley to find her friend giving her a helpless look. She turned back to Rosalinda. "Rosie..."

257

The Mexican girl looked at them imploringly. "These people who are disappearing don't have anyone to speak for them. If we don't get involved, then no one is ever going to hear a word about this, and they'll just keep disappearing. We can't just stand by and do nothing while that's happening."

Shayna had to admit that when Rosie put it that way, it was difficult to turn their backs on the situation. She looked at Riley questioningly. After a moment, the blond girl gave her a shrug as if to say, "what else can we do?"

Turning back to Rosie, Shayna gave her a nod. "Okay, we'll go up there with you."

Even as she said the words, Shayna found herself wondering if she should do this. If Madoc found out, he'd spank her so hard she wouldn't be able to sit down for a week. Well, maybe that was an exaggeration, but he would definitely redden her bottom until it glowed.

They took Rosie's car up to the mining company. When they got there, it was just in time to see the head of security, Bill Bingham, getting into his own car. Since it was around lunch time anyway, Shayna didn't think it all that unusual for the man to be going out, but Rosie said she thought they should follow him.

Shayna fully expected Bill Bingham to head toward town when he pulled out of the driveway, but to her surprise, he didn't leave the mining company's property at all but turned down a dirt road. Shayna was afraid Bingham would realize they were following him, but Rosie was actually very good at tailing the man, and when he stopped alongside a second car, she made sure to stop far enough back so that he wouldn't see them.

For a moment, neither Bill Bingham nor the person he was meeting got out of their respective cars, but then both car doors finally opened. The second man was tall and thin, but rather nondescript in the looks department, and Bingham glanced around furtively as he walked up to him. Shayna had never seen a more guilty look on a person's face in all her life. He was definitely up to something.

"I wish we could hear what they were saying," Rosie muttered.

Shayna silently agreed. For all they knew, the two men could be talking about where they wanted to go for lunch. But at the way Bill Bingham was gesturing, she didn't think so.

Beside her, Rosie took her eyes off the men long enough to dig around in her shoulder bag for something. A moment later, she came up with a small pair of binoculars, a notepad, and a pen. She studied the men and their vehicles through the binoculars for a few moments before flipping open the notebook and scribbling down the license plate of the second man's car.

"I'll run his plate number when I get back to the station, then let you know what I find out," she said, dropping everything back into her bag.

At that, Shayna saw Riley give her a curious look from the back seat, but neither she nor the blond girl made any comment about it as Rosie turned the car around and headed out to the main road. If Shayna didn't know better, she'd think Rosie was a cop and not just a girl who worked in the sheriff's office.

Back in town, Rosie dropped the girls off at their car, then promised again to let them know what she found out before thanking them for going up to the mining company with her. Shayna was just glad they hadn't gotten themselves into any trouble while they were there because she really didn't want another spanking like she'd gotten the other night in the barn. Playful, erotic spankings were just fine, but those serious bad-girl ones were definitely not her thing. Of course, it helped that they usually resulted in great sex, but she'd just prefer to skip the serious smacks and go right to the fun kind of spanking. In fact, just the thought of getting a sexy, erotic spanking made her want one right then. Maybe she'd ask

259

Madoc to give her one when she and Riley got back to the ranch, she thought with a naughty smile.

By the time Riley and Shayna got back to the ranch, Madoc and Cade had already finished shoeing the horses and were waiting for them out by the pool. Seeing her husband in a pair of swim trunks was all the invitation Riley needed to hurry upstairs and put on her bikini. Apparently, Shayna felt the same about joining Madoc in the pool because she went up to change into her bikini, too.

But while spending the day with her half-naked husband was more than a little fun, it also made Riley incredibly horny, and by the time they went to bed that night, she was ready to jump him!

Grabbing her shower gel and body lotion off the dresser, Riley gave Cade a sexy wink. "Stay there," she ordered him in a silky voice. "I'll be right back. And don't you dare think of falling asleep!"

Hurrying down the hallway to the bathroom, Riley took a quick shower, then put on her shorts and tank top. Back out in the hallway, however, she stopped when she heard giggling coming from Shayna and Madoc's room. Normally that wouldn't have been enough to make her stop, but it was the distinct and very familiar smacking sound that followed Shayna's giggle that made Riley come to a halt. It couldn't be, she thought. But then her eyes went wide as she heard another smack. Oh my God, she thought. Madoc was spanking Shayna! And going by the soft moan that her friend was letting out, Shayna was enjoying it!

Riley knew she should go back to her bedroom, but instead, she found herself edging closer to the door. From inside, she could hear another smack, this time a little louder. It was quickly followed by a squeal.

"Hey, that stings!" Shayna protested.

Madoc chuckled softly. "I'd better rub it and make it all better then."

There was silence, then another soft, throaty moan from Shayna. Riley's pulse fluttered wildly as she pictured her pretty, dark-haired friend draped over her husband's lap while he lovingly rubbed her reddened bottom. It was just like Cade did to her, Riley thought. And it sounded as if Shayna liked it just as much as she did!

"Oh yeah," Shayna breathed, the words barely audible through the door. "Touch me right there."

Riley felt herself blush, but still she didn't move away from the door. She felt as if her feet were glued to the floor; she had to stay and hear more. She couldn't believe how turned on she was getting! The thought of what Shayna and Madoc were doing just on the other side of the door had her pussy positively tingling. It was all she could do not to reach down and touch herself; if she weren't standing in the hallway, she probably would have done just that!

Just when it sounded like Shayna was getting into some serious moaning, there came the sound of rapid, solid smacks. *Oooh*, Madoc was spanking her again!

Those sounded like some pretty hard spanks, too, Riley thought, and she could just imagine Shayna's bottom getting all red. She pictured the other girl squirming and kicking her feet in protest as Madoc brought his hand down over and over on his wife's bottom. Whenever Riley did that, Cade usually held her legs down with one of his own, and she couldn't help but wonder if Madoc did the same to Shayna.

Thinking of her own hunky husband made her suddenly remember that Cade was still waiting for her in their room. Riley was torn for a moment between staying where she was and eavesdropping some more, or going back to her room. The throbbing between her legs made the decision for her, however. She needed some loving right now!

Whirling around, Riley practically ran down the hallway to her room. Opening the door, she closed it quickly behind her. Cade was lying in bed, his hands behind his head and he looked up at her entrance.

"I was just about to come find you," he said with a grin.

Riley didn't answer. Setting the bath gel and body lotion down on the dresser, she walked over to the bed, stripping off her tank top and wiggling out of her shorts as she did so. The way Cade was eyeing her naked body told her he approved of her quick, little striptease, which only excited her even more.

Throwing back the quilt, Riley climbed into bed and settled herself between her husband's legs. Giving him a sultry look, she leaned forward and took his rapidly hardening cock into her mouth.

Cade groaned, his cock going completely hard as she slowly made love to him with her tongue. She moved her mouth up and down on his shaft slowly at first, and then more quickly. Each time she went down on him, she took his cock a little deeper until finally the head was touching the back of her throat. She held him there for a long moment, and then very slowly slid her mouth back up his hard length.

Cade lifted his head from the pillow to regard her with awe. "Whoa," he breathed. "What got into you?"

Riley laughed. "Oh, nothing," she told him. "I was just thinking of doing this the whole time I was in the shower."

She could tell from the look on his face that Cade thought she was going to go back to lavishing her attention on his cock with her mouth, and though that was tempting, right then she needed feel him inside her. Giving him a naughty smile, she crawled up his body until she was straddling him. As much as she wanted to have his cock inside her, however, she couldn't resist teasing both of them by rubbing her clit over the head.

But apparently Cade could only take so much teasing because after a moment he grasped her hips and slid into her pussy in one smooth thrust. Riley gasped, still amazed at how incredible his cock always felt inside her.

As she slowly began to ride up and down on her husband's cock, Riley was surprised to feel the first tremors of

262

an orgasm ripple though her. Abruptly, she remembered what had gotten her so turned on, and she immediately began to fantasize about what was taking place in the room next to theirs.

Was Madoc still spanking Shayna? Riley pictured her friend over her husband's knee, squirming and wiggling as he brought his hand down over and over on her bottom. Suddenly, Riley's fantasy became more vivid and in it, Madoc had slid his hand between Shayna's legs to tease her clit. Riley could imagine the other girl's breath coming in quick, little pants as Madoc made his pretty wife come. And then, after her orgasm subsided, he would lean down and whisper in her ear, telling her to climb on his hard cock.

Riley moaned as much from the fantasy playing out in her head as from the pleasure Cade was giving her. Her husband's hands suddenly tightened on her hips, urging her to ride him faster. On the brink of orgasm herself, Riley gladly obeyed, bouncing up and down on his cock wildly until they both came. Her climax felt amazing and she couldn't help but wonder if her fantasies about Shayna getting spanked had something to do with how intense it had been. The images of Shayna's bottom getting reddened had been so vivid that it felt almost as if Riley had been getting spanked herself. God, she never realized she had such a voyeuristic streak!

Spent, Riley lay draped across Cade's chest his chest afterward. After a moment, her brow furrowed. Lifting her head, she gazed down at her husband. "Honey, do you think your brother spanks Shayna?"

Cade opened his eyes to regard her sleepily. "What would give you an idea like that?"

She shrugged. "When I came out of the bathroom before I thought I heard him spanking her."

Her husband chuckled. "No way. My brother's way too vanilla for that."

Riley could only smile. She knew that wasn't true, but she said nothing as she lay back down. If Cade only knew, she thought.

CHAPTER SEVEN

As she and Shayna were lounging by the pool the next afternoon, Riley really wanted to ask the other girl if that was spanking she'd heard coming from their bedroom the night before, but every time she tried, she just couldn't seem to make the words come out. She didn't want to embarrass the other girl or herself, so she decided it was probably better if she just didn't bring up the subject. She supposed she would have to keep wondering.

Riley was just settling back in her lounge chair again when she heard footsteps on the patio. Thinking it was probably Arlene, she was surprised to see Rosie coming toward them. On the lounge chair beside her, Shayna looked just as surprised.

"Arlene told me you were out here," Rosie said as she sat down on the bottom of Riley's lounge chair.

Riley sat up, as did Shayna. They both looked at the other girl expectantly.

"Were you able to find out anything from the license plate number you copied down?" Riley asked.

Rosie nodded, her dark eyes filled with excitement. "Yes, and it's really weird. That car belongs to a pharmaceutical company."

Shayna frowned. "What would someone from a pharmaceutical company be doing talking to Bill Bingham out in the middle of nowhere?"

The Mexican girl shrugged. "I don't know for sure, but I'm thinking that it must have something to do with drugs. I mean, what else would a pharmaceutical company be involved in?"

Riley's brow furrowed. "Drugs make sense, but what are they doing?"

"I have no idea," Rosie said. "None of the day-laborers who work at the mining company will say anything, either. But I know that a lot of them got picked for work today, which means that something big is going on up there." She looked at them expectantly. "I thought you girls might want to come with me to check it out."

Shayna's eyes narrowed. "Check it out how exactly?"

"I'm going to sneak up there and take pictures of whatever it is that's going on, then give them to my boyfriend," Rosie told them.

Riley looked at her in surprise. "Why? Is he a cop?"

The other girl nodded. "He's the deputy you saw me with the day you came to the sheriff's office."

Shayna gave her a frown. "Then if he's a cop, why don't you just tell him your suspicions and let him check it out?"

Rosie sighed. "Because Clay always thinks I'm imagining things," she said. "Which is why I need to get him proof."

"But wasn't your boyfriend the one who ran the license plate for you?" Riley asked. "Didn't he wonder what you wanted it for?"

The Mexican girl shook her head. "Actually, he didn't run the plate for me. I got his computer password out of his wallet while he was in the shower."

Shayna blinked. "Won't he be angry if he finds out?"

But Rosie only gave her a grin. "Probably," she said. "But I have Clay so wrapped around my finger he doesn't know which end is up most of the time."

If Cade caught her doing something like that, she would be over his knee so fast, Riley thought. From Shayna's expression, apparently she didn't think Madoc would be nearly as understanding as Rosie's boyfriend, either.

"So," Rosie said. "What do you say? Are you in?"

266

Riley looked at Shayna, who shrugged. She knew exactly what the other girl was thinking – they'd better not get caught, or they would be in for it.

"Okay," Riley told Rosie. "But our husbands can't find out about this."

Rosie grinned. "No problem," she said. "We'll just tell them we're going shopping."

Since they couldn't very well go with Rosie dressed like they were, Riley and Shayna went upstairs to change out of their bikinis and into more suitable clothes. When they went back downstairs, it was to find Rosie in the kitchen with Arlene.

"You girls have fun," the older woman said when Riley told her they were going shopping with Rosie.

As they left the house, Riley wondered if they should have let Arlene in on where they were really going just in case something went wrong and she and the other girls got caught snooping. Then again, if they did get caught, Bill Bingham would probably have them all arrested for trespassing on private property, which meant Madoc and Cade would find out anyway.

They drove out to the same location they had the day before and hid the car in a ravine. As they crept over the next hill, they saw that the area was crawling with people. Most of them seemed to be the day laborers Rosie had mentioned, but there were also a handful of men carrying rifles. It looked like they were the ones directing the work that was going on. It was hard to see exactly what they were doing with all the dust that was being kicked up, but Riley could see that there were several large trucks, as well as a bulldozer. The dozer had just finished digging what looked like a really deep trench.

Eager to see what was going on down in the valley below them, Riley and the other two girls carefully crept closer to the working men. They tried to move as stealthily as they could from one hiding place to the next. Within a few minutes, they had worked themselves to within a hundred feet or so of

267

the work site. From their vantage point behind a large rock, Riley watched as the day laborers unloaded plastic bags from the trucks and tossed them into the huge hole the bulldozer had dug.

"What are they doing?" Riley whispered to the other two girls.

It was Rosie who answered. "I don't know, but it's obviously not legal."

Digging into her bag, Rosie took out the digital camera she had brought with her and held it up so that she could use the zoom function to see better.

"Do you think they're burying drugs?" Shayna asked, leaning in close so that she could look through the camera, too.

"Maybe," Rosie said.

Riley's brow furrowed. "But why would they bury drugs? That doesn't make sense."

"Unless someone else is going to come and dig them up later," Rosie suggested.

They all fell silent for a moment as Rosie took some pictures. "I'd love to get a little closer, but I don't know if we dare," she said.

"And what the hell do you girls think you're doing?"

Startled by the gruff male voice, Riley jerked around to see two men standing behind them, a pistol in one of their hands and a rifle in the other. From the corner of her eye, she saw Rosie's grip on the camera tighten.

Riley swallowed hard. "We, uh, were just out sightseeing and..." she began.

"Like hell you were!" the second man snarled. "Get up!"

With two guns being held on them, Riley and her friends had no choice but to obey. She wondered for a moment if they should try and make a run for it, but then thought better of it. If they ran, the men would probably shoot them for sure. However, if they went along willingly, the men might let them go, or at least she and the other girls might be able to escape later. Apparently, Shayna and Rosie must have thought so, too, because when the men gestured for them to walk toward where the men were working, they went without protest.

Though the day laborers looked at Riley and the other girls curiously, they didn't stop unloading the trucks. But perhaps that had something to do with the half a dozen men brandishing guns, she thought bitterly. Bill Bingham, however, strode over to meet them as soon as she and the other girls were herded into the clearing.

"I thought I told you girls to stay away from here," he said, looking from Riley to Shayna. "But you couldn't leave well enough alone could you? And now you've involved your friend, too."

Rosie glared at him. "They didn't involve me in anything. I've been on to you for weeks now, you bastard! I knew you were doing something illegal and now I've got the pictures to prove it."

Bill Bingham's eyes narrowed as he took in the camera she had in her hand. "You've got nothing but pictures of a bunch of Mexican day laborers unloading plastic bags from trucks and tossing them into a hole in the ground."

"Plastic bags full of drugs, you mean," Rosie sneered.

Bill Bingham stared at her in disbelief. "Drugs? Is that what you think is in those bags?" He let out a harsh laugh. "Does that stench smell like drugs to you?"

Riley had been too preoccupied with their situation before to pay much attention to the smell, but now that she did, she wrinkled her nose. She didn't know what drugs smelled like, but she didn't think it was that.

"If it's not drugs, then what is it?" she asked.

He regarded her in silence for a moment as if deciding whether he should answer, then shook his head. "You really want to know what's in the bags? I'll tell you," he said. "A local pharmaceutical company is paying us to dispose of the lab animals they use for testing."

Riley blinked, her gaze going to the bags the workers had already thrown into the hole. There had to be hundreds of bags in there, she thought, sickened by the idea. She didn't like the thought of animal testing to begin with, and after seeing this, she was even more against it.

Beside her, Shayna looked just as disgusted. "This can't be the approved method of...of disposal," she said.

Bill Bingham shrugged. "No, but it is cheaper. And more importantly, it covers up how many animals they're actually killing in their testing. If the public ever found out how many of those cute, cuddly critters die just to make sure their mascara doesn't run, there'd be an international outcry."

Riley tore her gaze away from the growing pile of bags in the trench. "What about the body we saw floating in the stream the other day? That wasn't an animal."

His mouth tightened. "No, it wasn't. It was one of the laborers we hired. He decided he was going to tell the authorities what we were doing up here, anonymously of course, since he was an illegal. But either way, we couldn't have him doing that, so we stopped him."

"Killed him, you mean?" Rosie sneered.

Bill Bingham fixed her with a glare. "If you prefer," he said. "Which is exactly what it looks like we're going to have to do to you."

Riley felt her heart start to pound. "B-but you can't!" she protested.

"She's right," Shayna told him. "Our husbands are U.S. Marshals and they know we came up here."

Bill Bingham smirked. "Somehow I doubt that." His gaze went to the men standing guard behind them. "Shoot them and then put them in the trench with the rest of the trash."

"You can't think you're going to get away with this!" Rosie shouted.

But Bill Bingham was already walking away.

Cade and Madoc were just heading in from the barn when they spotted a sheriff's vehicle coming up the driveway. His brow furrowing, Cade came to a halt, as did his brother. A moment later, the SUV slowed to a stop and Clay Ericson got out. Cade and Clay had been friends since grade school, and while Cade had chosen to become a police officer in Dallas, Clay had decided to stay in the local area and become a deputy instead. Cade grinned at the other man as he and Madoc walked over to meet him.

"What brings you out here?" Cade asked, giving him a hearty handshake.

"I'm looking for Rosie, actually," Clay said. "She left me a message on my cell saying she was coming out here to see your wives. I'm going to be on duty for a while yet so I thought I'd come by and see if she wanted to grab some dinner."

Cade glanced at Madoc. "Rosie's not here. She went into Fort Worth to do some shopping with Riley and Shayna."

Clay's eyes went wide at that. "Shopping? Are you sure? Rosie hates to go shopping."

Cade didn't think he'd ever heard of a woman who didn't like to shop. "That's what they said."

Clay was about to reply when a woman's voice came over the radio handset attached to his shoulder.

"Clay, you there?"

The deputy reached up to thumb the talk button. "Go ahead, Marcy," he said.

"I think we may have a problem," the woman said. "One of Rosie's friends is here and she said Rosie went up to do some snooping around on Big Sky Mining property this afternoon. She says Rosie swore her to secrecy, but since Rosie's not back yet, her friend thinks she might be in some kind of trouble."

Cade's brow furrowed as he shared a look with Madoc. There was no way Riley or Shayna would deliberately go snooping up at the mining company after they'd specifically told the girls to stay out of it. What the hell was he thinking? Of course they would!

Clay swore under his breath. "Is the sheriff still there, Marcy?"

"He and his wife already left to go to Dallas," the woman said.

"What about Whitley or Michaels?" he said.

"Both of them are out on Old Mine Road about a domestic disturbance," Marcy said.

"Shit," Clay muttered. "All right. Get them on the radio and have them meet me up at Big Sky Mining."

"Roger that," she said.

"What do you think is going on?" Cade asked.

Clay shook his head. "I'm not sure, but Rosie has been going on about something shady happening up at Big Sky Mining for weeks now. I told her to stay out of it, but obviously she didn't, and now who knows what she's gotten herself into." His mouth tightened. "Or what she's gotten your wives into."

Madoc clenched his jaw. "Shayna and Riley probably didn't need that much persuading. They thought they saw a body floating in the stream when they went riding up near the mining company's property the other day, so they were already suspicious."

Clay frowned. "Absolutely wonderful," he muttered. "Well, as you heard, I could use some back-up. You boys game to help out?"

Cade had known his wife's snooping was going to get her into trouble, and now it seemed that he'd been right. He should have listened to her when she'd said they'd seen a body. If he had, then she and Shayna wouldn't be in this situation right now. But there was no time to beat himself up about it; they had to get out to that mining property, and quickly.

Apparently, Madoc had the same thought because he turned and disappeared into the house without saying a word.

A minute later, he came back out with two rifles, one of which he tossed to Cade.

"Let's go."

CHAPTER EIGHT

Oh God, this had been a really bad idea, Shayna thought. Madoc and Cade had been right; she and Riley should have minded their own business. But of course they hadn't, and now they were going to pay for that stupidity. She glanced frantically at Riley and Rosie to see that though both girls looked as frightened as she felt, they also seemed as determined as she was not to give in without a fight.

"You can't do this to us!" Shayna shouted, trying to jerk free as the man holding her began dragging her closer to the edge of the hole.

"She's right!" Riley added. "People know we're here!"

"They've probably already called the sheriff!" Rosie said. "He'll probably be here any minute!"

The men all laughed, obviously finding the whole thing amusing.

"If they called the sheriff, he would have been here by now, bitch," the man who was holding on to Rosie snarled. "Which means you girls are on your own."

"And about to become fertilizer," the man holding Riley sneered.

Shayna was dangerously close to the edge of the hole now. All it would take was one shove from her captor and she'd be in it, she thought. If that happened, she'd never be able to escape. Desperate, she began to fight more wildly, as did the other two girls.

Suddenly, Shayna heard police sirens. Jerking her head around, she saw not only two sheriff vehicles, but also a familiar dark SUV speeding down the dirt road toward them. *Madoc!* Thank God, she thought.

The man holding her tightened his grip, and for one fearful moment, she thought he was going to throw her in the hole anyway, but to her relief, he released her. Barking an order to the other two men to get the hell out of there, he and his companions took off at a run toward their one of the trucks. They weren't fast enough. though, and within moments, Madoc, Cade and the sheriff's men were out of their trucks and holding them at gunpoint.

Shayna's first impulse was to run over to her husband and throw herself into his arms, but she forced herself to stand beside him while he and Cade kept their weapons trained on Bill Bingham and his men so that the sheriff's deputies could handcuff them. Once that was done, Madoc immediately turned to her. Resting his rifle against the SUV, he took her in his arms.

Shayna leaned against his chest, hugging him tightly as she let the warmth of his body envelop her. All too soon, however, Madoc pulled away to gaze down at her.

"Are you all right?" he asked. "Did those men hurt you?"

She shook her head. "No," she said. "I'm fine. We're all fine. But thank God you got here in time."

Though Madoc clearly looked relieved that she and the other girls hadn't been harmed, his jaw tightened anyway. "What the hell were you girls doing up here? You promised you wouldn't get involved!"

Shayna bit her lip and looked away to find Riley getting the same lecture from Cade. Several feet away, Rosie was obviously hearing the same thing from her boyfriend.

She lifted her gaze to look up at Madoc. "I know, and we really had every intention of keeping that promise, but then Rosie had a hunch something was going on up here. Riley and I couldn't talk her out of it, but we couldn't just let her investigate on her own, either, so we came with her. We only meant to take some pictures, so that we could prove to you that there was something illegal going on, but then we got caught."

Shayna went on to tell him what she and the other girls had discovered, including the fact that they'd been right about the body floating in the stream that day.

276

Madoc scowled at her. "We are definitely going to talk more about this when we get back to the ranch."

Shayna suspected she would be over his knee for a good portion of that conversation, but she supposed she couldn't really say she didn't deserve it. If Madoc and the other men had gotten there even a couple of minutes later, then she, Riley, and Rosie would be dead right now. The thought made her shiver. She was so happy that she and the other girls were safe that she'd gladly submit to any spanking Madoc gave her.

Madoc's gaze kept drifting over to where Shayna and the other girls were giving their statements to the federal investigators who had arrived. While he was angry with his wife for putting herself in danger once again, he was also immensely relieved he, Cade, and the sheriff's deputies had gotten there in time. If they'd just been a couple of minutes later...he didn't even want to think about it.

With a sigh, Madoc turned his attention back to his brother and Clay to find them wearing the same grim expressions as they stood regarding their significant others.

"I don't know what I'm going to do with Rosie," Clay said, shaking his head. "Not only did she get involved in this whole thing when I told her to stay out of it, but then I find out that she stole my computer password so she could run a license plate check on the guy from the pharmaceutical company."

Beside him, Cade's mouth tightened. "Well, if she were my girlfriend, I'd put her over my knee and give her a spanking."

Clay's eyes went wide. "A spanking? You're kidding, right?"

Madoc had to admit that it was the same kind of advice he would give, thought he was definitely surprised to hear those words come out of his brother's mouth. Maybe his brother wasn't as conservative as he'd thought.

But Cade only shook his head. "No, I'm serious. In fact, when I get Riley back to the ranch, that's exactly what I plan on doing."

Clay looked even more surprised at that. "Really?" he said, his gaze going to his girlfriend. "A spanking...I don't know."

Cade shrugged. "It might sound old-fashioned, but believe me, it'll make Rosie think twice before she does something this foolish again."

"Cade's right," Madoc put in. "Though in Shayna's case, sometimes it takes several trips over my knee before she finally learns her lesson."

At his words, both men looked at him in surprise, but it was Clay who spoke first.

"You spank your wife, too?" he asked, then looked from Madoc to Cade. "What is it, some sort of family tradition or something?"

Madoc couldn't help but chuckle at that. "I don't know about it being tradition, since I didn't know Cade spanked Riley until he just mentioned it a few seconds ago. But I do know that it works."

The sheriff's deputy was silent for a moment as he considered the idea, but before he could say more, the girls walked over to them. While Madoc didn't know Clay that well, he had the feeling Rosie would be sitting a little gingerly that evening.

After the ordeal she and Shayna had been through, Riley wanted nothing more than to take a shower and curl up in her husband's arms, but when they got back to the ranch, Cade surprised her by taking her hand and leading her in the direction on the barn instead. He couldn't mean to spank her, could he? she wondered. As much as she knew she deserved to have her bottom reddened, she didn't think he'd put her over his knee the moment the got back to the ranch. But glancing over her shoulder to see Shayna and Madoc heading to the barn

278

as well, Riley relaxed as she realized Cade wouldn't spank her in front of the other couple. More likely, the brothers were going to give them a stern lecture, she thought.

Once in the barn, Cade and Madoc stood before the two girls with their arms folded across their broad chests, scowls on their handsome faces.

"You girls could have been killed up there this afternoon, you know," Cade said. "If Madoc and I hadn't gotten there when we did, you would have been."

She and Shayna didn't really need a reminder of how stupid they had been to go up there, Riley thought, but she said nothing as Cade continued.

"And if you've ever deserved to get a spanking for something, this would definitely be it," he said.

Riley blinked in surprise. She must have heard him wrong, she told herself, because Cade could not just have said the word "spanking" in front of Shayna and Madoc. But when she darted a quick look at the other girl, Riley saw that her friend was staring at them opened-mouth.

Riley swung her gaze back to Cade. "You're can't seriously be saying that you're going to spank me in front of them, are you?

It was Madoc who answered. "Don't worry," he said. "Shayna is going to be getting a spanking, too."

Stunned, Riley glanced at her friend to find the other girl blushing furiously and looking at Madoc in disbelief.

But Madoc merely shrugged. "Cade and I figured since you girls got into trouble together, it's only right you should get spanked together, too."

The barn was filled with stunned silence for a moment while Riley and Shayna both gaped at the men. Riley couldn't believe Cade and Madoc were actually going to spank her and Shayna in front of each other. But apparently that was exactly what they intended to do because Cade took Riley's hand and led her over to one of the hay bales while Madoc led Shayna over to another one.

Standing before Madoc as he sat down on the hay bale, Shayna couldn't help but glance over at Riley and Cade. While the idea of getting spanked in front of her friend was a little embarrassing, strangely enough, the thought of getting her bottom reddened alongside the other girl was also kind of thrilling.

"Push down your shorts and climb over my knee."

Madoc's deep voice brought Shayna's head around. "Wh-what?" she stammered.

Her husband regarded her patiently. "Push down your shorts and climb over my knee."

Shayna's gaze went to the other couple for a moment before she turned her attention back to Madoc. Getting a spanking in front of the other couple was one thing, but getting a bare-bottom spanking was quite another. "But..."

Madoc lifted a brow, but said nothing. Clearly, he wasn't going to change his mind, Shayna thought. Reluctantly, her hands went to the buttons of her shorts. Undoing them, she glanced over at Riley and Cade before pushing them down, only to see the other girl pushing down her own shorts to reveal a tiny pair of lavender-colored bikini panties. Well, at least Riley was getting a bare-bottom spanking too, Shayna thought.

With a sigh, Shayna wiggled her shorts down over her hips and obediently draped herself over Madoc's knee. Though she knew from experience that his strong hand on her back would hold her in place, she automatically put her hands down on the hay-covered floor to steady herself.

Even though she was focused on the spanking she was soon going to be getting, Shayna couldn't resist taking a peek at the other couple. She'd never seen another girl get spanked before and for some reason, she found herself watching in fascination as Cade guided Riley over his knee and settled his hand on her back. He placed his other hand on Riley's panty-covered bottom.

Shayna had been so caught up in watching the other couple that when Madoc rested his hand on her panty-covered bottom, she actually jumped a little. She turned her attention back to the floor, waiting for the lecture she was sure she would be getting, but Madoc surprised her by suddenly lifting his hand and bringing it down on her bottom in a sharp smack.

"*Owwwww!*" she yelped, then immediately bit her lip in embarrassment as she remembered the other couple.

She heard Riley let out a yelp of her own a moment later as Cade delivered a loud smack to his wife's upturned bottom. At least she wasn't the only one, Shayna thought even as Madoc brought his hand down on her other cheek.

Soon, the barn was filled with rhythmic smacking as both Madoc and Cade set to work reddening the girls' bottoms. While Shayna was grateful that Madoc had allowed her to keep her panties on, they didn't offer much protection, especially since they rode higher up on her asscheeks with every smack of his hand. Soon, her entire bottom was suffused with heat, and she couldn't keep herself from squirming.

"Honey, please," she begged. "That really stings!"

Madoc's hand didn't even pause as he answered. "Well, it's going to sting a lot more because I'm just getting started."

With a groan, Shayna darted a quick look at the other couple to see that Cade had stopped spanking Riley to pull down her panties. Shayna's own spanking forgotten for the moment, she gazed at the other girl's bare bottom, mesmerized by how red her friend's asscheeks were. Was her own bottom that red? Shayna wondered.

Shayna felt her pulse quicken in anticipation as she watched Cade lift his hand. It didn't seem right to want to see her friend get spanked, but Shayna couldn't seem to help herself. In fact, she was so captivated by it that she was barely aware of Madoc lowering her own panties.

As if sensing Shayna's eyes on her, Riley lifted her head to look over at her and Madoc. Embarrassed to be caught staring, Shayna started to look away, but then stopped when she realized that Riley was gazing at her ass with the same fascination.

Shayna felt her pulse skip a beat, but before she could even begin to think what it meant, Madoc lifted his hand and brought it down on her bare bottom. The smack seemed to echo throughout the barn and Shayna saw Riley's blue eyes go wide. A moment later, however, it was Shayna who was wide-eyed as Cade's hand connected with Riley's ass. She didn't think she'd ever seen anything so provocative before.

But even as captivated as she was by watching Riley get spanked, Shayna couldn't ignore the hard smacks Madoc was administering to her own bottom. He was concentrating on her sit-spots now, his hand coming down over and over on them with impeccable aim. *Ouch!*

The force of the smacks soon had Shayna kicking and squirming wildly, and she let out a squeak of protest after each one. When she had said she would gladly submit to whatever spanking Madoc gave her, she hadn't been thinking that it would be one quite this hard. Madoc must be really determined to teach her a lesson!

Amazingly, though, even while she was kicking and squealing, Shayna still found her gaze drawn repeatedly to the spanking Riley was getting. The other girl was putting up quite a fuss herself, kicking and wiggling so vigorously that her husband was forced to put a lot of effort into holding her still. *Oooh*, Riley's bottom was so red, she thought. Shayna was sure her own bottom never got that red!

Then, all at once, Madoc stopped spanking her. A moment later, she was back on her feet in front of him. Shayna automatically reached back to cup her throbbing asscheeks with both hands, only to gasp at how hot her bottom felt. Maybe her ass really was as red as Riley's. She suddenly had an almost uncontrollable urge to stand beside the other girl and compare!

Abruptly realizing that she didn't hear any spanking coming from the other part of the barn, Shayna glanced over her shoulder to find Riley standing in front of her husband, her hands cupping her glowing red ass. Shayna had to admit that seeing her friend's bottom all red like that was damn sexy! She couldn't wait to get Madoc alone; she was going to be all over him like a wild woman!

Madoc and Cade made her and Riley stand where they were for several minutes while they lectured them again on keeping their noses out of places they shouldn't be. Shayna wasn't really paying much attention to what her husband was saying, though because she was spending most of her time glancing over her shoulder to check out her friend's very red bottom. She had to smile when she realized that Riley was doing the same to her.

As they were all walking back to the house a little while later, all Shayna could think about was how much fun it had been to get spanked alongside Riley. She wondered if they could orchestrate a reason to make it happen again.

Riley must have been having the same thought because she smiled mischievously. "You know," she said, glancing at Shayna as they walked back to the house. "Without the mining company to bother us, there's no reason we can't spend lots of time up there looking for that Confederate gold now."

Shayna returned her smile. "I agree. Though I'm not sure the guys are going to be crazy about the idea."

Riley glanced over her shoulder to where the two brothers were walking a little distance behind them. "You're probably right," she said. "Of course, we'll probably get another spanking when they find out about it, you know."

Shayna laughed as she glanced over her shoulder at the two men. "I'm counting on it."

Blushing Books ® hopes you enjoyed this spicy, spanking novel by Paige Tyler. We have lots of other erotic novels and novellas available. For the "latest," you may want to check out our Internet websites, owned and operated by our Internet partner, ABCD Webmasters.

Bethany's Woodshed has been publishing erotic and romantic spanking novels since 1998. Each week the website is updated with six new novels or short stories, featuring adult romantic and erotic spanking stories. Every story published on Bethany's Woodshed is original, exclusive, brand- new, and all are written by paid professionals. Bethany's Woodshed is located at: http://www.herwoodshed.com

Spanking Romance is also a site which is updated weekly. At this site, we publish a completed novella – 4-6 chapters – every week. Again, all stories are brand new and exclusive, written by paid professionals.
Spanking Romance is located at:
http://www.spankingromance.com

Romantic Spankings is our eBook site. On this site there are literally hundreds of eBook novels and novellas, all available for immediate download.
Romantic Spankings is located at:
http://www.romanticspankings.com

Many of our longer books are also available in print through Amazon. Please check out the following titles:

A Glitch in Time by Judith McClaren ISBN: 978-1-935152-00-2
Master of Wyndham Hall by Sullivan Clarke ISBN: 978-1-935152-01-9
Barbarian Worlds by Sharon Green ISBN: 978-1-935152-02-5

Cindra and The Bounty Hunter by Paige Tyler ISBN: 978-1-935152-03-3
Victorian Brats Volume One by Melinda Barron ISBN: 978-1-935152-04-0
Princess Brat by Sharon Green ISBN: 978-1-935152-05-7
Mistaken by Laurel Joseph ISBN: 978-1-935152-06-4
Magic Spell by Paige Tyler ISBN: 978-1-935152-07-1
The Cutler Brothers by Paige Tyler ISBN: 978-1-935152-08-8
Simple Pleasures by Nattie Jones ISBN: 978-1-935152-09-5
DeAkeny's Bride by Darla Phelps: ISBN: 978-1-935152-10-1
The Friends Series, Volume One by Paige Tyler: ISBN 978-1-935152-11-8
Comanche Canyon, by Judith McClaren: ISBN 978-1-935152-12-5